The
NEVERSINK
CHRONICLES

Stories

By

John Dwaine McKenna

RHYOLITE PRESS, LLC

Published in the United States of America by Rhyolite Press, LLC
P.O. Box 2406
Colorado Springs, Colorado 80901
rhyolitepress.com

McKenna, John Dwaine
The Neversink Chronicles / John Dwaine McKenna
1st ed. January 2012

Library of Congress Control Number: 2011938269
ISBN 978-0-983-99520-3

PRINTED IN THE UNITED STATES OF AMERICA

1st edition

Cover design and book design by Donald R. Kallaus

Author photo, © Donald R. Kallaus, 2011
Cover art from original oil painting, *The Neversink River Gorge*, by D.C. Grose, 1883,
collection of the author.

CONTENTS

Preface

In the 1830s, having exhausted all of the sources in Manhattan and Brooklyn, the city of New York set out to find safe, reliable and abundant sources of fresh drinking water and deliver it to the city. Their search took nearly 140 years and carried them as far as 125 miles north and west, into the heart of the Catskill Mountains.

Along the way they built a total of twenty four reservoirs and 345 miles of underground tunnels and aquifers . . . a system so large and complex it has been called the eighth wonder of the world . . . a system that destroyed thirty eight towns and villages, displaced more than ten thousand people through forced evictions and killed several hundreds of construction workers.

The Neversink Chronicles are about, and dedicated to, the displaced people of Bittersweet, Aden, Old Neversink, Eureka, Montela and Lackawack . . . the lost hamlets and villages of the Neversink and Rondout Valleys.

The stories are all fictional, and products of the author's imagination. All of the characters are fictional and any similarity to actual persons, either living or dead, is unintentional and entirely coincidental, except for certain historic public figures. Locations and places are either fiction or used fictitiously, and are likewise products of the author's imagination.

And lest there's confusion . . . Sullivan County, New York, consists of fifteen townships . . . one of which is called "Neversink." The town of Neversink includes the village of Grahamsville and hamlets of Neversink, Curry, Claryville, Bradley and Willowemoc. If you Google their website, townofneversink.org, you will find a well organized, lively, fully functioning town administration and a thriving community. It is one of the most scenic, beautiful and bucolic areas of the Catskill Park . . . it's the place where I was born and raised . . . where my roots run deep.

John Dwaine McKenna
Colorado Springs, Colorado
August 2011

The Catskill area once had seven beautiful streams. New York City has taken five of them, only the Beaverkill and Willowemoc remain.

The Townsman
Grahamsville, New York
April 12, 1950

Eureka Poker Night

1932

Eureka Poker Night

Back in the '30s, before television and World War II refocused our attention, every Saturday was poker night over in Eureka, in the back room of Rocky O'Mara's service station. Normally it was a night of comradery and fellowship, some card playing, a little town gossip, rumor mongering, cigar smoking . . . lying and bragging. The wives all thought of it as the boys' night out. The town busybodies and prudes thought it was disgraceful. The boys themselves, those who pondered such philosophical matters, felt that Saturday poker night at Rocky's was their one opportunity to act disreputable and rowdy, but in a genteel way. They could revisit their youth and act out their Boys-will-be-Boys routines in a non threatening environment, and do some friendly grab-assing with lifelong friends at the same time.

It was the fall of 1932 . . . Roosevelt was running for president . . . it was the year John Dillinger was killed in July and a pair of young outlaws named Bonnie Parker and Clyde Barrow were robbing banks and killing lawmen down in Texas and Oklahoma. Halloween was two days away.

Rocky went home at five o'clock to wash up and eat supper. I stayed at the garage to get things ready for the game, which started around eight o'clock or so. I swept, using the big push broom, then hosed down the concrete floor, getting all the oil and grease cleaned off. I rolled the big wood spool that Rocky got from the telephone company guys into the garage bay and went next door to the firehouse for some folding chairs. Bobby Ryan was there.

"Hiya' Bobby," I said. "I come over for some chairs."

"Sure, Buddy. How many y' want?"

"Dozen or so I guess. Maybe a few more, say twenty."

"Okay, I'll help you. You expecting a crowd?"

"Dunno. Y'never know."

We got twenty wood folding chairs and carried them to the back-door of the garage. Bobby got four at a time but I could only manage two. We made several trips, and then he helped me turn the wire spool we used for a table on to its side.

"Thanks, Bobby. You comin' tonight?"

"Naw. I'm going to the movies with Alice."

"Lucky you."

Bobby grinned and offered me a piece of Wrigley's, which I took. Rocky got back at seven thirty, with a covered dish his wife, Betty, had sent for me. My supper was venison meat loaf and gravy, a boiled potato, stewed tomatoes and green beans from the garden, plus a big chunk of her soda bread and butter. I was living high on the hog for a twelve year-old orphan boy. I've always been lucky that way, in life I mean, except for Mommy and Pa getting killed in the car wreck when I was five years old.

Rocky found me standing by the wreck, looking for Mommy and Pa . . . I was walking back and forth, between the road and what was left of the old, patched-up car Pa was driving. I got thrown up in a bunch of blueberry bushes when he ran off the road and the car rolled over, down the bank.

I was lucky Rocky found me, lucky he and Betty took me in, when they already had two boys of their own to raise.

I finished supper and ducked into the little room in back where the oil drums and antifreeze and other stuff like soda pop was stored, to change clothes and comb my hair. This was my place, where I lived. I had a bunk, a dresser and my own footlocker under the bed where I kept my personal things like a lock of Mommy's hair and Pa's onyx ring. Like I said before, I was lucky. I had a place to stay, warm and dry, food to eat. I was a heck of a lot better off than others, who were stuck in orphanages or out on the road, begging for food and shelter every day and running away from the cops, bullies and pervs.

I took off my coveralls and put on my good pair of pants and the blue plaid shirt I'd got from Betty. She got them from Mrs. Greenburg whose boy had outgrown them. They fit pretty good too, after I rolled the cuffs up. I wiped my brogans off with a grease rag and was ready to go.

When I went out to the garage bay where the poker table was sitting, Dr. Murdoch was there. He and Rocky had put on the brown wool army blanket we used as a table cover and were smoothing the wrinkles out.

"Hello Dr. Murdoch," I said.

"Good evening, laddie. You're looking well."

"Buddy," Rocky said, "go get the bank and new decks. They're under the cash register in a cardboard box."

I went to the front room of the station where the soda pop and candy case was, and opened the back compartment of the cash register. I got the box Rocky wanted, the one with the walnut case of ivory poker chips and twelve new decks of playing cards. I closed the cash register and carried the stuff back to Rocky.

All the regular players started to come in at the same time.

Bill Green was first in the backdoor, then Jack Bonner the local surveyor and gunsmith. Ira Eastman and Hank Lockwood came in together, followed by Benny Dillman. Everybody was talking and laughing, come to have a good time. Rocky and Jack Bonner were already smoking cigars. It looked like Bill Green, who owned the hardware store a few doors down the street, was getting ready to fire one up too.

"You know what a cigar is?" Ira said.

"What's that?" Bill answered as he shook out the wooden kitchen match and dropped it on the floor.

"A Link Trainer for a cocksucker," Ira said with a grin. Everyone laughed.

"Aw, fuck you, Ira," Bill said.

"Best you ever had."

"Let's play," said Rocky.

The game was played with chips, and Dr. Murdoch was always the banker. White chips were a quarter, reds fifty cents and blues were a dollar. The buy-in was twenty dollars a head, a pretty good sum in 1932, but not enough to bankrupt any of the players. They were all merchants and businessmen or professionals like Dr. Murdoch, Jack Bonner and Benny Dillman, a lawyer from Neversink, four miles up the road.

The game started with seven-card stud because it allowed for more betting; at least that's what Rocky told me. They always played seven-card for the first couple of hours, eventually switching to five-card draw, which was a little bit livelier in the last hours as the number of players decreased. My job was to keep everybody supplied with Cokes and candy bars, and cigars if they wanted. The first cigar was on Rocky, his treat, sort of a "thanks for coming, glad to see you" gift. But after the first one, everybody had to pay, even Rocky. I carried a little notebook in my shirt pocket with their names and the number of candy bars, Cokes and cigars each one had consumed. It was an unspoken agreement . . . I wasn't to be questioned about the bill. If I said three Cokes and two cigars, it was three Cokes and two cigars, twenty-five cents due and payable, cash or chips, tips for good service gratefully accepted. I was proud of that and kept scrupulous track of everything. No one ever argued when it came time to settle up. Even the losers paid before they left, no questions asked.

I got pretty busy for a while, fetching Cokes and candy, passing out cigars like a new daddy instead of the kid I was. When I finally got a breather, I noticed there was a crowd — a lot more people than usual. The work bay where the game was being played was almost standing room only. They were all talking and waving their hands, or moving their heads around like people in groups do. There were still six players in the game, but I could see that Rocky and Ira Eastman had gotten up from the table. They were talking to the Redmond brothers, Otis and Charlie. I knew them because they stopped for gasoline every time they were in town. They were farmers who lived south, down the valley, almost to Montela. I went over to see what was going on.

" . . . pretty sure they was gov'ment cars. We seen at least two of 'em. Looked to me like they were shooting lines with survey instruments. When Otis and I went over t'ask them what they's doing, they got in their cars an' took off, down towards Lackawack," Charlie Redmond said.

"They haven't been here," Rocky said, "far as I know. They ain't bought gas or anything."

"What do ya' think they're up to?" Otis asked.

"Dunno," Rocky said. "You sure they were using surveying equipment?"

"No. It looked like it is all."

"Coulda been photographers," Ira said.

"Don't think so," Charlie said. "They just looked like they were surveyors."

"Surveyors have stick men and chain measures," Jack Bonner said. "I ain't heard of any other surveys up here."

"Maybe not. But Charlie and me saw them, and they looked like surveyors."

"I saw a black sedan, looked like a government type, over at the post office in Bittersweet about a week ago."

"They're from the city. Bet 'cher ass."

"Think they're lookin' for up here?"

"There's a car out front, with 'is lights on. Buddy, go see what he wants," Rocky said.

"What do we have that the city wants?"

"Water, you dumb fuck. They want our water."

I inched out the backdoor to see what the car out front was all about. Behind me the talk went on.

Out front by the gasoline pump was a pale yellow Model A Ford roadster with the top up and a steamer trunk stuck in the open rumble seat. I walked up to the driver's side and recognized the driver right away. I also recognized the car.

"Hi, reverend. How are you?" I said.

"Fine, Buddy. I'm just fine," Reverend Purdy said. "Do you think

I could get some gas?"

"Oh sure. I'll have to go get the pump handle and the padlock key."

"I . . . we're in kind of a hurry."

"Okay," I said. I ran to the office and got the pump handle out and the key to unlock the gas hose. When I got back out front, Reverend Purdy had shut the motor and headlights off. I could hear the hot manifold ticking as it threw off heat, and smell the exhaust fumes as they faded in the chill of the October night.

"How much do you want?" I asked.

"Try ten gallons."

I pumped the big glass cylinder on top of the gas pump to the 10 GAL GAS level on the glass, then put the hose in the tank.

"Be careful of the paint," Purdy said.

"Yessir," I replied, thinking, *This ain't the first time I put gas in a Model A.* The gas cap on a Ford is on the cowl, right in front of the windshield. I had to stand on the passenger's side running board in order to reach it.

"Hello . . . Mrs. MacWalloper," I said.

"Hi, Buddy," was all she said. She and Reverend Purdy both had on heavy fur coats and gloves, and she was also wearing a felt, snap-brim hat, pulled down low over her face. She turned away and looked out of her window, toward the front of the garage.

"It won't take quite ten gallons," I said to Reverend Purdy, "about nine and a half's all. You want me to check the oil?"

"No thanks Buddy." He gave me a five-dollar bill. "Here. Keep the change." He started the car and took off before I even had the gas hose back on the hook. I locked the pump and started back inside, wondering if I should tell Rocky about a $3.35 tip on $1.65 worth of gasoline.

When I went back inside, the cards had been put down and the talk had picked up.

". . . tell ya, there ain't nothing to it. There's been rumors about it for years."

". . . new road or something."

". . . houses, schools, farms, businesses, the post office."

". . . truthfully worried."

"Well shit. What the fuck are they gonna do . . . kick us all the fuck out?" Bill Green said.

"You are the most profane man I have ever met," said Benny Dillman, the lawyer. "But yes. They can force everyone out."

"Oh, my dying ass," Bill said.

"My family's been here for more than a hundred years," said Otis Redmond. "Aren't we grandfathered in or something? We've got title that goes clear back to the Hardenburgh Patent, the original land grant from Queen Anne."

"Doesn't matter. The city can claim 'eminent domain' and take the property." Dillman said.

"They can just take it?" someone asked.

"Yes. Prove a need, then take it," Benny Dillman said.

"They have to pay us, don't they?" Hank Lockwood asked.

"Oh yes. They have to pay fair market value."

"What's that?" Hank asked.

"Whatever it's assessed at by an appraiser," Jack Bonner replied.

"Whose . . ."

"Depends. Usually theirs. Although you could hire your own,

go to court about it." Benny said.

"Well that's a crock of shit," Bill Green said.

"True enough," said Benny, "but it's the law."

"The dirty bastards," said Bill.

Dr. Murdoch grinned at the foul-mouthed Bill Green, then said, "They are indeed a shower of fookers," in his soft Irish brogue.

"You mean to tell me, the city can come up here, a hundred miles away, and tell us what our homes and farms and businesses are worth, and then, they can force us to sell it to 'em and all's we can do is hire our own appraiser and our own lawyer? And take 'em to court?" Charlie Redmond said.

"I'm afraid so," Benny Dillman said.

"Not from me," Charlie said. "Not while I've got ammunition."

"Got plenty, over at my hardware store," Bill Green said. "Let them fuckers come and try to get my property."

I went back to work selling Cokes, cigars and candy bars. I was doing a pretty good Coca-Cola business because several pints, half-pints and silver pocket flasks were making quiet appearances in the crowd. The whole country was supposed to be dry but there were plenty of drinks in it. The election was still a few days away and Roosevelt promised to repeal Prohibition, the Volstead Act, as his first official act of office. He was predicted to win by a landslide.

The game was back on with plenty of commentary from the onlookers with their flushed faces and bottles of "Coca-Cola" in hand.

I was sitting on my bed, checking and adding up my Coke and candy sales when Rocky came in.

"What was that about, the car out front?" he said.

"Reverend Purdy needed gas."

"Purdy . . . what's he doing out?"

"He was driving Eugenie MacWalloper's car." I said. "She was in it."

"The Model A roadster?"

"Yeah. There was a steamer trunk in the rumble seat."

"Eugenie, and Purdy..."

Rocky was interrupted by Benny Dillman, who stepped in the doorway and stood there.

"Buddy, we need more Coca-Cola," he said. "Something going on?"

"Maybe," Rocky said. "Buddy was just telling me about our last customer."

I looked at Rocky, who gave a slight nod of his head.
"Reverend Purdy came and got gas," I said. "He was driving Eugenie MacWalloper, in her car. The yellow Ford roadster."

"Angus MacWalloper's wife?" Benny said. "From up in Bittersweet?"

"Yeah."

"Do you know, he owns over two thousand acres up there, all-in-all, about five and a half miles along the Neversink River?" Benny said to Rocky.

"Yeah," Rocky said. "I also know he's in his sixties and she's barely thirty, if that."

"Did Purdy say anything to you?" Benny asked me.

"No," I said. "But he was in a hurry, didn't want me to check the oil or anything. There was a big trunk, one-a those steamer ones, in the rumble seat. And he gave me five dollars for a dollar sixty five worth of gas and left."

"She say anything?"

"No. She just sat in the car. Didn't say a word when I said hello."

"When he left, which way'd he go?" Rocky asked me.

"South," I said. "He went south."

"Sweet Jesus on a bicycle," Benny said. "That takes the cake."

"Tell you one thing," Rocky said to Benny, "I would not want that old man hunting for me."

"No," said Benny. "Don't believe I would either. Jesus Christ if that don't beat the band." He went back out to rejoin the game, still muttering and shaking his head.

"Whad'a ya want me to do about the five he gave me?" I said to Rocky.

"Why don't you put two dollars in the register and keep the rest. It ain't like you're getting paid around here or anything."

"Thanks, Rocky," I said. "Thanks a lot." All of a sudden I felt prosperous.

I finished my accounting, tallied the notebook and went back out to where the game was. Benny Dillman was spreading the word about Reverend Purdy and Eugenie MacWalloper.

Bill Green said, "She was a real sweet-looking piece of ass, for damned sure."

"I don't think you ought ta talk about Mr. MacWalloper's wife like that," Hank Lockwood said. "No one here knows for a fact what she and Reverend Purdy were doing or where they were headed. Someone may be sick or dying. We don't know."

Green looked at him through eyes that glittered from an internal source, a source that was a degree plus or minus of the line defining the sane from insane among us. I never knew, as a child, or as an adult, which side of the line Bill Green looked out from. But at the poker game, he looked at his cards and then into Mr. Lockwood's face and said, "Sure. And they might also be doing the horizontal bunny-hop too. You know, hein' and shein' like young 'uns do. Fucking like minks. Wouldn't be the first time it happened."

"But you don't know, do ya?" Mr. Lockwood said as he folded his hand. He asked Dr. Murdoch to cash him out and Otis Redmond took his place at the table. You could almost see the tension flowing in the room like radio lightning bolts in the magazine advertisements. Everybody anted. Jack Bonner had the buck and was dealing five-card stud. He dealt the fifth down card, and the last round of betting started. Otis Redmond folded out of turn, and drew a glare from Jack.

"You're supposed to wait your turn," Jack said.

"Oh, sorry. I forgot."

Bill Green checked. Dr. Murdoch bet a quarter. The bid was Benny Dillman's. He said, "I'll see your quarter, and raise you a dollar."

Ira Eastman was next. "Too rich for me," he said, tossing his cards.

"Me too," Jack Bonner said, and folded his hand. He moved the Buck jackknife, which indicated who was designated the dealer, to his left, in front of Bill Green.

Bill had both forearms on the edge of the table and was hunched over his cards, careful not to expose his hand. He had the stub-end of his last cigar wedged in the corner of his mouth and one eye closed. With the other eye he was squinting at Benny Dillman like a Missouri Bushwhacker drawing a bead on the Virginian in Mr. Wister's book. He stared like that for the longest time, with Benny staring right back. All of us were watching, waiting to see the next move.

"I think you're jacking us around Benny," Bill said.

"Well, pay and play, Billy-Boy, pay and play. You look like you're layin' an egg over there," Benny said, then made a noise like a clucking chicken.

Bill Green kept squinting, but Benny Dillman just stared back, each of them guessing about the other one's hand. Bill said,

"Benny, you're as full of shit as a Christmas goose. I'll see Doc's quarter, and your dollar," tossing chips into the pot, "and I'll raise ya another two." He threw bright red chips on the pile.

"Boyo, you're too tough for me," Dr. Murdoch said as he mucked his cards.

"Looks like it's down to you and me Billy-Boy," Benny said.

The room began to focus on the game. All the conjecture, speculations, innuendo and gossip ground down and died as everyone's attention turned to the poker table and the drama unfolding there.

Bill Green didn't say a word, but I could see his jaw flexing ever so slightly. Perhaps he was getting a better grip on the cigar he was chomping like Mrs. Evans's bulldog with a pork chop, but I thought Benny's needling was getting him. He squinted. Benny stared at Bill Green and clicked his chip stacks like he had all night tonight and all day tomorrow to play. Neither one spoke as the tension mounted.

"I'll see your two . . . and I'll raise ya five," Benny finally said.

Bill Green looked like he was about to bite his cigar stub in half. He said, "I'll see your five . . ." And that's the exact moment Bobby Ryan crashed in the back door. "Doc. Doc Murdoch. You better come out here. I've got Wes Beaman in my car. He's bad hurt," Bobby said.

"What's a matter with 'im?"

"Wrecked his motorcycle,"

"Young Wes or old Wes?" Otis Redmond said.

"Young Wes, dummy. Old Wes won't be motorcycle driving," Charlie Redmond said.

Dr. Murdoch was headed out the door. Rocky sent me for the electric lantern we kept in the back where I slept. I got it and followed Bobby and Dr. Murdoch.

Bobby was driving an old Oakland four-door sedan with a large back seat; it was his family's vehicle and I'm sure it was good for courting.

Alice Conover was standing beside the front fender of the car, weeping, when I got out there. Dr. Murdoch and Bobby Ryan were in the old sedan, talking to Wes Beaman, who was lying sideways on the rear seat cushion. I could see a lot of blood and torn clothing. "Buddy, get in front and hold the light for me, laddie," Dr. Murdoch said.

I did as he asked and hopped in the front seat, holding the lantern up so Doc could see. All the card players, and Rocky, were still inside but about seven or eight rubberneckers had followed us out to see the blood and get in on the gory details for retelling their friends. When I held the light up, I could see that Wes was pretty hurt. His hands, arms, legs and face were bloody from sliding on the macadam roadbed. Dr. Murdoch looked in Wes's eyes, lifting his eyelids. He made sure Wes could move his arms and legs, then checked his neck and mouth.

My arm was getting tired from holding the light up in the air so I shifted around until I had both elbows on the back of the front seat and the lantern in two hands.

"Hold the light still, Buddy."

"I'm sorry, Doctor Murdoch," I said.

Outside, the gawkers were really getting into it.

"He gonna live?"

"Think he'll walk again?"

"Hey Doc, is he alive?"

"Christ! Look at the blood."

"He's crippled fer sure."

No one paid attention to Alice Conover, no one asked her if she was okay, or wanted to go inside or anything. I felt sorry for her. Doctor Murdoch looked up and said, "Why don't you all go back inside and let me help this boy. Go on. You should be ashamed of yourselves. Go. I'm asking you."

Wes was moaning and tears were leaking down both of his cheeks. I could see that the front of his pants were ripped almost to his knees and he was bloody.

"Wesley, listen to me," Dr. Murdoch said. "I'm going to take you to my office. I can't treat you here."

"Owww, I'm hurt. I'm hurt bad, Doc."

"I know it hurts. Brace up, boyo. I'll fix you up. You're gonna need some stitches down there."

Dr. Murdoch got out of the car.

"Bobby, take him to my office and wait. I'll be right there. Buddy, Alice, come with me."

"What about Alice?"

"I'll get her a ride home," Dr. Murdoch said. "Now go. I'll be right there."

I held the lantern up and followed Dr. Murdoch and the still-weeping Alice through Rocky's backdoor. I heard Bobby start up and drive away.

Inside, the game looked suspended, with the cards and chips lying facedown on the table. Benny Dillman and Bill Green both had their elbows on the table. I could see they were talking to each other, but couldn't hear the words.

I got a chair for Alice and sat her by the wall, next to the door.

"Alice, would you like a Coke or a candy bar?"

"No thanks."

"Are you okay?" I said. "Are you hurt or upset by how Wes looked?"

"I'm okay," she said between sobs, "I'm just scared. I was supposed to be home by ten o'clock. It took a long time to pick Wes up and get all the stuff off the road. I don't want to lose my reputation. My father will be going crazy."

"Where'd you find him?"

"Bobby was taking me home from the seven o'clock movie down in Ellenville. We were just about to Lackawack when we found him. Wes, I mean, down by the iron bridge."

Alice was hiccupping now, and sniffing and sobbing at the same time.

"Don't worry Alice. I'll talk to them for you."

I left her there and went to find Rocky and Dr. Murdoch. The players and the gawkers were all talking and watching . . . see what was going to happen next, I guess.

I found Rocky and Dr. Murdoch in the front room by the cash register, talking to Hank Lockwood.

" . . . sure Doc. I'll do it. Glad to," Mr. Lockwood said.

"Buddy," Rocky said. "Is Alice all right? What's she crying about?"

"She's okay," I said, "She's worried about her reputation and she's scared what her father's gonna do. She was supposed to be home by ten o'clock. They were on their way there when they found Wes."

"Where?" Rocky said.

"Down by the iron bridge."

"Hank will take her home," Dr. Murdoch said.

"I'll talk to her father too," Mr. Eastman said. "I grew up with her daddy. I'll tell him what happened."

Mr. Lockwood went to get his car. I went to get Alice. Rocky and Dr. Murdoch came in behind me and Dr. Murdoch raised his arms to get everyone's attention and hush them up. He said, "I'm leaving to go tend to Wesley Beaman. He had a motorcycle accident and was assisted by Bobby Ryan and Alice Conover. They found him on the highway down by the iron bridge. He has scrapes, bruises and contusions; he'll be fine in a few days. His most serious injury is a gash on his leg. I'm leaving to treat him now."

Then Rocky said, "We're gonna finish the poker game too, in just a minute."

I took Alice out the back again, holding her hand when we got outside. I said, "Don't worry Alice, it's gonna be okay. Mr. Lockwood is gonna drive you home and talk to your father, tell him what happened."

"Thanks, Buddy. Maybe now Daddy will let us get a telephone."

I walked her across the street to Lockwood's Coal and Fuel Oil and waited until he drove out from behind the coal sheds in his Studebaker sedan. I waved as they drove away, but I'm not sure she saw me.

17

As I went back to Rocky's, I thought to myself, *This is turning out to be one hellacious poker night.*

When I got inside, there was an argument going on, about the number of raises allowed. Apparently, Bill Green had called Benny's five-dollar bet and raised him another ten. That was the third raise and the last one allowed by Rocky's usual game rules. Benny Dillman wanted to raise again and that's what the arguing was about. It was already a huge pot, the biggest of the night. Bill Green didn't want any more raises.Benny did. They needed a tiebreaker.

Everyone in the room looked at me when I came through the door.

"Let Buddy decide."

"Good idea," Benny said. "Bill?"

Bill Green looked at me from his glittery black pupils with internal fire in them.

"Decide what?" I said. With about as much emotion as a monitor lizard, Rocky explained about the number of raises.

"Okay with you, Bill?" Benny said.

"Sure, why not."

I had a bad feeling in the pit of my stomach—like eating too many green apples, like I was going to be sick.

"Why don't you flip a coin?" I said.

"If Mr. Green wins, no more raises. If Mr. Dillman wins, then more raises are okay."

"Hold on," Rocky said. "If you guys flip and Benny wins, there needs to be a fixed number of raises, else this could go on all night. Agreed?"

"Sure," Bill Green said.

"Okay," Benny Dillman nodded.

"Are we agreed on a coin flip?"

They both agreed on a coin flip and a maximum of two more raises if Benny won. I flipped a quarter on the center of the table and Bill Green won. There were no more raises. All Benny could do was call or fold his cards.

"Call," Benny said as he slapped a ten-dollar bill down.

Bill Green turned over two jacks, diamonds and hearts.

"HAH!" Benny yelled and turned over two pairs, sevens and kings. He said "hah" again and reached for the biggest pot I had ever seen. There was still a crowd in the room and they all started talking again. I'd been so intent on the coin flip I hadn't realized the room was dead quiet.

Bill Green waited until Benny Dillman had arms out to rake in the pile before he said, "Hold on there. Hold on. I ain't done goddamnit."

Benny sat back with a face set in concrete.

Bill Green's cards lay in front of him, three down and the two red Jacks up. He gave a little smile and said, "And up jumps the devil," turning over the jack of spades.

Now the room was buzzing with energy.

"Damn. Did you see that?" Jack Bonner said to nobody in particular. Benny Dillman looked gut shot. Bill Green looked like he ate the canary. He pulled the big pot in and started to count the chips into piles, chortling and giggling to himself and making comments to Benny about his card playing.

He hadn't gotten very far when Benny said, "Hey Bill, I betcha a hundred dollars against that pot I can set my underpants on fire before you can count those chips."

"Aw shit," Bill said, "that ain't no bet. You'll take 'em off." He stopped counting and looked at Benny.

"Nope," Benny said, "I won't take 'em off."

We could all see there wasn't a hundred dollars in the pot. *For all we knew, there might not be a hundred dollars in the whole town,* I thought to myself.

Bill Green looked at Benny and relit his cigar stub, puffing out blue smoke. "Lemme get this straight," he said, "You wanna bet me a hundred dollars against this pot, you can set your shorts on fire, with you in them, before I can count the pot. That right?"

"Yes. I'll set my underpants on fire before you can count the pot."

Bill Green took another puff or two, looked up at the ceiling for a moment, then crossed his arms on his chest and looked right at Benny Dillman.

"Bet ya can't," he said.

Now all the rubberneckers got in the act, some with Bill Green, some with Benny Dillman and some just egging them both on to watch what happened next. Everyone in the room had an opinion, including me. I wanted to see if Benny could do it.

Benny pulled out his checkbook and started writing.

"Wait a minute, just hold on there," Bill Green said, "I ain't takin' no check for a bet. Shit too. You'll not make good when you lose."

"I'll cash his check if he loses," Rocky said. "I'm not taking sides, understand. Just cashing the check if needed. This is between the two a ya."

"Okay, Bill?" said Benny.

"Sure," Bill said.

Benny tossed the check on the table. Then he reached in his pocket and dug out four kitchen matches.

"Case I lose my nerve," he said. "I'm ready when you are Bill."

"I'm ready."

Rocky said, "Okay. I'll count to three. Ready?" they both nodded.

"One, two, three."

Bill Green started to stack chips as fast as he could count ten.

Benny Dillman just sat there, like he was having second thoughts. When Bill Green was about two-thirds done, he looked at Benny and laughed. That's when Benny stood up all of a sudden and pulled down his fly. He reached in and pulled out some of his underpants and twisted them up, rope-like. He held the twist in his left hand and grabbed a kitchen match with his right. He struck the match on the edge of the table and lit the twist, which started burning nicely.

"Oh Bill . . . my underpants are on fire and you're not done counting. Guess you know what that means."

Bill Green looked at Benny Dillman, who looked like he was pissing on the poker table as he stood there with his crotch pushed out and the smoking piece of his underpants pinched between his thumb and forefinger like a tiny phallus.

The room burst into bedlam. Otis Redmond, who started laughing while he was drinking Coke, was choking and sputtering soda all over his shirt and pants. Coca-Cola was running out of his nose. Rocky had his face in his handkerchief trying to smother his laughter. Jack Bonner, always ready with a stick when there was a wasp nest close at hand said, "He's gotcha Bill. Fair and square, you been snookered, boy."

A chorus of agreement started from the rest of the crowd.

Bill Green turned bright red. His face progressed from triumph to surprise, to embarrassment, chagrin and at last, anger. Even I could see the rage in his face as he leaned forward and shoved the chips in the direction of Benny Dillman, then stood up so violently he knocked his chair over and into Charlie Redmond who was several feet behind him.

"Fuck you Benny! And fuck you all. You all can go right to hell!"

He threw his cigar butt on the floor and shoved his way to the backdoor, which he slammed so hard the glass broke out, shattering all over the floor.

"Hate to see that boy when he's mad about somethin'," Jack Bonner said. "It just wouldn't be a pretty sight."

Poker night was over. Everybody cashed out with Rocky, who handled the bank after Doc Murdoch left, and then settled their bill with me. I'd sold a lot of candy bars, cigars and sodas, so it took awhile longer to settle up with everyone, and I made seventy-five cents in tips. It was more than I usually made, so I was feeling pretty good.

The last one to leave was Benny Dillman, our hometown lawyer and underpants arsonist.

"That was some switcheroo bet," I said to him.

"It's not what you say, Buddy, it's all in how you say it. I haven't pulled that stunt since I was in college."

"Everybody except old Bill Green got a big charge out of it," Rocky said.

"Yeah. Well, I guess he'll get over it sometime," Benny said.

"Wouldn't count on it," Rocky said. "I've known him all my life.

He's a proud man. Carries grudges."

Benny didn't say anything. I showed him his page in my book. He owed me for four cigars, four Cokes and two candy bars, a total of fifty cents. Benny was the big winner that night and had a wad of money.

"Tell me something, Buddy," he said.

"Okay," I said. "What?"

"What're your plans?"

"Plans . . . for what?"

"For life. What you're gonna do, what you wanna be."

"Well, I dunno."

"Finish high school?"

"Oh sure," I said, wondering what this was about. "Unless something happens to Rocky. Then I guess I'd run the garage for him. Until his sons were able to take over."

"You're plenty smart enough to do that," Benny said. "But did you ever think about going to college?"

"Sure. But it's a dream. Takes money," I said.

"True, it takes money, but it can be done if you've got the desire. If you want it enough."

"I guess so," I said. Benny gave me a dollar and said good night. I started sweeping the broken glass and cigar butts, as Rocky tacked a piece of canvas over the busted window. I put the money out of my pocket, less four dollars in tips, into the bank bag that Rocky took home every night. He said "good night," and I made sure the lights were off, then fell on my bunk with all my clothes on. I had to get the station open early for the morning church crowd.

I felt good. I had four dollars in my pocket . . . it was a fortune back then.

Rhyolite Mountain

1936

Rhyolite Mountain

In the far ten-mile distance, the mountain looks like God's own heap of diamond dust as it winks and glitters with ten million points of light. It stands like a beacon among its brother and sister mountains; its mystery drawing the viewer to investigate. As the mind and body get closer however, the mountain coalesces and loses its allure until, in the near one-mile distance, the eye and brain realize that the ten million points of light come not from diamonds, but from ten thousand junk cars.

Rhyolite Mountain is the name of this place, this mountain of glitter. It is only two miles as the crow flies from Bittersweet, the doomed hamlet along the Neversink River . . . soon to be flooded under twenty fathoms of water by New York City's Neversink Dam.

It is the home of Oliver and Irma Varley, their eighteen children, and ten thousand rusted, wrecked, inoperable and partially dismembered automobiles.

The Practice of Artful Deception

1937

The Practice Of Artful Deception

Chapter 1

It was Saturday, the kind of gloomy day you get in upstate New York in mid-January, overcast and gray, with wisps of snow and high-riding ice clouds blown in on an artic cold front . . . the kind with winds born someplace in the Canadian Rockies . . . the kind that numbs the brain and freezes the muscles, right down to the bone.

In the meadow, snow was drifted and crusty, a bit luminous in the weak afternoon light. It was high against the west side of our old farm house and barn, while entirely blown away, leaving bare ground on the east side. The year was 1937. I was in the kitchen of the house on Rocky Hill with old Mose and a black Border collie named Ella Allen. Mose had the wood box chock-a-block full of split maple and ash and there was a good fire in the old Home Comfort Range. An iron one-gallon teakettle of water simmered on the back, ready to make tea and putting some much needed humidity back in the air. An octagonal oak regulator clock on the wall by the backdoor ticked away the minutes and completed the scene of domesticity.

Ella Allen was sleeping behind the stove on a nest of burlap feed sacks. Mose, whose name was really Gino Scarlotto, was doing something with a box of leather harness stuff for Jack and Dolly, the draft horses that, like Mose and Ella Allen, had come with the hundred-sixty-acre farm when Daddy bought it for $400 back in 1934. The whole shebang was up in the Catskill Mountains, outside of a one-street town with the funny enough name of Neversink. Neversink was about a four-hour drive north of New York City, and about as different from the city as the North Pole was different from the Amazon Jungle.

I sat at the kitchen table, trying to read *Tortilla Flat* by a hot new writer named John Steinbeck, but I couldn't keep my mind on the pages. I was worried about Daddy, it was getting along toward dark and he still wasn't home. He'd left at dawn to go down to Ellenville. He hadn't told me why, just that it was "business," and I had sense enough to know he was in real danger whenever he was in Ulster County. That was where *he-who-shall-not-be-named*, the Lord High Executioner himself, Albert Anastasia, had a hidey-hole someplace. Who knew where? Who knew how many henchmen were around and about down there? And any damned one of them could put the finger on Daddy. The afternoon creaked by, every minute seeming like an hour, every hour like a whole day. Time was ever so slowly crawling into eternity. I closed my book and walked to the stove, added a piece of wood.

"Mose, want some tea? Coffee?" I said.

"No. Thanks Missy. I think I'll go down there and feed dem horses, milk the cow." Mose got up and put on his old army great coat and clamped a battered brown fedora on his head. He clucked once to Ella Allen, who beat him to the door, her tail fanning the air.

"Okay. Let me know if you change your mind. It's no trouble," I said, as the door closed behind him. Mose was unaware of Daddy's and my troubles, and Daddy had warned me many times to "keep it that way." Mose didn't, in fact, even know our real names, Daddy's and mine. He knew Daddy as Roscoe Evans, the name he'd bought the farm under, and me as Hattie Evans, his niece. *Keep it that way,* I thought, *keep it that way,* as I lit the oil lamps in the kitchen.

I stuck two more ash chunks in the stove and opened the damper on the chimney pipe a little bit to make the fire hotter. I filled the graniteware coffeepot with water from the hand pump and threw in a heaping cup of coffee grounds, put it back on the stove to boil. *Thank God for small things,* I thought for the umpteenth time, *it would really be miserable to have to carry water from the well house in this weather. But then too, I've gotten used to the outhouse. Pretty good for a city girl.* I was adapting to life on the lam.

It was full dark out now, a little after five o'clock, and I was really getting worried about Daddy. He should have been here a couple of hours ago. I thought about the comfort in routine as I went to the cellar and gathered an apronful of wrinkled winter potatoes from a wood barrel Mose and Daddy had stored last fall as we'd dug out the last of them. I got four white onions, big ones that had yellow shoots growing out of them. *We'll be out of potatoes and onions soon. Then it'll be rice, noodles, and store-bought stuff. Or canned,* I thought as I added a quart Mason jar of canned green beans from the garden to my apron. I headed up the cellar stairs, blowing out the lamp nailed to the stair post on the way.

I peeled potatoes and chopped onions on the big harvest table that stood in the center of the kitchen. Its surface was covered with dents, cuts, gouges and depressions from a hundred and some years of scrubbing and scraping, according to Daddy. We used it for everything from butchering—Mose did all that—to preparing bushels of garden produce for fall canning. Yessiree, I was turning into a real live farm girl. I got two big iron fry pans and placed them on the stove, one on the hot side, the other on the fender. I put three spoonfuls of bacon grease in the hot pan and tossed all the sliced potatoes and onions in, shut the damper and checked the fire, gave it a stir with the iron poker that hung on the side of the wood box. I threw salt and pepper on the potatoes and stirred them with a long-handled spatula. I wiped and dried the table, sifted two cups of flour in a big mixing bowl with one teaspoon salt, one tablespoon baking powder and one half-teaspoon baking soda. I added four tablespoons lard and three-quarters cup of buttermilk. I stirred the mixture until it was a big lump, spread flour on the table and kneaded the dough, rolled the mixture to about one-half inch thick. I cut biscuits out with a tin can I'd washed and put them on a greased cookie sheet and put it in the oven. I stirred the potatoes and onions, now brown, and added water from the iron teakettle, covered them with another cookie sheet, moved the pan to a cooler part of the stove. I opened the green beans, dumped them in a saucepan, put it on the stove next to the fry pan of potatoes and went to the cold room. The cold room was really a kind of cellar, built on the back of the house, partly underground, where a mountain spring bubbled up. It was concreted in a square tub, about three feet to a side, with a pipe through the side of the wall to carry off the overflow into a big trough outside. The room was cool, summers and winters. I took a small smoked ham wrapped in burlap down from where it hung on a wire, with the other cured meats.

When I got back to the kitchen I heard, then saw Mose through the kitchen window, coming toward the house, hunched over in the cold. Ella Allen was in front and Daddy was behind him. They were both carrying something. I was cutting the ham into slices and dropping them in the fry pan when the dog, followed by Mose and Daddy, came in the door. I threw a chunk of the ham rind in the beans, and wrapping my apron around my hand, pulled the oven door open to check the biscuits. They looked done, golden brown on top, about one and a half inches high. I grabbed a potholder and pulled them out, put the tray on top of the stove where the warming ovens are.

"Well Jesus H. Christ," Daddy boomed out in his loud voice. "It's cold enough to freeze the balls off a brass monkey. If I ever get another vehicle without a heater in it I'm gonna get my friggin' head examined. I'm freezing my arse off, I swear to God!"

"Sit down, Daddy. I'll get you some hot coffee. I just made fresh. Mose, coffee?"

"Thank you, Missy. I would," Mose answered in his old-fashioned way.

Mose was carrying a car battery. Whatever Daddy had was wrapped up in the old wool army blanket that he usually had over the seat of his '34 Ford pickup truck. I looked at it, but didn't ask what it was.

I got the small coffeepot and poured it full from the big one. I set it on an iron trivet on the table and got cups and saucers. I set the table, turned back to the stove, dying to know what he had, but damned if I'd ask.

*   *   *

My hands and feet ache—they hurt like hell—from being so cold for hours, coming home in the Ford pickup. I sipped some coffee and watched Arlene getting supper ready. Ham and fried potatoes was a helluva change from Delmonico's and Jack Dempsey's. Damn big change. But then too, it was a lot safer for us here than in the city. Cheaper too. Good thing, as I wasn't making three or four thousand a week anymore. I was happy just to be on the green side of the sod, that's more than I can say for the Dutchman and Berman. I know for sure that Otto warned that crazy sonofabitch Schultz: talking about taking out Tom Dewey was causing a lotta problems. Poor Otto. Never seen it coming. And Dutch Schultz, dumb bastard got shot with his pecker in his hand . . .

I kept watching Arlene. She had bowls and plates full of food coming, but I could tell, she was dying to know what I'd brought in. Wasn't gonna ask though. Good girl. Makes me feel thirty years old again. But damned Smart. Smart as hell. Good looking too. Damned good looking, I lit a cigarette and sipped my coffee. Warming up.

Thinking about later, when the lights go out, if she ain't wearing me out in bed . . . good way go though.

* * *

I take coffee. Watch Roscoe and the Missy. Her name she say is Hattie Evans. Roscoe niece. Hah! My English is not so good. Yes. But I am not so stupid. I see the looks they got each other. I know she not his sister girl. No. I know the names not right neither. But no more have to cook for myself. That's-a good."

* * *

Arle-a-Missy, how long before we eat?" I gave him a look. We both recognized the near slip-up with my name.

"A few minutes, Daddy. Hungry?"

"Yeah. Mose, help me untie the cord, remove the blanket."

Scarlotto got out his pocketknife and cut the twine. Daddy unwound the blanket, uncovering a walnut Zenith radio—a "tombstone" type, about two and a half feet tall—and fiddled around in the back of it for a moment.

"There," Daddy said, "the short antenna will do for tonight, we'll rig up a better one tomorrow. Mose, bring the battery over here."

Daddy pulled a rubber cord out of the back that had a red and a black wire. At the end of those were two clamps that he hooked to the battery. "Red one's positive," he muttered to himself.

The radio had three bands: broadcast, shortwave and police radio. Daddy set it on broadcast, then turned it on. As Mose and I watched, with a simple "flick of the switch," Daddy changed our lives. The dial lit up and with a hum that turned into an ear-piercing shriek, the Zenith was on. It settled down when Daddy turned the selector knob until he found a station that came in loud and clear, playing dance music by Fred Waring and the Pennsylvanians.

"Whad'a ya think of that, Mose?" Daddy asked with a smile.

"Just like-a the magic," Scarlotto answered in a low voice. "It's just like-a the magic."

Daddy laughed in his good-natured way. "Be damned if you're not right, Mose. It's just like-a the magic."

"It ain't magic," I said, "but supper's ready."

We ate a quiet dinner, enjoying the music. It was as if, like, the world outside was in the room with us. We, Daddy and me, were no longer isolated up here on the farm in Neversink. I didn't think the radio made the same impression on Scarlotto, "Mose," as Daddy called him.

Mose was probably sixty or sixty-five years old. He told us he'd been born on a farm in Italy sometime in the 1870's as best he could determine. He left in 1905, hunger and poverty driving him from his family and homeland. Somewhere, some way, he scraped up passage, and emigrated to the USA, a common enough story at the turn of the twentieth century. What was uncommon was that he landed in New York City and hooked up with a young Tommy Gallagher about ten years later. They were both working construction for the city of New York, on the Kensico Reservoir Project at Valhalla, New York. Scarlotto was a stonecutter, working on the sixteen-ton granite blocks used to line the face of the dam. Tommy was an Irish laborer, a "pick and shovel" man at $1.75 per day. Scarlotto, skilled, got top wages of $3.50 a day, but paid $25.00 per month for his cot and meals in the twenty-four man Italian-only barracks the general contractors had built. Ethnically separated, Italians, blacks, whites: each group had its own barracks.

By 1917, the Kensico Project was done. Scarlotto and Tommy Gallagher were both out of work and living back in Hell's Kitchen, on the west side of Manhattan, when fate intervened. The passenger ship *Lusitania* was sunk off the coast of Ireland by a German submarine, and America entered World War I. Scarlotto was exempt as a foreign citizen, but Tommy was drafted. He lasted three months before being sentenced to one year at Leavenworth Prison and a dishonorable discharge for striking an officer. He got out just as the war ended and the Volstad Act—Prohibition—came in.

Tommy Gallagher took to Prohibition like George Armstrong Custer took after the Sioux Nation, and by the early 20s he was making a lot of money. By the late 20ˢ he was a kingpin among the bootleggers and making a fortune. In 1928, he owned fifty Yellow Cabs, a dry cleaners, two restaurants and a 160-acre farmstead up in the Catskill Mountains. Tommy bought it in 1925 while up there selling hooch to a speakeasy in a place called "Lackawack." *Where do they think up these names?* I asked myself.

Scarlotto, who was Tommy's chauffeur and bodyguard, was getting pretty old to be in the rackets by then, so he agreed to go up to the farm and be the caretaker. Tommy's new driver was a tough guy, a mean little dago named Rico Mondini. Rico was as tough as whang leather and mean as a fifty-year blood feud. He had eyes so dark they looked like holes in his head, and a big scar on his left cheek. Those who saw Rico staring at them left and found business elsewhere. Rico was that menacing.

Tommy lost just about everything in the crash of 1929. The rest went in 1932 and 33, after the repeal of Prohibition. In 1934, down and out, broke and living on skid row, he sold the farm to Daddy for $400 and a case of twelve-year-old Canadian whiskey. Daddy was working for Otto Berman in the Dutch Schultz gang back then. He'd known Tommy from the beer wars of the early 1930's, when they were both aligned with Schultz against Legs Diamond, Charlie "Lucky" Luciano and the Italian Mob. "All water under the bridge," as they say.

As I cleared the table and washed the dishes, Daddy sat quietly, smoking cigarettes and drinking coffee. He looked as if he were lost in the ozone somewhere, thinking. Just as I dried the last dish, Mose stuck his pipe in his shirt pocket, stood up and said to Daddy:

"I think I cut the wood tomorrow, Roscoe. I take Jack and Dolly and the stone boat."

"Okay. That sounds good. I'll come up later, bring some coffee."

"All right. Thank you, Missy for the supper."

"You're welcome, Mose."

He put on his hat and coat, then left for his room in the barn, next to the tack room. Ella Allen stretched out on her bed by the stove, opened one eye and then closed it again with a sigh as she went back to sleep.

I got myself a cup of coffee and sat at the table by Daddy. He adjusted the radio and tuned in another station playing dance music. The program was *Your Hit Parade* and the band was just finishing "The Shoe Shine Boy." I watched Daddy take a deep drag off his cigarette while the announcer prattled on about Lucky Strike cigarettes in the green box. Then, as the orchestra took off on "It's *De-Lovely*," I touched his hand and said, "I was worried about you, honey. Really, really worried. This's been the longest damn day of my life. I love the radio, I'm really glad to have it and appreciate your thoughtfulness, but I was really scared when you weren't home before dark."

Daddy looked at me for some seconds before he said anything. I was hypnotized by those pale blue eyes that looked as faded as an old denim shirt. He had white hair and craggy black eyebrows that jutted out from his face and had to be trimmed by the barber. I was lost in those eyes when he finally spoke.

"I know you were Arlene, but it couldn't be helped, I had to go all the way to Kingston to get the radio."

"Kingston? . . . Kingston? Are you crazy? What if you were seen?"

"It's okay, don't worry. I was careful, and I was out of there before two o'clock. Besides, I look like a farmer in an old truck. Nobody's ever seen me in overalls and slouch hat before."

"Don't worry . . . worrying's all I've been doing all day."

"Arlene, listen to me, I was careful. Nobody saw me, I'm invisible looking like this, and besides, Roscoe Evans has three bank accounts down there. You know that. Those little savings accounts are the only way I can get safe deposit boxes. You remember when we first came up here to look at the farm, meet Mose? We had lunch in Kingston? I had you sign all those bank forms? Those were for savings accounts and lockboxes. The savings accounts don't amount to anything—less'n a hundred dollars in the three. Like a farmer in hard times would have. It's the lockboxes that're important, it's where the money is. You're the deputy on all three of 'em. Under Arlene Bradley."

"I forgot. It was three and a half years ago."

"I know you did, sweetheart, but listen. Things may heat up and we've gotta be prepared. I saw Ray Richards today."

"Mad Dog? That Ray Richards?"

"Yeah. I followed him down Broadway in Kingston for a couple of blocks. He was driving a blue '36 Chevy coupe with New Jersey plates on it."

"Oh jeez, Daddy. You think he's looking for you? Or me?"

"Me maybe. Hard to know. Those guys all think I might know where Dutch Schultz hid his treasure—that Otto Berman knew and told me."

"Daddy, it's been almost two years since the massacre—you think they're still after us? We've been laying pretty low. You think Edward Geary and Arlene Bradley are still of interest?"

"Hell yes, sweetheart. I'm always going to be hunted, as long as they live. You, no. I don't think so. Anything happens, you do the dumb bunny routine. And by the way, it's only been a little over a year. Fifteen months to be exact. They killed Otto and Schultz in Newark, New Jersey, on October twenty fifth, 1935."

"At the Palace Chop House. That, I remember."

I got up from the table, and put a chunk of hard maple in the stove, turned the damper.

"More coffee, honey?"

"Yeah."

Daddy got a bottle of bourbon out of the cupboard and poured a tot into each of our cups. As I put the coffeepot back on the stove, the radio orchestra finished up on "Cheek to Cheek" and swung right into "I'm in the Mood for Love." I took Daddy's hand and we danced, right there in the kitchen. The oak regulator read 10:40 when I turned the radio off and we went to bed. Daddy said he was tired out but I soon disproved that notion and had him purring like a big old house cat—snuggled under the feather comforter—when we finally spooned up and fell asleep.

Chapter 2

The winter passed in the slow, methodical way that I'd come to associate with living in the country, and our lives were filled with peace, quiet and routine; every day was pretty much the same as the one preceding it. There were unending chores to do—we had no modern conveniences—and the work was hard. My hands had become calloused and perpetually chapped. I rubbed them every evening with petroleum jelly, but they were always red and sore, my cuticles cracked and scabbed. The work never ceased. Clothes washing had to be done in a tub with hard brown soap and a metal scrub board; it took a whole day, sometimes more if there was a lot of wash because Daddy and Mose had been working in mud or grease, fixing machines or repairing fence, say. Cleaning out the barn was a daily chore, hauling and spreading manure on the fields. Feeding and watering the livestock took up much of each day for the men, and cooking and washing dishes took up much of mine.

Our daily lives were a grind, but it kept Daddy and me occupied up here in the boondocks, and safe, we thought. Some days, I was so busy working, so tired out at the end of the day, I would forget we were hiding up here. I'd forget, bad people were looking for us. People who thought we were holding a treasure, people who would do us harm.

Winter slowly gave way to spring. The snow and ice melted, shoots of green grass were appearing and yellow crocuses were coming up by the front porch.

Daddy and Mose clomped into the house for lunch. They took their boots off on the porch and came in the kitchen. It was the first week of May.

"Good boys," I said as Daddy poured coffee for himself and Scarlotto, who was busy washing up. "You took your boots off."

Daddy grinned. I saw him wink at Mose as he said, "We're trainable, honey, it just takes awhile. What's for dinner?"

"Venison stew. It's the last of the deer meat. We'll probably have it for supper too, if it's okay with you."

The men sat down while I got bowls of stew for all of us. I set them on the table with a plate of biscuits and a jar of apple butter. The radio was off because the battery was low and I wanted to listen to the Lux Radio Theater that came on at eight o'clock. As we started eating, I asked Daddy, "Are you going to town?"

"Day after tomorrow," Daddy answered. "You need something?"

"Yes. Staples, like coffee and sugar. I'm nearly out of flour. Some other stuff too. I thought I'd go with you."

Mose added, "I want to mail a letter to my cousin."

"You sure stay in close contact. Didn't I just send a letter for you?"

"Last-a month."

"I'm just joshing you, Mose. 'Course I'll mail it—I've got to go to the post office for the rest of the mail. I haven't picked it up for a couple of weeks."

"Oh yeah," I said, "the battery for the radio needs charged too."

"Well Jesus H. Christ," Daddy said with a mouthful of biscuit and apple butter. "Do you think I'll have time for the rest of my errands?"

He was smiling as he said it, so I knew he was glad I was going along.

As we started down the hill at seven o'clock on Thursday morning, Daddy was quiet, and didn't say much. We got down to Eureka and stopped at O'Mara's Garage. Daddy got out and hoisted the radio battery from the wood box he'd put in the pickup bed and carried it into the station. It was a regular car battery that we had to get charged every couple of weeks, depending on how much we'd played the radio. I sat in the pickup, enjoying the early morning.

After awhile, Daddy came back out with Rocky, who owned the place. I rolled the window down and said, "Hi, Rocky. How's Mrs. O'Mara and the kids?"

"Hi Missy. They're fine. Growing like weeds they are."

"Please say hello for me, would ya?"

"That I will. That I will," Rocky said as he turned the gas pump on and put the hose into the gas tank.

"Ten gallons, please. And check the water and oil would ya?" Daddy said. He got a dollar bill and some coins out of the leather pouch he carried and closed the metal clasp with a "snick". "This damn gas is gonna be up to twenty cents a gallon soon, way it's going," he added. Rocky just smiled and said, "Oil's okay Roscoe," as he took Daddy's money. He touched the bill of his SOCONY hat and went back inside his garage. Daddy and I stopped at the post office where he got our mail and sent Scarlotto's letter. Looking at the electric poles, I could still see remnants of the condemnation notices the city had plastered all over the Rondout Valley last year. The city of New York was claiming by "right of adverse possession," all of the land and property in Eureka, Montela and Lackawack. The city wanted to dam up the Rondout and Chestnut Creeks, then send the water down to Manhattan for drinking. People of the valley, some of whom had lived here for generations, were being evicted. Even though I was a city girl at heart, I felt more sympathy for the folks up here than I ever would for the New York City Board of Water Supply. The BWS it was called. The town folks had their own name, calling it the "Big Wad of Shit." The more I thought about it, the more unfair it seemed.   I mean, just because you want something doesn't mean you have the right to take it. Does it? Didn't we all learn that in Sunday school or from our mothers and fathers? "I need it" isn't reason enough to take someone's heritage, is it? Taking another's property against their will, no matter how it's justified, is just theft. Theft by another name, "right of eminent domain," is still theft. Back where I was raised, theft is theft. Stealing is stealing. Pure and simple.

Daddy, who'd been the taciturn one all morning, reached over and touched my hand. "You okay, sweetheart? You look like you just lost your best friend."

"I was just thinking about the condemnation notices, that's all. I feel bad for all those people losing their homes and farms and businesses. Just doesn't seem fair."

"It's not." Daddy said in his simple, direct way. It was one of the things I loved the most about him. Even with the twenty-five year difference in our ages, he was in touch with my feelings. He understood.

We were on the state road, Route 55, headed south. We'd passed through Montela, a hamlet of a few hundred people, and were just going past a construction site. Traffic was slow. I asked Daddy what they were doing.

"They're getting ready to sink some caissons, down to bedrock. Here is where the dam will be built, right at the county line. We'll be in Ulster County as soon as we get past the construction. It's called Lackawack."

"I know. I feel sorry for the people here . . . losing their homes and all."

"Businesses too," Daddy said, "and farms, schools, property and history."

"Nora Temple told me the people here are calling it 'The Taking.' She said a lot of them were resentful, felt they were being screwed by the city, the prices they were being offered."

"I know they are," Daddy said.

"Anyway," I said, "there's nothing they can do about it. These are real, live ghost towns; they will be gone from the earth pretty soon. They're dead. They just haven't died yet."

Daddy looked at me from the corner of his eye, but didn't say a word. Well, it made sense to me . . . we didn't know then that

World War II was going to come along and delay everything for ten years. We headed on south that day, not knowing the future, not even guessing how things would turn out. Daddy had insulated and protected me, but it was going to change soon. "Bidness," as they say, was about to pick up.

I did the food shopping while Daddy went to the bank. We ate a late lunch at Pinto's an Italian restaurant in an old stone cottage just outside Wawarsing, where we had a delicious Scaloppini de Pinto and a bottle of good Chianti. I worried about being seen, but Daddy told me the wise guys never went to restaurants before nine or ten o'clock at night. He was his old self in there, enjoying our first meal out in a long, long time. I kept watching, looking around as if my head was on a turntable.

On the way back to Eureka, Daddy turned serious. "Arlene," he said, "listen to me. There's been a lot of activity down here. Civilians were talking about all the city guys up here with suits and big fancy cars, guys with too much money and too much attitude. They stick out. The locals notice it. I heard it at the bank, both banks, in fact, and the hardware store. Something's up, but I don't know what."

I felt as if something icy had just touched the base of my spine, then my bladder, finally settling in my stomach. I had an urge to pee.

"Are we in danger?"

"I honestly don't know," Daddy said. "I got five thousand out of the safe deposit just in case. It's all in old fives, ones and a few tens from the numbers games up in Harlem. Don't ever take more than a few dollars out at once. I'll put the rest of them in the bookcase."

"Underneath the false-bottom shelf. I know."

"Do you think you can drive by yourself now? Are you confident?"

"I think so. Guess I won't know until I do."

Daddy pulled off the road, under some trees. "Okay. You drive."

I slid over under the steering wheel. Daddy got in on the other side. I started the Ford pickup and pushed in the clutch, moved the floor shift to the bottom left of the "H," just like he'd showed me, that's where first gear was, gave it some gas and let the clutch out. At which point I stalled it with a lurch.

"Forgot to release the hand brake. Better check for traffic before you pull out too."

"I know that," I said. "I just forgot is all."

He looked out the window, didn't say a word. *Good thing too,* I thought.

I drove us all the way back to Eureka where we stopped at Rocky's for the charged-up battery, more gasoline and a quart of oil.

We got back to the house in the late afternoon. I scrambled around for dinner fixings, frying up some hamburger steaks and potatoes for a quick supper. I was just finishing drying the dishes while Daddy, with Scarlotto watching in his silent way, hooked up the Zenith radio and turned it on.

When he did, we heard for the first time that the giant German airship, *Hindenburg,* had burned, then crashed, at Lakehurst, New Jersey, that very afternoon, May 6, 1937. We were riveted to the radio, listening to the replays and updates, until late in the night. By the next day the disaster was common knowledge everywhere —thanks to the radio. It may even have been the first-ever on-the-scene reporting of a disaster as it was happening, for all I knew. It sure gave me the shivers when I heard it.

Nineteen thirty-seven, my second year in hiding from the

syndicate, was a year full of surprises, world changing events, tragedies and personal heartache. In just a few weeks during May, June and July, the *Hindenburg* crashed; the Golden Gate Bridge opened in San Francisco; the Duke of Windsor, who would have been the King of England, abdicated the throne in order to marry a commoner, American divorcée Mrs. Wallis Simpson; Amelia Earhart disappeared over the Pacific Ocean while circumnavigating the globe in her twin-engined airplane; the Japanese army invaded China; and SPAM, the ham-based mystery meat in a tin can was introduced in grocery stores across America.

Down in the city, Thomas E. Dewey, the federal prosecutor for the Southern District of Manhattan, obtained grand jury indictments against Dixie Davis, who was Dutch Schultz's crooked attorney, George Weinburg and Harry Schoenhaus for policy racketeering —a numbers-based form of illegal lottery—up in Harlem. The three were almost the last members of the Schultz gang, and the keys which would allow Dewey to go after Jimmy Hines, the Tammany Hall politician who'd been on Schultz's payroll. That left only Daddy, Edward J. Geary himself, as the last man standing of the Schultz mob. That was mid-July.

Three weeks later, the body of Walter Sage, a Murder, Inc. hit man "bellied up like a dead fish" in White Lake, New York, not more than twenty-five miles from our farm in Neversink. He'd been stabbed twenty-seven times with an ice pick, garroted and lashed with bailing wire to a slot-machine frame. At almost the same time, only a few days later, on a Saturday so perfect it could have come straight from God's very idea of Eden . . . Daddy disappeared.

He had started out around six thirty in the morning. It was

the same as most other Saturdays: errands, some shopping, take the battery to O'Mara's for charging, go to the bank . . . all the minutiae of ordinary lives. We both forgot, for only an instant, that our lives weren't ordinary; we were the hunted, the chased, the prey. We let our guard down. Now, we were paying the price. Daddy was gone.

He went to the hardware store in Kingston while I was at the grocery. I had the pickup. Daddy walked three blocks over to the Hudson Valley Hardware on Water Street. He waved, walking backwards, said he'd meet me back at the Ford pickup in a half hour or so and we'd have lunch on our way home. That was the last time I ever saw him. I've seen his image a million times in my head, smiling and walking backwards; I didn't know he was stepping out of my life forever.

I looked and looked, all that afternoon and evening. I drove up and down alleys and side streets, searched the hardware store, the barbershops, the bars and restaurants, I even walked along the docks down by the river, trying to find Daddy, trying to find someone, anyone . . . who'd seen him. It was all for naught. There wasn't a trace of him. It was as if he'd disappeared into the ether, rode a radio beam out beyond the stars and landed in another dimension. Daddy was gone and I knew somehow, he'd never return. I was certain of it. I was also certain, somehow, he was no longer among the living; our psychic connection was broken.

I made it back to the farm in Neversink late Sunday night, hungry, exhausted and broken-hearted. I left the pickup in the front yard under the big sugar maple, the forgotten groceries still on the passenger seat and on the floorboards. The house was empty, dark and hot. I curled up in the porch glider and fell asleep.

I woke cold and stiff. The dawn was just breaking and Ella Allen was licking my face while Scarlotto gravely watched from his seat at the top of the porch steps. The early morning dew was heavy on the grass and sparkled in the rising sun. I sat up, ruffled Ella Allen's fur. She wagged her tail, cautious, her head tilted to one side like she was concerned and confused at the same time.

Scarlotto said, "What's-a the matter?"

"Everything's the matter. The fat's in the fire for sure. I can't find Daddy. He's-been-missing-since-Saturday-morning-when-he-went-to-the-hardware-I-went-to-the-grocery-he-never-came-back-I've looked and looked and . . . Oh, Jesus. Sweet Jesus, he's gone." And then I started to cry and I just couldn't. Stop. Crying.

"I go make-a the fire," Scarlotto said. After some minutes of weeping, from sorrow or self-pity or maybe both, I gathered myself up and went to the kitchen where I busied myself in life's little routines.

I made coffee and realized I hadn't eaten since Saturday morning. I made a big breakfast, pancakes, eggs and ham slices from one of the smoked hams in the cold room. I ate like a farmhand at haying time. I started getting back to the hard, hard business of living.

While we were at breakfast, I told Scarlotto everything. I told him about Daddy's being involved with Otto Berman, and Otto being Dutch Schultz's right-hand man. The shoot-out, the fight between Schultz and Lucky Luciano over Schultz's plan to assassinate Thomas E. Dewey and last, I told him about Schultz's supposed hidden treasure, including the fact that Daddy had absolutely no idea if or where any treasure was hidden, but some of Luciano's syndicate guys were convinced he did . . . and that that was the reason we were hiding out up here. I even told him our real names: Edward Geary and Arlene Bradley.

Scarlotto wasn't much when it came to conversation, but he was an excellent listener. He nodded with old-world dignity at certain points during my narrative and confession. He didn't say a word in fact, until I had spilled my guts, as Daddy used to say, telling the old man everything but my bra and panty sizes. When I'd finished, Scarlotto said something I'll never forget, even though his meaning wasn't clear to me until much later.

"I'll be-a goddamned," he said, and then genuflected, making the sign of the cross on his chest and forehead.

Scarlotto stared off into space, taking a sip of cold coffee now and then. Finally, after ten or fifteen minutes of silence, he spoke.

"What you want-a do?

"I'm not sure," I said, "I haven't had time to think about it much, but I don't have anywhere else to go. I haven't any living relatives that I know of. They died in the influenza epidemic in 1918. I was twelve at the time, been on my own ever since."

"That's sad-a story."

"Oh, I ain't the first one to live through hard times. Won't be the last. What if we just stay here? Until Daddy comes back." I said with more hope than expectation.

"I don't think he will be back."

I agreed with him but I could not say it out loud. I just looked away, my eyes brimming with tears at what I knew in my heart was true.

Somehow, I made it through the rest of that awful Monday and the day that followed. I couldn't go to the cops. What would I say?

"Hi. I'd like to report a missing person, his name is Roscoe . . . no, Edward . . . we're ah, hiding out up here under assumed names?" Oh, yeah. That would go over like bathtub gin at the Women's Christian Temperance Union meetings. Besides, I think, truth be told, at least half the cops in the state work for the gangsters. All I could do was wait, and hope. Maybe even pray.

Somehow, the days melted into a week, then the weeks went by and fall came. Scarlotto ran the farm, I ran the house and just existed. I lied like a four-year-old full of cookie crumbs about Daddy's whereabouts. I told the folks over in Eureka that he was working in the city. I knew everyone was gossiping about me but there was nothing I could do. I just endured, only half-aware of the gossip, only half-caring about any of it. I went through the motions of living, but truth was, I only existed for the rest of 1937. I cooked and cleaned, washed clothes and dishes. I listened to the radio but it no longer held the same joy. My contact with the outside world was limited: Rocky at the garage, Frank Chambers at the post office and Cody and Lorna Smith at the grocery store in Eureka were the sum total of my social set. And those were limited to short weekly or biweekly conversations. No wonder I was going nuts, little by little, day by day, hour by hour.

I cooked a turkey for Thanksgiving even though it was just me and Scarlotto. It was a small turkey, only a bit bigger than a plump chicken, but we still ate turkey meals for the rest of the week.

I got depressed when Christmas came without Daddy. We hadn't had even a hint of him. I gave Scarlotto a wool hat and a can of Sir Walter Raleigh smoking tobacco and made us a big pot roast. He gave me a precious carving of a seated collie dog that looked for all the world like Ella Allen. It was about ten inches tall, well made and lifelike. Scarlotto had carved and whittled it from a piece of soft pine firewood.

"Scarlotto, I had no idea you were so talented," I said. "Thank you ever so much, I love it. It's beautiful."

Scarlotto, taciturn as ever, gave me a small smile then puffed on his pipe and gazed out the kitchen window. I put the statue on the table, poured us each more coffee while the radio played "O Holy Night" and other carols through the afternoon.

And so, Christmas 1937 slipped into the past.

The New Year came in, and I was still in a funk. I had my thirty-second birthday by myself on February twentieth, got a bit tipsy all by myself, and cried for a while, thinking about Daddy. In the second week of March, my world was tipped upside down once again . . . when Scarlotto came down with a cold.

We'd had typical March weather. It was warm, in the high sixties, with bright sunshine one day, then the clouds would roll in, rain would start, then sleet, ice and snow and the thermometer would drop down in the low twenties. We were in the middle of maple syrup season, tapping the maple trees with a drill bit, then pounding in a three-inch metal spike—sort of a miniature faucet—with a hammer and hanging a ten-quart sap bucket to collect the sap that dripped from the tree. In wet years like this, we'd put a little piece of tin "roof" over the top of the bucket to keep the rain out. Scarlotto or I would go out every day with Jack, the big draft horse, who pulled a farm sled with twelve, forty-quart stainless steel milk cans on the back that we emptied the sap buckets into. After the sap was collected, we took it to the sap house where it was boiled off in a series of pans until it became maple syrup. It took about forty gallons of sap to make a quart of maple syrup. We did it because it was a cash crop that we sold to produce income.

The sap house had to be constantly watched. As each pan of the raw sap was boiled down, the concentrate was drained and put in a series of smaller pans until it became pure syrup. The series of pans was to make the process continuous, from a one hundred gallon pan for the raw sap down to a six-gallon industrial cook kettle for the syrup. It was hot, demanding work. In addition to keeping the fire stoked, the boiling sap had to be constantly skimmed to remove the foamy crust that rose up to the top, as well as other impurities, like wood ash or charcoal. The day dawned nice, but had, all of a sudden turned wet—rain, then a snow squall caught Scarlotto in the middle of the collection run. His teeth were chattering and his lips had turned blue by the time he unhooked Jack's harness at the end of the shed.

Scarlotto came in wet to the skin from collecting sap.

"You'd best get some dry clothes on, you look drowned and frozen."

"W-w-will as soon I dry Jack, put him in-a his stall."

Scarlotto led the horse to the barn and dried him with a burlap feed sack. He made sure there was fresh straw on the floor, fresh water, hay and grain. Then, the old man went to his room and dried himself off, changed his clothes and came up to the sap house. I had a pot of hot coffee, and poured a cup, handed it to him. "Here. Drink this and sit here, next to the fire."

Scarlotto took the cup, nodded thanks. He looked shrunken from the drenching he'd received and continued to shiver uncontrollably. He didn't look good. I had a fry pan, eggs and bread and a place on the edge of the firebox under the evaporator where I could cook. I fried a couple of eggs and made him a sandwich. Scarlotto took a bite, drank some coffee.

"Are you warming up?" I asked.

"Yeah."

His eyes were bright but not feverish and he looked like he was getting warm.

"You tend the fire for a while," I said. "I'm going to get the sap cans unloaded and in the tank. This batch is about ready to be drained."

At the time, I thought I had everything under control. At the time, I had no idea how wrong I was.

By the next morning, Scarlotto had a runny nose, constant cough and a sore throat. His condition worsened all day and he grew feverish. I did what I could for him, kept him warm and made hot broth, but he just got sicker. No matter how I nursed him with aspirin, soup and hot plasters. Nothing much helped. Five or six days after the storm his lungs were badly congested, his temperature was 104 degrees and he was dying from pneumonia. I had him on a pallet in the kitchen by then, so I could keep him warm and as comfortable as possible. I wasn't getting much sleep myself — a few minutes here, a half hour there — trying to do all the farm chores and be a nurse too. Then Scarlotto started to hallucinate, talking to ghosts, childhood friends and all of a sudden, out of the blue, he was talking to Daddy. He was talking to Daddy not as Roscoe, his fake name, but as Blackie, his real nickname from when he was Edward Geary – Otto Berman's right-hand man.

As I listened to the mutterings and ravings of the feverish old man, I realized that Scarlotto wasn't who Daddy and I thought he was either. To my increasing horror, Scarlotto was implicating himself in Daddy's disappearance and death. He was a spy for the syndicate, the Italian gangsters we were hiding from. Those bastards! They had known where we were all along. Scarlotto's letters in Sicilian weren't to his cousin — or whoever — they were reports about us, Daddy and me. The bad guys had known all along where we were ...

I believe my revelations to Scarlotto on the Monday I came back from losing Daddy were what finally convinced him Daddy and I didn't know, had never known, about Dutch Schultz's supposed treasure. That was the reason for Scarlotto's "I'll be-a goddamned" comment. I had inadvertently confirmed what he, and others of the Murder, Inc. mob had tortured out of Daddy. All of the hiding, the worrying, the hardship had been for nothing. I had lost Daddy for nothing.

Then I cried, listening to the ravings of that treacherous old man. I could only interpret what he was ranting about; it was impossible to interrogate him. I was repulsed and curious all at the same time, as if I had happened on a big smash up on the highway, then realized the victims were my own family members.

But as Scarlotto began to rave more about Daddy, about what they were doing to him, I went from grief to anger in just a flash of the imagination. I had hoped to endure the mental torture long enough to find out what they'd done with Daddy after ... after he died, but I was too weak.

My anger grew in a flash of self-imposed images into a white-hot explosion as all the neurons in my brain exploded. God help me, save my immortal soul ... I picked up a pillow and smothered the old son-of-a-bitch. Not only was he Judas Iscariot right here under my own roof where I had cooked for, and cared for, and worked beside him, he was the murderer of the man I loved with every atom in my body. The rage I felt consumed me.

Afterward, I was oddly calm. An inner peace descended on me as I went to his room and packed his few possessions into bindles I made from the bedclothes. I carried everything out to the farm sled and loaded it, then I hooked Dolly, the other draft horse, up to the traces. I pulled up to the house, dragged Scarlotto out and loaded him on the sled. I filled four one-gallon vinegar jugs with coal oil and set out for the wood lot up on the very top of the hill. It was the most remote place on the farm.

Up there was a huge pile of slash, the limbs and branches from all the wood that had been cut last summer and fall. I put Scarlotto's body and all of his possessions on the slash, poured the coal oil on and lit the pyre. It burned most of the night and left a sick smelling odor.

I went back up a few days later and raked out all the bones and teeth. I used a two pound sledge hammer and a flat piece of iron I'd found in the shed to pulverize everything to a pulp. Then I scattered the pulp all over the mountain on my way down. *See if they ever find him!*

All that was forty-some years ago. I could see the priest in the confessional was restless, whether from the length of my confession —or its contents—I couldn't tell. I had deliberately gone down to the city to confess, seeking anonymity. Now that my days were numbered, after four decades of living in fear of retribution, I sought absolution; I didn't want to meet up with Scarlotto on the other side of the great divide.

There was silence for some while, then, the priest coughed, and said, "This is a very serious confession. It breaks more than one of the commandments, and God considers *Thou shalt not kill* to be the most serious mortal sin. I'm going to check with Monsignor Falcone."

A bolt of fear shot through me. "Would that be Pietro Falcone by any chance?"

"Why yes, yes it would. Do you know him?"

"I've heard of him."

"He's well known in church circles, and he's been here for fifty years. Begin your penance by reciting the Rosary. I'll be back in a few moments."

The small door that allowed me to speak to him slid shut, and I heard the priest's door open and close as he left the confessional.

By the time he was gone my heart was in my throat, pounding with fear, I was gasping and my body was covered in the cold sweat of a full blown panic attack. I realized I'd made a huge mistake coming here . . . Pietro Falcone was Scarlotto's cousin . . . the one he wrote to every month. I hugged my purse to my chest and slipped out of the booth, quiet as a cat burglar, and hurried away from the confessional hoping, just hoping, to get away before they caught me. I was near hysteria. My footsteps echoing on the marble seemed to be saying, *She's . . . Here . . . She's . . . Here . . . She's . . . Here, Here, Here.*

Irma and Studebaker

1946

Irma and Studebaker

Studebaker Varley was enjoying himself in the afternoon sun, running back and forth along the length of his mother's clothesline, to which he was attached by a seven-foot length of old cotton rope. The clothesline ran fifty feet, out over the grass of the flat side yard and was secured on each end by a six-inch pulley wheel that squeaked when turned. The clothesline and pulleys allowed Irma Varley or one of her daughters to hang the daily washing without having to walk off the porch. It was a small but great convenience for them, and much appreciated, because with twenty people, more or less, to wash and cook for, there was plenty of work to go around.

* * *

The oldest girls, Auburn and Buick, will be married in a few months and leave to start families of their own. Dusenberg, sixteen, and Essex, fifteen, will follow in a couple of years, but Impala, eleven, and pretty little Mercer, only seven, are already helping with chores and dishes. But Lord, help me, Irma thought, *the babies keep coming. God bless Oliver, the insatiable goat.*

* * *

Studebaker was chasing a white cabbage butterfly. He ran to the far end of the clothesline and made a hard turn to the right at full speed. When he hit the end of his tether, the old line broke, sending him face-first into the grass, which was nearly as tall as he was, and it tickled. Shaken by the sudden turn of events he blinked several times, but did not cry, then pushed himself to his feet. Confused at first, he turned around where he stood, realized he was free, and trotted up the dirt driveway as fast as his bare feet and chubby legs could take him . . . looking for more butterflies to chase.

He went a hundred yards or so and was almost at the end of the driveway, where it joined the paved county road, and stopped. He shoved at his sodden diaper with both hands and managed to spring one of the safety pins open, bent over and pushed until he could step out of the wet thing. He couldn't remove his blue polo shirt with the yellow lamb on the front because it was underneath the leather harness his sister Mercer had buckled on him right after lunch. It was originally meant for a Welsh corgi but was just the right size for eighteen-month-old Studebaker. Three feet of gray cotton clothesline tied to the harness trailed behind him as he scampered up the county road toward the woods with his penis bobbing in the sunshine, chasing those elusive butterflies. Having a great time, he was laughing when he went in the woods.

*   *   *

Sweet Jesus, Irma thought. *Sweet Jesus, sweet Mary, blessed thou . . . no, that's not right. Not right.* She sat in the nursing rocker in the bedroom, hers and Oliver's, looking at the wall where the old wallpaper was peeling, showing the lath and horsehair plaster underneath. *Thirty-eight years old, married twenty-two years . . . more than half my life. Eighteen children, all but Studebaker born here in this house, in that bed.* She thought about Studebaker. *The night he was born, breeched, Oliver away somewhere, Mattie taking me up to the hospital in Liberty. The awful, awful pain. The blood. The relief, hearing the baby's first cry.* She blinked, looked at the weary old dresser with the cracked and faded mirror, looked at the kingsize bedstead. *It barely fits in the room.* She thought, *the only piece of new furniture Oliver ever bought.* She stared at it. *So big. So imposing. Like Oliver.* She remembered the afternoon after Studebaker was born. *Oliver, in a rage, dragging me out of the hospital, his size and ferocity scaring everyone, even the police. Oliver yelling, saying, "No kid of mine is gonna be born in a goddamned hospital."* I told the officers, *"No. No charges, no complaint, no signature. No."* She shuddered. *I cannot imagine what he would have done then. It's a miracle the stitches hadn't torn out.* She thought. *I would have bled to death. Right there, in that oversize bed.*

*   *   *

The woods were shady and cool. The woods beckoned and he answered their call. The dry leaves crushed under his feet as Studebaker ran farther in . . . where it was darker.

Something skittered in the leaves and a partridge thundered into the air. Studebaker stopped. He was frightened by the noise and movement. He turned in a small circle, looking, put his left thumb in his mouth for comfort. Where was Mommy? He was alone and scared then, so he sat down and started to cry; the dry leaves were scratchy on his bare behind and he was hungry and tired. He cried harder, and louder, tears and snot covering his face.

He cried for a time, until he started to hiccup and gasp for breath, then he laid down on his side in the dry leaves and slept.

*   *   *

Irma felt too heavy to move. Her arms were granite, her legs marble.

Her body felt like concrete, her head was of poured steel. She was more tired than she could ever, ever remember. *I can't do it.* She thought. *I can't lie in this bed any more. I can't have another baby, can't cook, and wash, and feed them anymore. I just . . . can't.* She raised the prescription bottle and took its entire contents in her mouth, then raised the water glass to her lips. She drank, swallowed and swallowed again.

*   *   *

A horsefly biting his right thigh woke Studebaker. He screamed and rolled over, crying and grabbing his leg. He managed to get to his feet and started running, frightened, alone, bawling at the top of his lungs. He ran out of the woods onto the two-lane county road; he'd been running parallel to it the whole time. His bare feet hurt from the hot asphalt and tar stuck to them. Winded, he sat down on the side of the road. He sat there crying, with his thumb in his mouth, until the old truck with screechy brakes stopped. Studebaker Varley reached up with both hands as strong arms picked him up and comforted him.

Memory and the Nature of Friendship

1949

Memory and The Nature Of Friendship

Claudie and I came up North in the summer of 1949. We left North Carolina and Mister Bailey's tobacco farm, sharecropping, Jim Crow laws, separate drinking fountains, midnight riders, lynchings, those cross-burning Klan sons of bitches, as well as our mothers, Granddaddy Littleton and a host of kinfolk down there in the heat, humidity and fine red dust a few miles outside of Durham. We left. We left everything and everyone. We left what we knew and headed straight into what we didn't know, determined to have a better life, and convinced our future would be better than our past. We said our good-byes, and caught a bus headed north, and neither Claudie nor I ever looked back at tobacco road, or missed Dixie, and the storied land of cotton further south. We headed up north, our thoughts and dreams on our future potential rather than a past built on property rights and the enslavement of one human being by another.

I think, but I'm not sure, it was Sunday when we got off the bus in what seemed like the world's biggest, noisiest, dirtiest, most crowded and confusing bus depot, somewhere in the middle of Manhattan Island. When we stepped off after riding for four days, we were hot and tired, and still wearing the same clothes as when we'd left. I gathered our three bags and asked the driver where we could get coffee, maybe a sandwich. He jerked his thumb over his right shoulder, never turning from the bus compartment where he was grabbing and throwing luggage to the side.

"Back there," he said between bag throws, "in the waiting room."

"Thanks," I said, handing the little bag to Claudie and taking the two big ones. We headed for the lunch counter at the far side of a waiting room that had at least a 150-foot ceiling. It was the biggest room either of us had ever seen.

I didn't see the sign for colored, finally had to ask a brother cleaning out the big ashtrays that were placed along each row of seats.

"Hey man, where the colored section?"

"You just get off the bus?" he said, then he answered his own question before I could say anything. "You sit where you want. You north of the line, man."

"Oh. Yeah," I said. "Thanks, just forgot. Tired, that's all. Too long on the bus."

He nodded and moved to the next ashtray. Claudie and I made it through the crowd, getting bumped a few times before making it to the far corner of the lunch area, where she sat in the last booth. I piled our bags in and sat opposite her.

Claudie finally spoke. "Honey, I'm not sure about this. This place I mean. More people than I've ever seen. None our own kind."

"They here, baby. Uptown a few miles. Harlem. That's where colored folks live," I said.

"Don't care, Joseph. I'm not liking this city much. Don't think I wanna live here."

"You just tired. Lemme get us somethin' to eat. We'll both feel better," I said.

I walked over to the counter and ordered two coffees with cream and sugar, and two hamburger sandwiches. I put a dollar bill on the counter. The grill man took it and put two cups of coffee on the counter. I told him to keep the change. He said he'd bring our sandwiches.

I was concerned that Claudie had used my whole given name. When she said "Joseph" instead of "Joe" or "Honey," it was her way of showing she was upset, and was serious about what she'd said. The only thing worse was when she said my given, and Christian names together, "Joseph Washington Cooley," like that. Then I knew it was time to surrender. I had my manly pride, but there were times, Claudie was the boss.

I was concentrating on the coffees, trying not to slop them into the saucers. I was halfway across the room, trying not to bump into people before I saw him. Some zoot-suited nigger in a white snap-brim hat and two-tone white and brown wingtips was sitting in my seat. As I got closer I could see the tooth pick in the corner of his mouth and a long silver chain that hung from his pants pocket down to the floor. He was saying something to Claudie. Had his hands on the table, reaching toward her.

Claudie saw me and looked up. Her eyes were wide open and her mouth was set, her teeth clenched.

"You in the wrong seat," I said.

"Who you?"

"The lady's husband. You best move on."

"And if I don't want to move on?" he said.

I stared at him for a few moments as I set the coffee down. "Then," I said, "we have a beef."

He stared back at me. Then took the toothpick from his mouth. He looked at my blue denim shirt and old dungarees. I had my weight mostly on my right foot, behind me, left foot forward, the basic combat stance I'd learned in the army. I waited.

"Feisty little nigger, ain't cha?" he said.

"Feisty enough," I said.

"Wouldn't want that," he said. The zoot-suiter stood and tossed his used toothpick in my direction. He touched the brim of his hat, nodded to Claudie, and said, "Momma, another time," then strolled off into the crowd. I watched him go.

"Joseph, please sit, honey. Let's have some coffee," Claudie said.

"You all right, honey?" I said.

"Of course."

"You sure?"

"Yes, honey. Take more'n a hustler like him to hurt me."

"Two-bit motherfucker," I said.

"Don't talk like that."

"Sorry, Claudie. I'm sorry, honey. It just made me mad. I'se only gone five minutes . . ."

"It takes two to boogie, honey, and you're my dance partner, always."

The counterman brought two hamburger sandwiches wrapped in wax paper and two cardboard containers of french fries on a tray. He left everything on the table without saying anything and went back to his grill.

"Friendly folks here," I said as I took a hound-sized bite out of my sandwich. Claudie grinned at me as she chewed the end of a french fry, looking around at the crowd of people. I could tell she was thinking, didn't interrupt her. She ate slowly and continued watching the noise and commotion, not saying a word.

We didn't have a plan when we left North Carolina. Despite all our hopes and dreams, despite all of our talks while riding the bus and despite all of our ambitions and our intentions, we had no idea what we should do next, where we would live, work or what we could do. We huddled together in the booth, looking at the people in motion around us, feeling alone.

I thought Claudie was sleeping, she'd had her eyes closed for some while. I'd gone through two cups of coffee and was starting to think about the restroom when she opened her eyes and said, " I know."

"You know what?" I said.

"I know this city ain't for us," She said. "I know we're country folks and that's where we need to be. I been praying about it and I know."

"You sure?" I said.

"Sure as can be, honey. The Lord told me. Yes, I am sure."

Claudie was a God-fearing woman. She had fifteen cloisonné pins from the Freedom Baptist Church back in Brownsburg attesting to fifteen straight years of perfect Sunday school attendance to prove it. And she put into practice what she learned there. Although I couldn't claim, not for an instant, to be the equivalent Christian man, I respected Claudie's wishes, right down to my bones.

"You're sure," I said.

Claudie looked at me. She looked me right in the eyes, but didn't say anything until I looked away.

"Yes," she said, "I am sure."

"Okay," I said, "let's go find the country. But first I got to find the restrooms."

I found the bathroom without difficulty, but then I found a real treasure: the shoeshine man. See, white folks don't know it, but the shoeshine man is like the Delphi Oracle and the *Encyclopedia Britannica* all rolled up in one. All day long he's keeping his head down, shinin' them shoes for all them important white folks, just a-shinin' and a-shinin', and all the while he's shining, he's listening. He listens and hears. He hears market tips, inside information, political intrigue, even a few nefarious schemes and illegal acts by good and bad guys. If he's not shining shoes and listening to the rich and famous, he's reading. Someone's always leaving a newspaper or magazine after a shine. Some days there's two, three different newspapers to choose from. I know because I shined shoes for a time, before I went in the army, back in '43. Anyhow, I found the shoeshine man, and he was a kindly old gentleman with a wealth of knowledge. His name, I found out, was Bill Burton.

Mr. Burton told me that here in New York City, the country was about one hundred miles north, a place called the Catskill Mountains, in Sullivan County. He also told me there was a lot of work up there; the city was building a couple of big water projects at a place called Neversink, and at a place called Lackawack. The last thing he said was, "And don't let'em give you no shit neither. It's a gov'ment job. They gots to hire minorities at the same pay as the white folk. The racial crap ain't quite as bad up here, but it's here, all the same. They just ain't as apparent about it. God bless you, boy. And good luck." I thanked Mr. Burton and gave him a half-dollar for the shine and tip.

Claudie and I took turns sleeping on the waiting room benches and watched the sun, rising orange and red over the high Palladian windows of the depot. At 8:10 the next morning we boarded the Short Line bus, bound for Middletown, Monticello and Liberty, with a half hour rest stop at Suffern. We were second or third on the bus and sat toward the front . . . a novel experience for us. We were as excited as a couple of ten-year-olds at a carnival.

The bus chugged uptown and made a series of turns at Lexington Avenue and 125th Street, and we crossed the Hudson River on the big George Washington Bridge.

"Look, honey, you can see boats," Claudie said. "I wonder how high we are?"

"High enough," I said, trying not to look out or down. I felt sweat run down my underarms and back. I do not care for heights. Not me, not one bit. I had sweat on my lip, and my gut was doing backflips with a full twist by the time we crossed over. Safe on solid ground again, I let out a sigh and drew in air.

"You okay, Joey?" Claudie said.

"Oh yeah, Claudie. Too much bus riding and lack of sleep I guess."

"Too much road food too." She said, "I'll get 'choo fixed right up soon's we get a place to stay."

"Uh-huh," I said. I was looking forward to Claudie's cooking, because she was renowned for it. I mean, that woman can cook. Her biscuits so light and fluffy they damn near float off the table. Her fried chicken so good the chickens fight with each other to get cleaned, plucked and dipped in flour by Miz Claudie. I mean, DAMN it's good. Just thinking about it made me feel so fine, I snuggled up next to Claudie and fell asleep. I woke at Suffern, where we both went to the restrooms and bought a couple of nasty looking, desiccated ham-and-cheese sandwiches and Yoo-Hoo chocolate sodas that we ate for lunch. I leaned on Claudie and fell asleep again.

As I slept I started dreaming. I was back in the army, at the Bulge, slipping in the snow, ice and fog all around me, freezing, freezing in the forest . . . then gunfire everywhere, small arms, artillery shells screaming in, trees shattering, falling right at me, Tiger tanks coming through the woods, ground shaking, shaking.

"Joey, wake up. You're having those bad dreams again. Wake up honey."

Claudie's voice soothes me, I know where I am, fall asleep again. I dream again. Crossing the Rhine on pontoon bridges the engineers have laid down. I know somehow, that I'm in Germany. The war, over. I wake again, sweaty, panting, groggy. We're in Liberty. We're in the Catskill Mountains.

Claudie is excited, chirping like a mother robin with her first egg.

"I knew Liberty was the right choice" she said, "there's hills and trees, green grass and animals. We been going past farms. I seen barns and cows, hay and fields. This place is gonna be good, honey. We'll do okay here."

"Sure honey," I said. "I'm sure we will." Liberty, for all of its name appeal and implied promise of freedom, looked to me to be an old small town. Not as old as European towns I'd seen, but older than most places. From what I could see, I'd guess five to ten thousand people. The buildings were a mix of old, older and oldest. The exception was the post office. It looked like one of those New Deal ones that FDR built before the war. One thing was certain though: the faces I saw were of the white kind. I didn't see any brothers or sisters.

The bus dropped us in the center of town at a small depot that doubled as a taxi stand. It was the middle of the afternoon.

"Let's head over there," I said, pointing to a storefront across the street that had a neon sign that said "EATS" in green letters.

"You always hungry, baby. 'Sides, we need to find a place to stay, least for a few days."

Truth was, I was nervous, and worried. Were we the only Negroes in Liberty? Had we managed to stumble right into a northern enclave of what we'd fled from, down south? We made it to the café across the street, still carrying our suitcases.

We sat in the café for ten minutes before the waitress came out of the kitchen and took our order for coffees with hamburger sandwiches again because they'd sold out of the luncheon special. The waitress didn't refuse to serve us, but made it plain she wasn't happy about waiting on us either. I looked at Claudie and shrugged. Her face was a study of impassivity, but the hurt in her eyes hurt me. Then again, what's new . . .

We ate slowly and took stock. I still had my savings and mustering out pay, close to $1,200 sewn into the lining of my shirt, another $18 in traveling money, mostly ones and a couple of fives spread around in various pant and shirt pockets, and Claudie had a couple of ten dollar bills . . . our emergency money . . . in her brassiere. We needed to find a place to stay and a bank to put our money in.

The waitress had left our check when she'd brought the food. When I turned it over the total was $1.50 for the exact same meal we'd had the day before in the city for ninety cents. Mr. Burton the shoeshine man had told me the Catskills were a summer tourist area. "Be aware," he'd said, "they hike up the price of everything in the summertime."

"Why?" I'd asked.

"Take advantage of the tourists."

"Oh," I'd said.

Now I remembered. *Welcome to the Catskills,* I thought as I laid down a dollar bill and two quarters. I didn't leave no tip either.

We'd gathered our things, and prepared to get a taxi over at the bus depot. As we stood at the curb, waiting for the traffic to clear, an old sedan with old-fashioned wire spoke wheels and a tarred canvas roof stopped and a voice called out the open window, "Hey, brother. Y'all needin' a ride?" It was the moment Claudie and I met Harold Jones, Junior. He was driving a 1928 Model A Ford four-door sedan that looked like Ernest Hemingway had used it for ambulance duty during the Spanish Civil War. There were dents everywhere, rust holes and metal patches made from flattened tin cans that were fastened with metal screws. Driving it was Junior Jones, the sole owner and proprietor, driver and chief mechanic of the Snappy Cab Company. I knew this because it was written in pencil on the cowling. The man driving was the blackest Negro I had ever seen.

"Ah know," he said, "she ain't good to look at but she getcha any place yuh want. C'mon. Hop in. Traffic be backin' up. People be honkin' an' shit."

I looked at Claudie. She gave a little grin and reached for the door handle. I chucked the bags up front with the driver and followed her.

We were barely into the backseat when Junior took off and made an immediate right turn followed by another one into an alley, where he stopped. I thought he meant to rob us, but he turned toward us and said, "I just loves puttin' it to them white boys over at the bus depot."

"Stealing fares?" I said.

"Hell yes."

"Don't the other cab drivers get mad about that?" Claudie said.

"Bout like a tomcat in a tub of wash water," Junior said, then added, "course its like old man Caywood say, "Catchin' come before hangin'. I ain't intendin' on bein' catched, neither. Ah'm faster than bad intentions. Now, where can I take you-all?"

With his help we found a quiet place to live, near a corner store where we could get some groceries and the necessities, that was within easy walking distance. It was in a neighborhood of old houses, most of them lived in for a long time, by Negro families. Our one-story frame house had two bedrooms and a kitchen, living room, indoor bathroom and a front porch. It was way better than what we were used to in North Carolina, and best of all, it was two streets over from the main road so we didn't get all the dust and noise from the trash haulers going to the town landfill of a day. The place came with some furnishings, enough to get by with anyway, and Claudie started right in cleaning and sweeping, making it her own. She sent me to the store with a list of things to get.

I got to the store with Junior's help. I just went ahead and hired him for the whole next day, figuring I'd have plenty of errands, and more importantly, get the layout of the town.

Junior was waiting for me at the curb when I came out with a couple of big boxes full of groceries, canned goods and paper goods.

I said, "Junior, where's the liquor at? I didn't see none in there."

"That's the A&P," he said, "they don't sell no alcohol. Whatcha want, wine, whiskey, shine . . . ?"

"Beer. Just some beer."

"We'll go to the liquor sto'," he said.

He took me to another street, a bit farther uptown, where I bought six bottles of Knickerbocker beer, because I liked the funny name.

We went back to the house, where Claudie cooked up a mess of pancakes and eggs in a borrowed frying pan over an open fire in the weedy backyard because there was no gas in the propane bottle under the kitchen window. Junior and I sat on the back steps, and watched Claudie cooking, while we drank Knickerbocker out of brown bottles wrapped in paper bags. Then the three of us ate pancakes smeared with apple butter and fried eggs from paper plates, sitting on the back steps. We watched the moon rise, and drank the last of our beers. It was a good first day.

The next morning broke overcast and wet with a constant light drizzle. It wasn't heavy enough to call it rain, but it sure as hell wasn't dry either. I put it down in my mind as "northern" weather. Claudie made me some cold cereal in a bowl with milk and some hot coffee in a pint mason jar.

Junior showed up at a few minutes after nine.

"Wet this morning," he said as he came to the door.

"Maybe it won't last."

"Wouldn't count on it."

"You-all go for the propane first thing," Claudie said.

I told her I would and we took off in Junior's Snappy Cab.

I paid cash to the gas man, who promised to deliver it before noon, and put the deposits at the electric company and fuel oil company so we'd have heat when fall and winter got here in another few weeks. I was starting to get the layout of the town from my errands. Junior was keeping up a stream of chatter, some helpful, some not. Helpful was when he said, "So this here joint, the 22 Tavern, you wanna stay out of there. It's all redneck ofays. They'll hurt you. You can go to Larry's Bar, over on High Street, it's okay. But the 22 is where they'll stomp your ass for the fun of it. Won't nobody see nothin' neither."

"Sounds like down South."

"It is. Don't go thinkin' it's all great up here, 'cause it ain't. Not as bad as them southern motherfuckers that'll cut your nuts off and hang ya, but don't let'cher guard down neither."

"I hear you," I said. "I ain't really much of a drinkin' man anyway but I like to play cards and throw the bones . . ."

"Cards and dice at Shorty's barbershop. Mos' any time. In back. You can say my name. It's okay. They know me."

"Where do our people go?" I said.

"Mostly to the Downtown Lounge. You like eye-talian food," he said, "we'll go there and have lunch."

Junior drove out of town a ways and pulled into a big dirt parking lot next to a white stucco building. It looked like it had been built before the First World War, had an arched top, like the Alamo down in Texas. A weather-beaten sign on the front spelled "Downtown Lounge" in red neon letters.

"Used to be a hotel," Junior said.

"What happened to it?"

"Went broke during the war. One of the few that never caught fire."

"Caught fire?"

"Oh yeah," Junior said. " It's a epidemic up here. They calls it Jewish Lightning.

"Jewish Lightning?" I said.

"Its spontaneous 'bustion. Happens when mortgage papers rub 'gainst the fire insurance."

"You mean spontaneous combustion?"

"What I said," he answered. "C'mon, let's eat."

We went in and had meatball sandwiches and a couple of draft beers, and I met Little Al and Ruby Duncan who owned the place. Nice folks. I could see why their place was successful . . . great food and friendly owners, nice atmosphere. It reminded me of some Paris cafés I'd been in when I was on leave in 1946. Little Al invited me back on a weekend night when there would be live entertainment. I thought Ruby and Claudie would like each other, said I'd bring her. When Junior and I left we were in good spirits.

I wanted to go to a bank next, to deposit the cash I had sewn in my shirt. I also needed to find a car to drive, so Claudie and I could get around. When I asked Junior if he knew of any cars for sale, he thought about it for a moment before saying yes, he did.

Junior said, "You care what kind of car?"

"Nope. Want one that runs okay and don't cost a whole lot. Don't want too new or too old."

"I know where one at. Had my eye on it for a while, 'bout ten, 'lebben years old. Belong to a friend of mine, didn't come back from North Africa in 1943. Car's been in a garage over at his momma's."

"Think she would sell it?"

"Not sure. Mebbe if I ast, I'll go see if she's home, while you at the bank."

"Okay," I said.

Junior dropped me off at the bank, right on Main Street; where I went to open a savings account; where I got my first lesson in living among the white folk up North.

I had $1,180 left from my army savings. I figured I'd put $750 into a savings account. When I stepped up to the teller's cage a young, mousy-looking white girl was sorting bills in a drawer under the counter. When she finished, she looked up and gave an involuntary start, like when the unexpected happens in the movies, and stepped back a half step.

"Yesss. . . can I help you?" she said.

"I'd like to open a savings account," I said.

"Oh. You'll have to talk to Mr. Cohen. "His office is over there." She pointed to a man sitting at a desk across the lobby by the front door. "I'll call him."

I went back to where he was sitting. He hung up the phone and rearranged some papers on his desk. Then he motioned me over. I sat down, said I wanted to open a savings account. I saw a wood and brass plate on his desk that said, "ELLIOT COHEN, ASST. V.P.," wondered to myself what an "Asst. V.P." was.

"We don't open accounts for less than ten dollars."

"I have more than that."

"How much more?"

"Seven hundred forty."

"Where'd you get it?"

"Saved it."

"Where from?"

"Combat," I said, "with the United States Army. Two Corps. Europe, 1944 to 1945, from the Bulge to Berlin. Then the army of occupation, 1945 to 1948. I mustered out as a sergeant, E-6, Purple Heart and Bronze Star. Anything else, or you ready to open my account now?" I noticed the teller and another customer looking at us, hadn't realized I'd raised my voice.

"No offense mister . . ."

"Cooley," I said, "Joseph W."

We got the paperwork out of the way then, and I got a blue passbook with my deposit printed on the first line. I told Mr. Cohen I would bring Claudie in next week to put her on the account too. He said that would be fine. I got up to leave, we didn't shake hands and I left. *Nice doing business,* I thought. *Yeah. You betcha. Some things don't change with geography.*

Junior was parked just down the block and he pulled right up as I stepped to the curb.

"Did you have fun in there?"

I didn't say anything.

Junior was diplomatic, and kept quiet for a couple of minutes.

"Welcome to Sullivan County," I said.

Junior snorted, giggled and took off up Main Street.

"Where are we going?"

"Auntie's house to look at Ray-Ray's car," Junior said. "Her name is Louise Wray. She be like fambly to me. Her son Ray-Ray and I grew up together. He the one in North Africa. Place called Kaisserine Pass."

"Where the big tank battle was?"

"Yeah."

"That was quite a soirée'" I said.

"What that . . . sore-way?"

"Soirée'," I said. "It's French for dance, kind of a party dance. Like that."

"Oh," he said.

"Sorry Junior, I was being sarcastic. The Kaisserine Pass was a helluva battle. Lot of good men died there, broke the back of the

Afrika Korps. They lost a lot of their tanks."

"Yeah."

I felt bad for being so insensitive. Me, the guy just up on his high horse, feelings hurt and all pissed off over some white guy being an asshole, making racial comments, acting like such a dumbass to a guy who was bent over backwards being a friend to me. I shut up and looked out the window at the scenery. It had stopped raining.

Junior drove us to a part of town I hadn't been in. We stopped in the driveway of a two-story bungalow with a porch in front.

"This be Auntie Louise house. I told her you my friend, just move here an' need a car. All the locals been hot fo' it, she don't want to sell it to any of 'em 'cuz she think they tear it up. And all the other guys be mad at her. She don't want to show favorites. You be a good choice, bein' a nonlocal." Junior said.

"Okay, Junior, I'll do whatever you-all think best if I like it well enough to buy."

"Oh, you'll like it. Guaranteed."

We went up to the backdoor by the kitchen. Junior knocked and a white lady about fifty years old came and opened it.

"Hello, Harold," she said. "Is this your friend about Raymond's car?"

"Yes, ma'am. This is my friend Joe Cooley. I'm helping him and his wife, Claudie, get settled in. They came by bus so he needs a car."

"How do you do, Mr. Cooley?" She said.

"How do you do, ma'am? Please call me Joe."

"Joe it is. Has Harold told you about the car?"

"No ma'am, he hasn't," I said.

"I figured I'd let him see for himself, Aunt Louise."

"Okay. Why don't you go look at it? I want you to know Mr. Cooley, I won't sell it for any less than two hundred fifty dollars. Cash."

"Yes, ma'am. I understand," I said.

She gave Junior the keys to the car and he took me to a garage that stood next to the house. It was a big one with double doors that swung out on hinges. The doors had big wooden Xs on them, painted white to contrast with the green of the house and garage. Inside was a maroon 1937 Ford five-window coupe with chrome-tipped dual exhaust pipes that stuck out below the rear bumper. It didn't have a scratch or dent that I could see, as it was covered with dust. Inside, the mohair was like new under the red plaid blanket that covered the seat. I noticed a big red and white marble on the gearshift lever that stuck up from the floor. The odometer read 31,127, and it still had an "A" gas ration stamp on the front windshield. My heart gave a little flutter and surrendered on the spot, right there in the dusty garage. I was in love. I had to have her. I opened the hood with Junior's help; he showed me how to turn the handle on the hood.

"It's got an eighty-five horsepower vee-eight. Back in the day this be the cat's nuts," Junior said.

"You know much about this car?" I said.

"Oh yeah. I was here the day Ray-Ray pulled it in here. This car was his pride an' joy."

"You think it'll run okay?"

"Change oil and drain old gasoline out, this car run like a watch," Junior said.

"Needs tires, these are all cracked."

"Sho'. Still cost two-fifty though."

"Okay," I said. "Let's go pay Mrs. Wray."

"Good idea."

The sun came out as we went back to the screen door and knocked. I told Mrs. Wray I'd like to buy the car.

She asked me again if I had cash. I told her yes, and would pay her now if she had the papers. She told Junior and me to go sit at the picnic table in the yard. She came out in a few minutes with a cigar box and Coca-Colas for us. She wrote a bill of sale and gave me the registration papers.

"Thank you for selling the car to me, Mrs. Wray. I'll take good care of it," I said.

"You're welcome, Joe. It was time, "she said, and went back in the kitchen and shut the door. Junior and I closed and locked the garage and headed back downtown.

"You know where I can get the car fixed?" I asked.

"Headed there now," Junior said. "Take you to Gatemout's Flying A. He's what keep this beauty running so fine. He a brother too. Price be right and job be done right. He honest and treat you good."

I noticed that Junior slipped in and out of black idiom or "street patois" sort of at will, but I didn't say anything about it. "Okay," I said.

Bobby "Gatemout" Franklin was built like a giant grouper fish: nearly as thick as he was tall, and a mouth that looked like it belonged on an American bulldog. I saw right away why he was called Gatemout.

Junior introduced us, and I told Gatemout about the car, gave him the keys.

"I'll get it and take care of it fo' you. You're pretty lucky. Every cat in town been after dat car. I'll fix what it need. Y'all come by tomorrow afternoon," Gatemout said. "Should be done by then."

I thanked him, and Junior and I decided to call it a day.

"Maybe I should let Mrs. Wray know that he's going to pick the car up."

"Done told her already," Junior said, "called her while you was talkin' with Gatemout."

"Hot damn, Junior, you-all think of everything."

Our house was on the south side of town, not far from the garage, so I had Junior drop me off. He refused my offer of beer and a potluck supper, but agreed to hire out for one more day of errands while the Ford Coupe was being worked on. I thanked him for all his help. He was saving me tons of time and money.

I went in to tell Claudie about my day and hear about hers. I could smell something good cooking the minute I opened the door. The house was clean and neat . . . I could see Claudie had had a busy day too.

The following day was frustrating. Junior came to get me around nine a.m., and we made the rounds of the insurance agent and "Department of Motor Vehicles". Anyone who's been there with an eight-year-old auto registration and tries to buy license plates will know all about frustration. I was no exception. But after three visits, explanatory and notarized signed forms and the all-important physical inspection to verify the serial number, I finally had a pair of shiny new license plates and a New York State driver's license.

We made it back to Gatemout's at five thirty, just before he closed at six. He had the car out front, by the old-fashioned gasoline pumps that had to be cranked by hand.

Gatemout waddled over to meet me and Junior, by the Ford Coupe.

"Boy, you are one lucky man, you got one hell of an auto-mobile there. That motor run smooth an' quiet as a jeweled pocket watch."

"Thanks, Gatemout," I said.

Junior slapped me on the arm. "Tole ya so."

"What all did you have to do to it?"

"Listen," said Gatemout. He sat in the driver's seat with the door open and hit the starter. The engine barely turned over when it fired up with a throb, then idled at a whisper, until Gatemout goosed the throttle a few times and it responded with a throaty rumble from the twin exhaust pipes that gave me chills.

"We changed the motor oil and greased her," Gatemout said. "We changed the grease in the rear end and transmission too. We checked the brakes, put in new points and plugs, fixed the carburetor and drained and flushed the radiator, filled it with antifreeze, changed the windshield wiper blades and a taillight bulb. We put on four new tires and tubes and checked the toe-in. Oh yeah — we drained the gas tank and blew out the gas line, put a gasket on the fuel pump and filled her up with high test gasoline."

Pausing for breath, Gatemout said the bill was $110. While I paid him, one of his apprentice mechanics went out and installed the license plates for me. The kid had also washed it after the mechanical stuff was done. When he came back in the office I gave him a half-dollar tip.

Just as I was about to leave, Gatemout said, "Oh shit." He turned to me and said, "I'm sorry son. I forgot, we put a new battery in too. The old one was dried out and fried. It's another twelve dollar and fifty cent. Comes with a four-year warranty too."

"Okay," I said, and paid him. I was getting pretty damn close to broke. I needed to quit spending and start making money. I did get Gatemout to throw in a new can of car wax at no charge, though.

I drove home at a sedate pace with Junior following in his taxi. I was anxious for Claudie's approval; she hadn't even seen the car yet. Cars were scarce and hard to find right after the war, and it was impossible to buy anything on the cheap. I had spent nearly half the base price of a new '37 Ford on a twelve-year-old one. But that was the way it was back in 1949 as factories struggled to change over from war material to consumer products and catch up with demand. Auto dealers couldn't get enough cars for the customers who wanted to buy them, so they marked up the ones they could get in order to make more profit. I was starting to worry about money as I drove back home like a near-sighted octogenarian.

Claudie loved the car. She wanted me to take her for a ride.

"Okay with you, I ask Junior to go?" I said.

"Sure, if he want to," she answered.

I went over to where Junior was sitting in his car, waiting.

"Junior," I said, "why you-all just sittin' here? Come on an' ride with me and Claudie. You was sure right about this car. Man it's a peach. I can't believe how good it run an' drive."

"Naw, man. You-all go 'head. I rode plenty enough in that car," he said.

I noticed then, Junior had a long face and wouldn't make eye contact. I realized it was a bittersweet moment for him. He was coming to understand, a part of his life was over and done with. His friend and pal wasn't coming home. With the car being sold, a portion of him had to move on, had to look ahead instead of back, and get on with the business of living. Ray-Ray was dead.

"You sure, man?" I said.

"Yeah, I gots to get to work, quit messin' 'round."

I settled up with him and added a nice tip.

"Thanks, Junior. I couldn't have done this without your help. I won't forget it either. I see you 'round."

"Yuh. I see you later," he said and drove off in the Snappy Cab.

There was a parking space alongside the house, next to the kitchen window. After I took Claudie for a ride we parked beside the house and necked for a while, just for the hell of it.

Next day was Thursday. We got up early and spent the morning cleaning and polishing the car. I rubbed and waxed on it until it shined like a fire truck in a St. Patrick's Day parade.

Claudie cleaned and brushed the insides so much I thought the mohair would wear out. She even cleaned around all the instruments with a toothpick. The '37 Ford was our first car and we were proud of it. Satisfied the car was as shiny and clean as we could make it, we went in for a quick lunch of onion and liverwurst sandwiches and coffee. I washed up and changed into a clean pair of dungarees and white tee shirt, then put on a pressed denim work shirt with double breast pockets while Claudie made the sandwiches and coffee.

"Why you change clothes, Joey?"

"I'm going to look for a job," I said.

"Right now?"

"Good'a time's any. 'Sides I'm about outta money."

"Honey, you gots seven hundred fifty dollars in the bank."

"That's our savings—our nest egg. I ain't gonna spend it," I said, "why I gotta find work."

"You don't think the white folk keepin' all the jobs for theirselves?

Jus' like always?"

"Don't know, Claudie, 'till I go see. Mr. Burton, the shoeshine man, told me about a government construction job where everybody gets same pay for the same job. He said they're obligated to hire so many Negros too. I'm headed there now, soon's I leave."

"Well good luck with that."

"We'll see honey." I said, "we'll see. President Truman integrated the armed forces last year."

"I'll believe that when I see a black general," she said.

I kissed her on the neck, right under her ear where she likes it.

"Be home soon's I can."

I headed out in my "new" thirteen-year-old Ford car seeking my fortune, so to speak, looking for the Neversink River dam project like an old-time prospector hunting for Eldorado.

My hunt took me ten miles east on State Route 55. I found the Neversink River and the dam worksite a few miles past Bradley, a little four corners hamlet that boasted its own tavern. The road wound through a birch and maple woods, going downhill until you suddenly broke out of the forested area into a mile-wide cleared basin. The road crossed the river and rose up on the other side where I could see construction activity. All up and down the valley, dump trucks, bulldozers and road graders were working, about to work or had been working. There were tracks, and dozed or graded newly turned earthworks everywhere I looked, as well as great piles of trees, brush and limbs as the valley was being prepared for the flooding that would come when the dam was finished and the Neversink River was impounded. Away off to my right, as I followed the road across a temporary bridge and headed up the east side, was the dam itself, stretching about a mile across the valley. Men were everywhere, working on what I learned was called the core wall, a concrete barrier drilled and dug down to bedrock, then concreted up in a seventy-five foot-high wall. As the core wall was being laid, motor-driven earth scrapers were laying dirt in front of, and behind it. Then, giant iron "sheepsfoot" rollers pulled by D-8 caterpillar bulldozers compacted the new laid earth. Giant rocks would be laid across the earthen dam as part of the finishing process. But that was months, years maybe, away. Today, I was just a guy looking for a job.

I followed the road across the wooden bridge, shifted the car down into second gear. The Ford Coupe walked right up the hill on the east side purring like a lady lion after a big meal. A lady lion named Calpurnia . . . old Julius Caesar's third and last wife . . . the name Claudie had given our maroon Ford coupe. It was in honor of Claudie's great-grandmother Calpurnia, born into bondage in North Carolina on the Bailey family plantation, just before the Civil War. The old lady had died the year before Claudie and I came up North; she was ninety-something and always favored maroon colors on her clothing.

There was a stop sign at the hilltop. The road intersected back into State Route 55 again, from the detour I'd taken in Bradley. A highway sign across the road read "Neversink 2 Mi" and pointed left, and "Hasbrouck 5 Mi," pointing straight ahead. I turned right, on a temporary dirt road of loose gravel, toward the construction site.

I bumped through a parking lot filled with mud-splashed cars and trucks of every size, shape, color, year, make and model imaginable, dodging potholes and big, moving pieces of heavy equipment. I parked at the edge of a field next to a ditch and walked over to a house trailer with a sign marked "Office". I put my "humble southern Negro" persona in place while walking, figuring it would be all white folks in there. My pride swallowed, *I need a job* my only thought as I went in the door.

Inside, there were desks on one wall, tables on the other, file cabinets and blueprint cabinets filled the third wall, a hallway the fourth. I stepped up to the first desk and waited until the middle-aged woman looked up, then said, "Ma'am, I'm looking for work . . ."

"You've come to the right place. We've got plenty. Fill this out, take it to the last desk," she said, and pointed with her finger.

I filled out what was a standard employment form and went over to the last desk where another mid-aged white woman sat. I noticed she had a couple of yellow pencils stuck in her hair bun. She had on gold wire-frame glasses. Again, I waited until she looked up.

"Uh, lady told me give this to you, ma'am," I said, looking at the floor like old Step 'n Fetchit hisself as I handed the employment application over.

She took the paper and glanced at it, then took out some other paper from a file in her desk drawer. She asked me my social security number and number of dependents, wrote them down. Then she said, "Print your name, address and number of dependants in the box here, sign and date it on the bottom, wait here."

She got up from her chair and went down the hallway. People worked at their desks, not much conversation happened. No one spoke to me. I stood. I waited.

I noticed a wood and brass nameplate, partly hidden by papers on her desk that said "KATHLEEN HENLEY, BOOKKEEPING." There was a little ceramic leprechaun sitting on the end.

I waited about ten minutes before Mrs. Henley came back, holding an armful of personnel files. She looked at me and said, "Take your application and W-2 form, first door on the right. Mr. Walden."

"Thank you," I said, careful to keep my eyes averted. I saw that she wasn't looking at me either.

The interview with Henry Walden was brief.

"What kinda job you looking for?" he said.

"'Bout anythin', sir."

"Worked construction?"

"Yas, sir. In North Carolina."

"You drink?"

"I do. Have a beer at night befo' supper. Heps my di-gestion."

"Honest, are you?"

"Yes, sir."

"Arrested ever?"

"No, suh."

"Were you in the service?"

"Yas suh. Army. Nineteen fo'ty-fo' to nineteen fo'ty-eight."

"You in combat?"

"Yas, suh. Bastogne to Berlin."

"Then what?"

"Army of occupation, to fo'ty-seben."

"Damn. You were in the shit."

It was a statement, not a question, but I answered anyway, dropped the Step 'n Fetchit routine.

"Yes, sir, I was some."

He eased up too.

"What was your discharge date and rank?"

"Seventeen October, 1948. Staff sergeant, E-6."

"Were you decorated?"

"Two Purple Hearts, Bronze Star."

"I was on Sicily, and the Italian campaign. Hit at Monte Casino."

"That was a scrap, for sure," I said.

"It all was," he said. "You start Monday. Swing shift. Be here two o'clock for equipment and locker draw. You have to see the shop steward. His name's O'Brien. Trailer behind this one. You're a general laborer, a dollar thirty an hour, time and a half, all over forty hours. Get here late, lose your job. Drunk, same thing. Fighting, stealing or not following foreman's orders you will lose your job. Immediately. No appeal. You understand?"

"Yes, sir. I understand."

"Okay. Welcome to Fraser-Davis. Step over to the wall, put your feet on the marks. I'm going to photograph you, for your file."

I followed instructions, got photographed and went out back to find O'Brien, the shop steward, whatever that was.

I found O'Brien in a silver camping trailer, and he was a real piece of work. Turned out the shop steward was a union representative, kind of a political appointee. I had found him there purely by chance because he was only in for a couple hours each day. If you had a grievance or pay dispute, O'Brien was the go-to guy. He signed me up as a dues-paying member of the International Brotherhood of Laborers and Hod Carriers for $3.50 and gave me a celluloid button with the two crossed horses heads of the Teamsters Union and told me to always wear it on my coat or hat. It showed that I was a paid-up member in good standing. The dues were $2.50 a month, payable on the first, and the button color changed every month so the steward could tell at a glance if your dues were up to date. I saw in the union book where your paid-in dues were recorded, that all the officers and directors had Irish surnames like McCallan, Boyle, Hanofee and Durry. Proof positive, I told myself, that the construction trades were dominated by the Irish laborers. "Joe Cooley" fit right in there if you overlooked my very dark tan. I almost broke into a few bars of "Oh Paddy Dear" and a little jig step.

Instead, I minded my Ps and Qs, thanked Bill O'Brien and drove home to Claudie to tell her all the good news, and show her my new union button. I spent the evening and the weekend with Claudie, working at "honey-dos" . . . cleaning up the car, putting up curtain rods and shelves, fixing a faucet that dripped . . . stuff like that.

On Sunday evening I took Claudie to a movie uptown. I can't recall what we saw, but it was probably a comedy or a musical because she liked those a lot. I was thinking all that evening about my soon-to-start job, wondering how hard the work would be, how I'd measure up to the other guys and what I'd be doing all evening. I'd explained to Claudie about swing shift, the one from four until midnight. I was also trying to reset my biologic clock to a later schedule so I slept in until nine o'clock Monday morning, late for me, but I was all slept out.

I was well rested and jittery to get started too. I dressed in dungarees and army boots, T-shirt and denim work shirt. I took a flannel overshirt too, figuring it would be cold once the sun went down.

Claudie made me a big breakfast of toast, eggs, grits and chitlins. While I ate and drank coffee she packed me a lunch and thermos of coffee.

"Honey," she said, "you nervous as a tied-up hound in a roomfull of rabbits. Can I get you anything? Why don't you just sit here and read the paper."

"Thanks, Honey. Don't need a thing."

I sat and read the paper, even the comics, which I never do. By one o'clock I couldn't take it anymore.

"Claudie, I'm gonna get started."

"So early?"

"Yeah. They told me to get there a couple-a hours early. I have to get some equipment."

"Okay. I put extra food in your dinner bucket, case you get hungry."

"I won't be back till after midnight."

I gave Claudie a hug, kiss and a rub of her left breast to remember me by, then left for my first day of work on the Neversink Dam.

I drove slow, and thought about the city of New York and the series of water dams they had built north, and now west, of the city. I figured there must be eight or nine, maybe even ten million people living in the Bronx, Queens and Manhattan. If each person used twenty or twenty five gallons per day, what with washing clothes, dishes and bodies, drinking and toilet flushing . . . heck, that would be around 200 to 250 million gallons of water every day. No wonder the reservoir was so big. There were a bunch of them already built; the Neversink and Rondout just coming online and a couple more to come north and west of here. Damn. That was a lot of dams and water. I wondered, *What happened to all the people and towns along the river?* and *Why didn't the City just take the water out of the Hudson River?* It was inexhaustible, free, and ran right by the place, so no pipelines to build. I'd have to think about all of those things. I was glad I'd taken the time to read up on the dams at the library on Saturday. For right now, I was happy to have a job and work that paid a $1.30 an hour. Damned happy.

I drove right in and parked like I owned the place. Went to the office, then to the shop steward's trailer, then to the supply trailer where I was issued a Bakelite hard hat and black rubber hip boots with yellow steel toes. After that, I went up to the "hog house" where I got a locker assigned to me and learned some of my new routine.

Roll call and muster up was fifteen minutes before shift start. The foreman took names and wrote the day and start time in a little book he carried in his shirt pocket. Then the foreman, whose name was Lyle Buchanan, gave us our work assignments. I was paired up with a great big Irishman named Dan Mahan. Everybody called him "Big Dan" because he stood about six foot four or five and weighed about 250 pounds, all of it muscle.

There were eight men in our crew that day and we were tasked with shoveling concrete in the cut, down at the base of the dam where the spillway was being built. The cut was about 125 feet deep at that point and crews were setting forms and pouring concrete around the clock down there. They were reinforcing the base and sides of the spillway, which is where the excess water would flow out of the reservoir and tumble back down to rejoin the Neversink River. The spillway was one of the most important, and hardest to build, parts of the entire dam project. It was definitely the highest and deepest part being built.

The other guys were old hands and comfortable in their work and with each other. They smoked and grab-assed as we got ready to go to work. Nobody talked to me; I was the new guy. I was the only black guy too. That may have had something to do with it.

The men walked over by a large crane. The boom was swung out over the edge of the cut with its cable going down toward the bottom. When it came back up, I saw a metal basket about eight feet square and four feet high was on the end. It had an iron U-shaped handle that was bolted on two sides; the basket itself was some kind of square three-inch iron mesh.

I figured it was for taking tools and supplies back and forth. It was a "mucker" used to haul wet mud and gravel up out of the cut. As I watched with growing apprehension and mounting horror, six of my newly met associates piled in the basket and held the iron bar over their heads. The crane operator raised the basket a few feet, then swung out and dropped them into the abyss.

Sweat broke out all over my body. I was sick at my stomach, thought I was gonna puke. Big Dan looked at me and said, "You okay? You lookin' a little green around the gills."

"Fine. I'm fine," I said.

"Don't worry, I've rode her down lots a times."

"That's good."

The basket came back and settled to the surface. I was nailed to the ground where I stood, paralyzed at the thought of climbing in and going in the air. I was starting to pant, breathing in shallow gasps. I could feel my heart pounding, and blood rushing in my ears. Dan climbed in with the nonchalance and ease of a veteran while I was rooted where I stood, a sheen of sweat on my face and the stink of animal fear on my person.

I told myself that fear was in the mind. *You'll be alright*, I told myself and took the first stiff-legged step toward the waiting basket. *Steady*, I told myself, again, *steady.*

"Come on," Dan said, "we ain't got all day."

"Sure," I said as I jake-legged over and climbed in, my heart tripping like Krupa tattooing the double snares in Carnegie Hall. I kept thinking about how good my wages were going to be if I held on to my job.

I barely had both feet in the bucket when it took off. It rose up in the air, turned and swung over the cut and dropped straight down, heading 140 feet to the bottom. That's when I freaked out. All rational thought left my being and the "fight or flight" instinct kicked in. I screamed like a hog being butchered, moaned, and made noises like I was speaking in tongues . . . all at the same time I was trying to jump out of the basket. Trying to escape from what I feared the most. I was a wild animal without sense or reason. All I had was panic and an overwhelming need to flee.

That's where fate, or luck, or divine intervention, or whatever you want to call it, stepped in. Before I could throw myself out of the moving muck bucket, Dan Mahan grabbed me.

"Quit it you goddamned fool," he said. He grabbed me in a head and arm lock. Had me over the left shoulder, and under the right arm from behind. All I could see was sky and granite rock moving past as we descended. Dan had one arm around the basket handle and the other one around me with his hands and fingers locked together. The more I fought, the tighter he squeezed. Every time I yelled more air went out of my lungs that wasn't being replaced. And yes, he was that big, and yes, he was that strong. It was like being wrestled by Conan the Cimmerian. I was starting to see stars and black stuff when the basket, with both of us still in it, touched solid ground, and your father let go a me.

*   *   *

Joe Cooley stopped his narrative at that point and took a long pull of his beer, gazing off into the middle distance, lost in thought. Neither he, nor the young middle-aged white man said anything for a long while. The old man sat thinking, the young man sat respectfully, knowing Joe would resume when ready. They sat in companionable silence, at a weathered picnic table in the old man's backyard, sipping beer.

"Until I met your father, and knew him for a while," the old man said, "I never knew the potential of friendship. I never had any true friend before then. There was strangers, there was family, there was white folks, and seemed to me they's all trying to get something away from you. Your money, your time and labor, maybe even your love and affection, but something. Always tryin' to get somethin' from you. Granddaddy Littleton used to say, "Big 'uns 'ud 'et the lil' 'uns." And that's what I thought, " 'Et or be 'et," about the whole world. Then your Daddy give me his hand in friendship that day and he never took it back. Never expected nothin' for it either. That's one of the things I most liked about him. Be his friend or not, once he held his hand out to you, he never took it back. Never."

The young man stared at the table, pulled the label from the beer bottle in his hand, then said, "You and Claudie were always special to me. I couldn't think of my childhood without thinking of the two of you. And the funny thing is, now that I'm a grown man, I don't have any friends like you and Pop."

"You mean black friends?"

"Yeah."

"Things are different now, that's all. Society is different. People are different. What you do is different. Black people, white people, all different now. It's the times we live in. You ever notice, pro sports all them black an' white boys workin' together on the field for a common goal . . . to win the game. Off the field they be segregated as 1950, by choice. Hell, they don't even sit the bench together. You watch, you see what I mean."

"I will."

Claudie came outside then, and sat beside her husband. She took a sip of his beer. She said, "Danny, I want you to know how sorry I am about your father's passing. He was a good man and a true friend."

"Thanks, Claudie. It means a lot to be here with you and Joe. I know he's in a better place."

"I was trying to tell Danny about his father and me. About the nature of friendship when you came out," Joe said.

"Ummm-hummm. Y'all might oughta talk about football or somethin," she said.

"Where's Mattie?" Danny said.

"She went to the powder room."

"Crying?"

"Yeah. Funerals will do that," Claudie said.

"I know," Danny said, "Pop loved her from the day I brought her home, when we weren't even engaged yet"

"We all sad today," Joe said. "You won't ever have another father. I won't ever have another friend like him."

"Yeah. What happened to you and Pop after you got down to the worksite that first day?"

"Well, there ain't really that much more to tell. Your daddy never said a word about me blowing a fuse up there in the basket, or bucket or whatever you want to call it. He asked me if I was okay as we got out the bucket. I told him I was and he said, "Don't let any-a these sons-a-bitches know or they'll ride you to death. I seen 'em do it."

"Thanks," I said.

"Smoke?" he said and offered me a Camel cigarette from his pack.

"Thanks," I said, taking one, even though I wasn't much of a smoker.

"Your Dad and I worked side by side for the next two and a half years on the Neversink Dam and Tunnel portal, and we've been friends for thirty-some years since then. See, your dad let me keep my dignity, and my self-respect. He never teased me about being afraid of heights or that first time I rode down on the muck bucket. I respected your dad for that. I think he respected me for coming back to work and riding down again. It never got any easier either. I learned to keep my eyes closed and that helped while the bucket was in the air, but truth is, I near shit the bed every morning when I woke up and remembered I'd have to ride her down again."

The Facts of Conjecture

1950

The Facts of Conjecture

The news flashed through Neversink like an electronic shock wave.

"Didja hear about the Varley boy gone missing?"

"Oh, yes, and the mother . . . the same day 'n all. My God."

" . . . searching for him all over Rhyolite Mountain . . ."

" . . . always said there was strange goings on up there."

"The guy with all the kids named for cars? The one with the car salvage? That guy?"

"Didja know they're alphabetical too? The girl Auburn is the oldest, baby Studebaker is the youngest."

"The poor woman . . . no wonder all those babies, one right after the other, can you imagine?"

"How'd she ever stand it? . . ."

Facts were few but rumors were many. Gossip and conjecture filled in the gaps, real or imagined, until at some point truth became a victim of imagination.

" . . . Gypsies, yeah, keeping it quiet . . ."

" . . . fishy, I tell you what, they're keeping it all hush-hush."

"Couldn't find their ass with both hands."

"Big crazy bastard . . ."

" . . . not want 'im mad at me for sure . . ."

" . . . cannibals . . . witchcraft . . ."

"Heard 'e's gone crazy with grief."

" . . . sold him. Uh-huh, you'll see . . . "

The gossip raged all over Neversink. The fabrications got more fantastic and the conjecture more outrageous with each retelling, but there was no foundation of truth in any of it.

The facts of the Varley family tragedy were few: Irma Varley had taken her life with an overdose of prescription painkillers. On the same day Studebaker Varley, age eighteen months, had disappeared from his family's yard up on Rhyolite Mountain. All the men, some women and most of the senior high school boys from Neversink had searched the woods and mountains in the area for the next five days without success. The Board of Water Supply police force, Sullivan County Sheriff's deputies and state troopers were also actively engaged in the search. Other than a soiled diaper, no trace of the baby had been found. He had vanished, as if he'd never existed.

Fear set in. The whole town suddenly got security-conscious. Almost overnight, new hasps and locks appeared on most every house and barn, shed and chicken coop. Long-time neighbors eyed each other with suspicion, doors and windows were checked and locked at bedtime. Strangers or out-of-town relatives come to visit were kept under close observation by the townsfolk. No child was left untended, no baby out of sight. Xenophobia was pandemic and most houses sported loaded shotguns close to hand.

Without results, the number of active searchers diminished until at the end of week two, only Oliver Varley and his two oldest sons, Cadillac and Franklin, seventeen and fourteen, were still looking, trying to find the little boy.

Every inch of Rhyolite Mountain had been searched; every culvert, ditch, bridge, stream, cave, hollow and animal den, and each and every one of Oliver's 9,847 junk cars and trucks had been looked into, under, around and down. Bloodhounds were employed. They sniffed out a trail that ended at the county road when it started raining, eliminating any further hope of using the tracking dogs.

The *Daily News* sent a reporter and photographer up from the city and an article ran on page three of the paper, but the human-interest story fizzled out quickly and more current events took over. The public's attention span was short and soon lost interest in the story of Studebaker Varley's mysterious disappearance.

The Shanachie

1954

The Shanachie

At the bottom of shaft two, 850 feet below ground, the Hogs had just about finished the bell chamber when the lights blew out. The bell chamber was where giant valves would be installed in the twelve-foot diameter West Delaware Tunnel, a connecting link in the New York City water system. It was sixty feet wide at the base, forty-five feet high and shaped like an old-fashioned beehive, or an egg, standing on one end. Now it was nearly finished, and the Hogs were prepared to start driving tunnels north and south from shaft two that would connect the Rondout distributing reservoir at Lackawack, New York, with the big collecting one at Cannonsville, thirty miles to the north. The men were trapped almost a quarter mile underground in total blackness, in a dark so dark, they couldn't see their own hallucinations. Without electric, there were no lights, no fresh air was being pumped down the shaft and there was no telephone to the shaft house. No phone meant no signal to talk with the surface, so they couldn't call for help. The good news was that their air would last eight to ten hours . . . according to the standard emergency manual all eight Sandhogs got when they hired on.

As soon as the lights went out, Ralph Corey, who was closest, hit the kill switch on the hundred-horse diesel air compressor that powered the eighty-pound jackhammers Bobby Michaels and Davey Slater were using to bore holes in the rotten shale. Shale is fossilized clay that hardened into rock over the millennia; it flakes into fragments easily, and has to be stabilized. The rotten shale in shaft two had groundwater running through it, making conditions even worse for the Hogs.

Curt Hightower and Tad Henry were attaching steel mesh, using six-foot by one-inch expansion bolts, then spraying a concrete fixative over it to hold the ceiling in place long enough to set steel and pour the concrete for a permanent wall and roof.

Safety drill called for them to get a head count and injury report. Common sense told them all to gather together along the outside walls just in case something crashed down the shaft. Grady Daggitt was the foreman. He called across the sixty-foot chamber, "Anybody down, hurt?" No one answered at first. He called each man by name, just as he did in the Marine Corps in Korea. "Bobby Mike?"

"Here."

"Slater?"

"Yo."

"Tad, Mike, Curt, Ray, Johnny Mack?"

Each one answered; there were no injuries, outside of a skinned knuckle where Tad Henry had run a drill bit into the rock face when the electric failed. His right thumb and index finger looked broken.

"I want all you guys to form on me." Grady held up his old Zippo lighter, the one he'd carried from the amphibious landing at Inchon, Korea with the 1st Marine Division in 1950, to the armistice at Panmunjom in 1953 when the cease-fire was declared. Scratched and dented where it had been hit by shrapnel from a Chinese mortar, the old cigarette lighter with the USMC world and anchor embossed on it still worked, perfectly. Grady was never without it.

Click-snap, click-snap, click-snap, the lighter counted cadence in the absolute dark.

Click-snap, click-snap, Johnny Mack and Mike Antrim made it over to Grady. They'd been nearest, shoveling muck from the last blast into the giant bucket that hung from a one-inch steel cable that went up 900 feet to the hoist house. When the bucket was full, it would be winched up, emptied and lowered to be refilled.

"You guys okay? See anything?"

"Yeah," said Johnny. "The cable's slack and we were getting all beat to hell with dirt and rocks when the power went off."

"How much dirt?"

"Enough that we were moving away, outta the shaft."

"That's right," Mike said. "It was so noisy with the air compressor and drilling racket we didn't hear a thing, just moved from instinct."

"Good instinct!"

The rest of the men made it, one by one, to the click-snap of Grady's lighter until they all huddled together on the south end of the chamber, in the driest spot. There was a constant drip and trickle of water into the chamber; without pumps the water was rising. It was a matter of time, or a question of fate, whether the eight Hogs would be asphyxiated or drowned . . . in a heart of darkness Joseph Conrad couldn't have imagined.

"Okay," Grady said. "Anybody got a light? Any kind of light?"

Mike, Johnny, Bobby Michaels and Slater all had cigarette lighters. The others, nothing.

"When's the lights comin' back on, Grady?"

"Just a couple minutes or never, how the fuck would I know? Slater, Curt, Bobby and Mike, start bringin' some ties from the stack over here, so we've got someplace dry to sit. Johnny, gather up the dinner buckets and water jugs. I want them all over here by us. Take Tad with you. You guys use your lighters and stay out of the shaft. Ralph you stick here with me. Help anybody gets in a pickle." They all set to their assigned tasks, accompanied by the click-snap of Zippo lighters. The percussive beat, click-snap, click-snap was accompanied by the melodic dripping of falling water, gathering in ever widening, ever deepening puddles.

Johnny and Tad returned first, arms full of tin dinner buckets and thermos bottles.

"Put 'em here at my feet then help the guys move ties."

Gradually, using main strength and ignorance as well as luck, pluck and Yankee ingenuity, they assembled a three-foot high platform of railroad ties, built from the electric train tracks. The train would run the "Jumbos," big four-hole rock drills, into the tunnel and the excavated rock and mud out of it. The men were sloshing around in toe-deep water by the time they finished, but now sat on a dry platform and for the first time since the lights blew, had a chance to think about their situation. They all started talking.

"What happened?"

"Think we'll be here much longer?"

"Darker than hell."

"Naw, hell'd be lit up from all the fires."

"Grady, water's getting deeper; it's over the toe a my boots."

"I hope the friggin' lights come on. Think it'll be long Grady?"

The yammering and dumb questions kept on until Grady spoke out, "You guys shut the fuck up! I don't know any more than you do. I'm ready to get my ass outta here too; I'm sure the bosses are figuring it out as we speak. We've been in the dark about two and a half or three hours as best I can tell. The good news is the air doesn't seem any staler to me, so we must be getting some down the shaft. The bad news is the place is gonna flood if we don't get the goddamned pumps back on. That's all I know. Don't ask me any more. I can't tell ya anything."

It was a shock, hearing the usually quiet and efficient foreman burst out like that. The tension was rising with the water. Anyone who works underground knows in his heart . . . it's dangerous down there. Men die. They usually get crushed by debris, rocks and mud from cave-ins, or blown up from methane gas explosions, crushed by equipment, electrocuted or who knew what-all. Those Hogs who worried about it didn't last much longer, they'd go topside and work for less money in the open air. When a man started thinking about getting killed underground, he always thought it would happen fast, he wouldn't see or hear it coming. At least he hoped so. He'd be here one second, and then BAM, just like that, gone. It was getting to all of them in the darkness, listening to the slow, steady drip, drip, drip of water, filling the chamber where they sat helpless, trapped, waiting.

"Somebody gimme a cigarette," Mike Antrim said. He lit his Zippo so Curt could see to pass one over. The dark seemed darker somehow after Mike lit up. The glowing tip of the Camel cigarette made arcs in the blackness as he dragged on it. After a few moments he said into the gloom, "I ever tell you guys about my uncle, Cyril McCready? He was my pop's older half-brother. After Pop came over in 1923 and worked for a while, he sent Uncle Cyril a ticket and sponsored him to get him into the US. This woulda been about 1925. Anyhow Uncle Cyril gets over here and follows Pop up to Neversink. Pop was with the Board of Water Supply by then. He was a policeman, patrolled the dams and tried to keep the hell-raising down to a minimum among the construction men. Well, Uncle Cyril worked on the Ashokan Dam down by Kingston as a laborer . . . but he wasn't too dependable . . . on account he was a drinking man. So they fired him after awhile and he went off into the woods up north of Neversink and lived by himself, in a little cabin up on Peekamoose Mountain, where he hunted and fished for a living. But he'd go get a job every now and then to get money for stuff he couldn't catch or shoot: ammunition, coffee, flour, salt and most important of all, whiskey. He'd buy a case of it if he had the money and carry it back up to his squatters cabin. Then he'd get blistering drunk. See, he was homesick for Ireland. He'd think about Ballycumber, back in County Offaly, and all the folks he wouldn't see again, and just get soused. This one time, he'd just got a whole case of cheap whiskey and had an attack of homesickness at the same time. He started in drinking and polished off a whole quart, up there on the mountain crying to himself, so he opened a second one and drank most of it too. By now he's pretty well paralyzed but still conscious, hadn't passed out.

"So he's laying out there by the firewood pile, can't move 'cause he's so drunk, when a small copperhead . . . one-a those orange-reddish ones . . . comes along out of the woodpile next to Uncle Cyril. The snake wiggles around for a while, then goes for Uncle Cyril, who couldn't move, and the snake bit him, on the arm."

Mike stopped talking and took a last drag on his cigarette and flicked the butt in a long arc out toward the center of the bell chamber. It was quiet for a moment then Ralph Corey spoke up.

"Is that it?"

"Oh, no," Mike replied. "Uncle Cyril had so much alcohol in his body that that snake dropped dead as soon as he stuck his fangs in."

"Aw-w-w-w, that's bullshit," Slater said.

The rest of them were still laughing and talking when Mike added,

"Poor Uncle Cyril died that winter . . . drank himself to death. Couple of hikers found him the next spring. He'd drunk so much alcohol that his body was in perfect condition, sitting in his chair, one he'd made by weaving green willow branches together. The critters hadn't even chewed on him, 'cause he was as hard as a granite rock from drinking so much. The undertakers were scared to cremate the body 'cause of the alcohol . . . thought maybe he'd blow up or something . . .

"They couldn't get him straightened out neither, he was sorta melted into the chair. Finally they just buried him in it, sitting up. Pop wanted to put on his tombstone, 'Here is Cyril McCready, still sitting on his ass drinking,' but Mother wouldn't let him. So it just says the usual."

Even Grady, who was always serious, sniggered at that one. But the truth was, they'd been in the dark for more than five hours, the water was about fifteen inches deep, they hadn't heard from the surface, and to a man they were growing more alone and afraid by the minute. Not that any one of 'em would admit it. They sat quietly and for a while no one spoke, as they all thought about their personal "shouldda-coulda-wouldas." A few of them smoked, a couple offered up silent prayers, asking for absolution, for deliverance, for hope during what St. John of the Cross called "the dark night of the soul." That had been the subject of Father James Burke's homily after the mass of a few months ago. *It's funny,* Mike thought, *that I'd think about it just now. Maybe that's why I go to Mass every week,* he mused.

Grady got up from the edge of the platform and discovered water up his calf, nearly to his knees.

"Tad, how many more of those ties are over there?" he asked evenly.

"We brought over about half of 'em."

"Okay. Get the rest of 'em over here. We gotta move the pile. Make haste you guys."

The Hogs waded out to the tie pile in the muck and started retrieving timber. Grady directed them to start cribbing ties more toward the center of the chamber and close to the shaft. Grady placed timber as they brought them and had the new platform rising up about eight feet when they exhausted the supply of ties. One of them grumbled under his breath, "Why all the extra work?"

"Because," Ralph said in his quiet way, "because this room we've been diggin' out is shaped like a bell. It's bigger at the bottom, smaller at the top. The higher the water gets . . ."

"The faster it'll rise," Tad said.

The Hogs were quiet as each one thought about his loved ones and their chances of living through the night. The steady drip and trickle of water continued unabated as they thought their thoughts, sitting atop the stack of ties . . . alone and in the dark.

"Oh. Shit! Shit. Shit. Shit!" somebody cursed. The water was about six feet deep. And rising. Rising slow. Rising steady. Rising inexorably.

Mike Antrim said, "Speaking of shit, did I ever tell you about the time my grampa over in Ireland came home drunk one night? . . . it was long, long after he was supposed to be there. It was payday see, but he didn't have any money on him other than a few pence. Coins.

They use British money in Ireland. Anyway, my grandma and my dad and one or two of his brothers tried to sober Gramps up . . . find out where the money was. Wha'd he do with it? They needed to buy food and pay rent. After awhile they figured out where he'd been and backtracked his path, looking for the money. Couldn't find it anywhere. Finally, my dad looked in the outhouse. Sure enough, the old man had gone in there drunk, took a 'shite' as they say, and wiped his ass with the British Pound notes. It wasn't too long after the Easter Rising in 1916 you see. The money had the king's face on it."

"Damn! That's sad and funny, all at the same time."

"What happened to the money?"

"My Dad fished it out with a couple of sticks while my Uncle Liam held a lantern for him. They took it up to the house and washed it with soap and water. My grandma was happy to find it and probably got a charge outta paying some English prick with all that filthy money."

The Hogs had been underground about ten hours. The water was still coming up and they hadn't heard from the surface. Nobody said it out loud, but hope was a diminishing commodity. Water was most of the way up their perch. Still rising.

Bobby Michaels said, "You got any more, Mike? Any more stories?"

"Yeah, Mike, tell another one."

"About Ireland."

Mike Antrim was from a family of shanachies . . . historians and poets in the oral tradition from before the Irish had a written language . . . he was a natural-born storyteller.

"C'mon, Mike."

"Okay, okay sure then, I saved this one for yez. One time around 1910 or '12 in Dublin, tuberculosis was a pretty big problem and the authorities were convinced public sanitation was the cause of it. Some smart doctors and college professors decided that TB, or consumption as it was called, had to do with germs. And furthermore, these germs were specific to, and spread by, houseflies because there was a lot of them around. Lots'a TB plus lots'a flies . . . must mean TB comes from flies. So they decided to have a fly-swatting contest."

"Fly-swatting contest?"

There were snorts, giggles and rude comments all around as the talk started.

"No. No shit, sure enough they had a fly swatting contest. I know, because my two uncles, Rory and Jimmy, won it. The contest was sponsored by one of the Dublin newspapers. I think it was *The Sunday Independent*, but it could have been *The Irish Volunteer* or *The New Ireland* too. They had a lotta, lotta newspapers back then, some Republican, some Loyalist."

"What's that?"

"Oh, the Republicans advocated a free Ireland . . . independent from Great Britain. The Loyalists were just that . . . loyal to England. There was a ton of newspapers and ten tons of opinions back then. Anyway, one of the papers advertised they was gonna have a fly-swatting contest with ten pounds to the person who got the most flies, six pounds for second most swatted and four pounds for third. It was a helluva bunch of money back then and everybody got all worked up. A pound is about two US dollars by the way, and the unemployment rate was probably thirty-five or forty percent. The newspaper figured they'd get a big boost in circulation from the excitement, and being Irish, they came up with a whole set of rules about what, where, why, when and how to swat flies. They even had official contest fly swatters made up with the paper's name on them that you could buy at the newspaper stand. They were made out of wire, like coat hanger wire and window screen . . . that's where they printed their name. As soon as the paper came out the whole city was buzzing about it. People could really use ten pounds; it was about a month's wage for a working man.

"Well, being Irish, Rory and Jimmy started skiniving, that's a combination of 'skin 'em and conniving,' about how they were going to win the contest. Of course, all over Dublin, twenty-five thousand other skinivers were doing the exact same thing. Jimmy got them both officially registered and Rory got official fly swatters from Muldoon's, where they sold *The Sunday Independent*. Now, part of the official rules was that the contestant had to present the fly carcasses for counting. This was done with the aid of a tin measuring cup, each cupful was assumed to hold a set number of flies. It was important therefore not to mash 'em flat. Rory and Jimmy found that out right away. All over the city, flies were being exterminated by the dozens, the gross, the peck. Everywhere you went you found someone swatting flies. In a couple of weeks, two to be exact, the contest was over and hundreds lined up for the count-off. There was so many people there that the newspaper had six tables for official tallying . . . supervised by various editors of the paper. My uncles waited until almost all the counting was done; folks showed up with quart jars, gallon jars, cigar boxes, shoe boxes, grocery bags . . . just about anything you could think of . . . full of dead flies. Then, just before the contest deadline, when time expired and the winner declared, Uncle Jimmy and Uncle Rory show up. They had bushel baskets full of dead flies. Rory had six and a half bushels and Jimmy had five bushels. Rory had his right arm in a sling for emphasis, and they were declared the instant winners by the astounded judges. When asked how they managed to kill so many, they both answered, 'perseverance.' 'We never took a break,' 'wore out me elbow it did,' and the like. The judges smelled a rat of course, but couldn't figure out any way to prove that the rules had been broken. After conferring for thirty minutes in 'Executive Session,' they awarded Rory ten pounds for first place and Jimmy six pounds for second place. The two skinivers collected their winnings and scampered off to celebrate at O'Boyle's Pub and split their winnings. See, before the contest started they'd agreed to divide their take right down the middle. If, when they got to the judging it looked close, they'd enter just once with all eleven bushels. When they saw it wasn't gonna be close, they split their haul in order to take first and second prize. The lads retired to O'Boyle's to celebrate, each with eight pounds after they'd pooled their winnings. Well, one pint led to another and by late evening Rory and Jimmy were double shit-faced. All their friends and cousins and such have gathered by now, and O'Boyle asks Jimmy,

'How the hell'd yez kill so many of them little buggers?'

Well, Jimmy looks at Rory, and Rory rolls his eyes up, gives an exaggerated shrug with his palms up and they both commenced to laughing. They laughed until tears streamed down their faces and then laughed some more. They couldn't stop laughing in fact until they both got the hiccups. They'd barely get control of themselves, and then take off laughing again. O'Boyle, he don't know whether the lads are laughing at, or with him. He don't know whether to be mad or laugh along.

"Finally Uncle Rory gets enough control to gasp,

"The dumb fookers. The poor, dumb, pitiful, ignorant fookers." And he laughs then hiccups, then blurts out, "We trapped 'em!' And takes off laughing again until he falls over on the bar in a fit of giggles.

"O'Boyle, thinking he's somehow the butt of the joke, roars out like a foghorn, 'What fookers would you be talking about?'

"Jimmy was first to get some control and says, "The judges, Pat, the judges. See, me and Rory never touched a fly with a swatter. We trapped the little bastards in jars.'

" 'Jars?'

" 'Yep, old food jars. We put a coupla holes in a lid with a nail, with the sharp side down. Put some garbage in, fish head or guts and leave the jar out somewheres like the stables and presto, baskets full of flies.' And he gets the giggles again while Pat O'Boyle thinks about it.

"Well, wouldn't you know, there was some sore losers in the crowd and they started to mutter amongst themselves and, as crowds will do, to egg each other on. The muttering turned louder, insults became curses, push came to shove and the fat was in the fire. It turned into a real donneybrook. Fists flew, then chairs, then glasses, ashtrays and anything not nailed to the floor. The peelers showed up and started to restore order by kicking people in the ass and whacking 'em with batons. When the commotion had died down enough to be able to hear, the duty sergeant asked O'Boyle who started it, O'Boyle pointed at Rory and Jimmy, who were grabbed by four big coppers and hauled off to jail. Two days later, the magistrate fined them five pounds each for drunkenness, disorderly conduct, fighting, disturbing the peace and being general nuisances at large. Since they only had a couple pounds and a few pence left they spent the next fifteen days at the county farm working off their fines. When they finally got out, my aunts were so mad at them for losing all the prize money, they had to sleep in the barn for another week. On top of that, O'Boyle never let them into his pub again . . . they had to go to Muldoon's over by the stables to have a glass."

"I guess that's what they mean by luck of the Irish," Slater said.

"Thanks for a good story, Mike."

"Yeah. Thanks. Makes the time go by faster."

All eight of the Hogs were standing back to back for warmth in the center of the platform, water halfway up their thighs, and rising faster now. They were all showing signs of hypothermia from being underground and wet for so long. It was twelve hours and some minutes since the lights went out. Nobody said a word but they all knew their situation was fast approaching the critical stage.

"Does anybody else feel like praying?" Tad Henry asked in a quiet voice.

He must have spoken for all the men because when Ralph Corey said, "Our Father," every one of the Sandhogs joined in. "who art in heaven," spoken as one voice, "hallowed be," was interrupted by a shudder and far-off boom like thunder in the night, followed by what sounded like an out-of-control freight train coming down the hole. It was as if all the hubs of hell had been disconnected and thrown down the 850 foot shaft number two. A few seconds later, seconds that were an eternity to the shivering men trapped in the bowels of the Catskill Mountains, a roar was followed by a leviathan splash as something big and heavy fell into their sanctuary. A huge wave almost knocked them all from their perch.

"What the fuck was that?"

"Something big and ugly."

"Heavy, too."

"You guys knock it off for a second," Grady said. "I think I hear something."

"Look. Look there—light in the shaft."

They could all see a faint glow that was getting brighter. As the light improved they could see a yellow Caterpillar bulldozer smack in the water below the shaft opening. It was lying on its left side in the water with the right track and some of the blade sticking out.

"Holy shit, lookit that!"

"A dozer."

"D-6."

Then a muck bucket with somebody in it, and a big light popped out of the shaft. "You boys having a swim?" Bill Henry said. The Hogs all recognized his voice. He was foreman on the midnight, or graveyard shift. "Anybody hurt?" he asked.

"Tad has a broken hand, I think. No other injuries. We're all freezing our asses off though," Grady said.

"Okay. Tad first, I can take two of yez at a time."

"Tad, go now. You'll have to swim for it," Grady said. "It's about twenty feet. Slater, you go after Tad."

Tad swam to the bucket where Bill Henry pulled him in, then grabbed Slater by the collar and pulled him in. He spoke into a walkie-talkie taped on the bucket chain and was hoisted out with the first two survivors.

"Don't go away you guys. I'll be right back."

It seemed like forever to the men left below, but he was back in less than twenty minutes.

Ralph Corey and Bobby Michaels were next; both swam the twenty-five feet to the waiting bucket through the cold water like Olympic champions.

"Don't worry guys, I'll be back in a flash," Bill called out. "Dr. Conrad is up there taking care of Tad. Father Burke is on his way from the church too. We'll have you outta here in a few minutes."

Mike Antrim went as soon as the bucket dropped back into view. He was numb with cold but managed a sidestroke long enough to reach Bill Henry's hand and make it into the bucket.

"I'm not a real good swimmer," Curt Hightower said as he took off his tunnel boots with the yellow steel toes. "And I'm really cold."

He went into the water and started a nervous dog paddle toward the bucket. About eight feet out, it was apparent he was in trouble . . . he started to hyperventilate and thrash in the water. That's when Johnny Mack went in. He already had his boots off when Curt started and that saved them both. He managed to grab Curt behind the shoulder and sidestroked eighteen feet to safety. Bill pulled Curt in first, then muttered, "Aw, screw it," and grabbed Johnny Mack too.

"You're gonna have to hang on the bucket handle, Johnny. Can you manage that?" asked Bill. "Can you stand on the edge of it?"

"I th-th-think so," Johnny said through chattering teeth.

"I'll be right back, Grady," were the last words Grady Daggitt ever heard. Less than ten seconds after the hoist started up the shaft, a twenty-five ton chunk of rock fell on him. The men in the bucket knew it was bad when water surged all around them, filled the mucker and inundated them all. No words were spoken; none could be said to help what they knew had happened in the miserable black and wet hell beneath them.

The morning sun was throwing long shadows that collected in the valleys when the surviving Hogs were pulled out. They were greeted with somber enthusiasm by the graveyard and day shift men. Everyone had heard about the swing shift and came to help their brother Sandhogs. They all knew it could have been any one of them trapped down there . . . just as they all knew what the rumble under their feet meant.

The surviving Hogs were sitting on benches in the hog house, wrapped in wool blankets and sipping hot coffee; all had the "thousand yard stare" of survivors everywhere.

Bill Henry, along with the walking boss and safety officer, went back in the shaft. They emerged about an hour later looking grim. No hope was forthcoming: "He never had a chance — never knew what hit him. The whole ceiling collapsed where it wasn't bolted yet, about fifteen feet high, fifty feet wide. Grady Daggitt is buried down there."

The superintendent himself cleaned out Grady's locker the next morning and told Mike Antrim, who lockered next to him, "Just go to work." Which is exactly what Mike did. "Do yer job or someone else will" was the mantra. After all, the BWS brass figured *a man a mile* would die in the tunnels, and figured it was an acceptable loss. But Sandhog crews are like family. They were back next shift, Ralph Corey was made foreman and seven men did the work of eight. It was a good deal for the contractors, they didn't complain. The tunnel went on, just as before. Eight million city-folk need water after all. So the Hogs labored on. They went down in the shafts and tunnels.

They drilled, and blasted, and mucked until an inch of tunnel became a foot of tunnel, then a yard, then ten yards until foot by foot, the project was done. But none of the survivors from that day ever heard the snap-click of a Zippo lighter without thinking of Grady Daggitt and the day the lights went out 850 feet underground. They never gathered for a beer that their first sip didn't remember "absent friends."

Rest in peace, Grady Daggitt, rest in peace. You are not forgotten.

The Empire of Automobiles

The Empire of Automobiles

Lance Corporal Cadillac Varley, USMC, was home on leave for ten days before his unit was due to ship out for Korea.

He was leaning on the right front fender of a 1948 Mercury sedan drinking Ballantine Ale, watching his father, Oliver, who was standing on the Merc's front fenders. The car's hood had been removed and placed on its roof, the radiator was in the front passenger's seat and all of the transmission bolts, linkages, hoses, cables and wires were removed, as was the transmission itself.

"Motor mounts unbolted, Pop?"

"Yeah," Oliver said. "This ain't the first time I done this yuh know."

"Sure. Just makin' sure."

"Gid outta the way," Oliver said. He pulled the chain that was bolted on the left and right sides of the flathead V-8 in each hand. He squatted some, then gave a deep groan, almost a primeval battle cry, and yanked the chain with all his might. He lifted and threw the engine out of the junk car, over onto the grass on his left, never losing his balance on the front fenders.

"Chrissakes Pop, I can't believe you haven't busted a nut doing that."

Oliver jumped down beside his oldest son, who handed him a clean shop rag to wipe the sweat pouring off his face.

"Give me one of those beers. Take more than this to pop my nuts, but not a whole lot more." Oliver grinned at Cadillac and drank off half the bottle of ale in one long swallow.

"Seen you do it a couple of times but I still don't believe it. It's inhuman." Cadillac said.

Oliver drank the rest of his ale in two gulps, then said, "Back the truck up here and quit your jabber."

Cadillac walked to the edge of the field and backed an old Chevrolet pickup that had no doors or front fenders down the row of disabled and partly disassembled cars, stopping where his father waited alongside the newly liberated Ford motor.

"Okay son. Help me set this engine in the pickup."

"Hey, I don't wanna get grease all over my pants."

"Take the front then. Come on, I need to get it down to the house before they come to pick it up."

Oliver pulled out a plank that was in the truck bed, and lowered one end to the ground. Then he and Cadillac wrestled the V-8 motor over to it; Oliver jumped up in the pickup bed.

"Hand me the chain." Oliver bent and took the chain in hand and put the toe of his left shoe on the plank. He groaned and heaved the chain, sliding the engine up the board. Cadillac, of equal stature to his father, lifted and pushed from the low side. Together they slid the thing up into the pickup bed.

"Good thing I was here, Pop."

"Sure," Oliver said as he closed the tailgate and secured it with chains fastened to each side. He climbed back into the pickup bed and wedged the salvaged motor in one corner with his feet. He sat on one side of the bed, bracing the engine with his size seventeen shoes.

"You drive, Cadillac. And hand me another bottle of beer."

As his oldest son drove down the mountainside from what was

once a forty-five acre hayfield back when Grandpa Solomon Varley was prospering in the dairy business, Oliver Varley drank ale from a green bottle and surveyed his empire of automobiles. They were lined up in precise, military-straight rows from tree line to tree line, each row composed of two lines of cars parked back-to-back with a driving lane in between. Oliver planned it like that to get the maximum number of cars in the least amount of space, and he noted with satisfaction it was working just fine.

The truck bounced over a rut, causing Oliver to spill beer and hit his teeth with the bottle.

"Hey! Slow down, damnit. I'm getting my ass kicked back here."

"Sorry, Pop."

Oliver was obsessive about his empire, he knew the exact number of cars in this and four other smaller hayfields as well as the cow pastures where he had mounds of tires, wheels, mangled body parts too damaged to be used and piles and piles of iron . . . things like springs, bumpers and axles, front and rear ends, batteries, generators and transmissions as well as barrels filled with nuts, bolts and screws from dismantled cars. Every piece that came off of every car was accounted for. Nobody was allowed to remove a car part but Oliver, and his other operating rules were equally simple: the price was the price, he didn't haggle. Cash only. No checks, no credit, no commercial accounts. It was an easy system to remember and it worked fine for Oliver, and although it was a bit inconvenient for the customer, no one seemed to mind much, and as the cars got older, the parts harder to find and more expensive, the line of supplicants seeking to do business with Oliver increased by geometric progressions.

On this day, however, as he drank beer and looked over his rows and rows of automobiles shining and glittering, refracting and winking in the afternoon sun, Oliver was content. He wiped sweat from his face with the tail of the red plaid shirt he was wearing . . . the one with the sleeves torn off at the shoulders.

When they passed through the abandoned barnyard where the cows used to gather at milking time, Oliver leaned out and told Cadillac to "park over there," pointing with the empty bottle. He belched long and loud as Cadillac parked in the side yard and shut the truck off. It was the place where the clothesline had been; the very spot where little Studebaker Varley had disappeared, ten years earlier.

The Travelling Mooneys

1957

The Travelling Mooneys

It was the summer of 1957 and the Cold War was going full-tilt. It was a time when Strategic Air Command bombers armed with nuclear missles were in the air twenty four/seven and General Curtis LeMay warned that "The price of freedom is eternal vigilance." We kids had monthly "atomic war drills" in school; we were ushered into the hallways, where we sat with our backs against the wall with an open book on our heads until the principal announced "all clear" and we went back to class. It was when *Howdy Doody* and *The Lone Ranger* were all the rage, and *Lassie* was not to be missed every Sunday night at 7 p.m. It was a time of prosperity and a time of worry about Communism, about the "military-industrial complex" and about whether or not the New York Yankees were the greatest baseball team of all time. Nineteen fifty-seven was also the year the Soviet Union, our most frightening adversary, stunned the world on October 4, by launching *Sputnik One*, ushering in the space age.

* * *

School was out and I was looking forward to a long summer of fishing in the clear, cold mountain streams around Neversink with my best friend, Terry, bike riding, hiking, and playing baseball in the evenings with the rest of the kids on the sandlot by the town's only stoplight. I dreamed of afternoons swimming in the Chestnut Creek and the "Little World's Fair" at the local fairgrounds in August. I couldn't wait for the lights, games, prizes, cotton candy like pink clouds, hot dogs, orange sodas and the nightly fireworks. I was ten years old, and the world was my oyster, just waiting to be shucked. Looking back, through a fifty-five-year lens, I believe I was at a perfect age, in the right time and place . . . too young for responsibilities, but old enough to observe and remember in detail the events which took place in the summer of '57.

I remember, it was mid-June, about six o'clock in the evening, and we were just sitting down for supper. A new, fancy white Chevy pickup truck turned up our dirt road and pulled in the driveway. My dad was watching through the kitchen window as the truck stopped by our mailbox and a man got out. He came to the door where Dad went to meet him.

"Who's that?" My little brother, Kevin, asked.

"Don't know," Mother said. "Finish your supper. You too, Jesse."

The man on our porch was a stranger, dressed in a khaki shirt and pants. He was just about to knock when Dad stepped into view behind the screen door. Dad was big, about six-two, and the porch was six inches lower than the entry, so he towered over the stranger who looked to be about average height. He looked up at my father and said, "Hi, mister. My name is Frank Mooney. I'm a general contractor. Is this your place?"

"Yeah," Dad said. "All 160 acres of it. What can I do for you?"

"I'm in the roofing business. I put galvanized finishes on tin roofs . . . like your barn over there." Frank hooked his thumb over his shoulder, pointing toward our aged dairy barn with the rusting tin corrugated roof on it.

"I've got a crew working over at the prison farm in Woodburn putting our special galvanization on their barn and. . ."

"I don't want to buy anything," Dad said, cutting him off. Truth was, he'd been worrying about the rusting tin roof for a couple of years.

"Hang on a second," Frank said, "let me finish. Then I'll go. I'm sorry, but I didn't catch your name. I'm Frank. Frank Mooney," and he stuck out his hand.

"Flynn. Thomas Flynn," Dad said as he opened the door and shook hands, stepping out on the porch.

"Well, this is a really nice place you've got, Mr. Flynn. Pretty as I've ever seen, and I've seen quite a few."

"Tom," Dad said. "Everybody calls me Tom."

"You milking Holsteins Tom?"

"Some, Jerseys, mostly, and four Guernseys. Mixed breeds."

"Say, that's pretty smart, makes them more disease-resistant, doesn't it?"

"I guess, but with the lack of rain we've had this summer I don't know if we'll get much production or not. We've been okay so far, but we've got to get rain so we can make hay, so I can feed them next winter."

"I didn't know you-all were having a drought. I'm always on another job somewhere. Don't get to see much of any one place."

"Don't know if I'd call it a drought," Dad said. "It just hasn't rained much, so far this year."

"Good thing, too. Looking at that barn roof," Frank said as he looked at the barn with his hand shading his face like a visor. "How's about taking a look?"

*   *   *

Kevin and I cleared the table, and I washed the dishes while he dried

141

and put them away. Mom put the leftovers, and a plate for Dad, in the refrigerator. I could see him and the man named Frank Mooney through the kitchen window as I scrubbed the pots and pans. They were walking up the driveway, talking and pointing at the barn. First Frank, then Dad, would point, then nod or shake their heads while talking in an animated way. They walked around the barn and out of my sight. Just as I was rinsing the last pot, Frank Mooney came down the driveway and got something from his truck, then disappeared back up the driveway behind the barn. I was dying to get out there, but Mom, with a mother's intuition, told me to "stay here," unless Dad called me. Burning with curiosity, I got out the book I was reading and sat on the porch glider, where I was soon lost in deepest Africa with Bomba, the jungle boy. Bomba was lost in a cave, fighting a giant serpent with his bare hands and a rock he'd managed to pick up, when my dad and Frank Mooney came back down the driveway. I heard Frank say he'd "see Dad tomorrow" then he got in his truck and left. Dad came up on the porch and gave the glider a little nudge, making it rock, as he went in the house with a grin on his face, like he was in a really good mood.

*   *   *

Dad went in, and Mom got busy reheating his supper. I know they were talking, but I couldn't hear everything they were saying. Kevin came out and started playing with a big yellow dump truck in the middle of the lawn. It was still pretty light out, so I went back to my book. It looked like Bomba would survive the snake attack, but he still had to find his way out of the cave he was lost in. I had my ears perked up, of course.

I got so engrossed in the book I didn't even notice the discussion inside had turned rancorous until Kevin huddled up on the glider next to me, with a worried look. He nudged me and turned his eyes up toward the open kitchen window. We could hear bits and pieces, snatches of conversation, getting louder.

" . . . discount deal . . . " Dad.

" . . . listen . . . what . . . " Mom.

" . . . know what . . . " Dad.

" . . . tomorrow . . . " Dad again.

" . . . don't . . . bank . . . can't . . . " Mom.

" . . . third . . . done . . . telling you . . . " Dad.

Kevin was getting pretty worried, and so was I. We knew something was up, but it wasn't a good idea to get caught eavesdropping. I motioned to Kevin, and we went down to the apple orchard and climbed up in our favorite tree. We stayed there, pretending we were pirate lookouts, until Mom called us just before dark. We went up to the house, on our best behavior and went straight to bed.

We got up early the next morning, but Dad was already gone. He'd milked the cows and turned them out into the lower pasture where, down by the pond, we could hear their bells clinking and ringing as they noshed deeper into the grass. Mom made us toast as Kevin and I got our bowls and spoons for breakfasts of Wheaties and Trix.

"Where'd Dad go?" I asked Mom. I'd heard him leave in the doodlebug, which is what we called his old maroon '48 Ford car, because it looked like a big round beetle.

"He went to town. To the bank," Mom said, "to borrow money. There's going to be a roofing crew here later, and I don't want either of you getting underfoot. Understand? Keep out of the way."

"Aww, Mom, we're not babies," Kevin said.

"STAY OUT FROM UNDER FOOT," Mom said kind of loud, like she did when she was serious about it. We knew it was her "I'm not kidding" tone. We ate quietly and went outside to play, soon forgetting her admonition. We went up to our "fort," which was a stand of three sugar maple trees on the hill overlooking the house and barn, where we were the last two of a company of Bengal Lancers defending the Khyber Pass with stick rifles until Gunga Din or Tonto and the Lone Ranger could bring reinforcements.

By late morning, we were out of water and low on ammunition, when we saw the doodlebug kicking up a rooster tail of dust as it came up the driveway a little too fast, as our father usually did. "Comanches!" screamed Kevin, as he was a little confused about the type of Indians we were fighting.

"Naw, they're Mussulmen," I said, using the British Army term for the Muslim tribesmen, "coming down from the Hindu Kush to wipe us out. How's your leg and ammo holding out?" Kevin had been wounded in the leg by a stray bullet, but fortunately, I was able to bind it up with his bandanna. We always wore our red bandannas around our necks when we played, just like all the TV cowboys. Good thing too, it saved his leg from having to be amputated. I gave Kevin the last sip of water from the mayonnaise jar we'd filled up at the kitchen sink, and crawled up to the edge of the lawn to reconnoiter. Our lawn sloped down toward the house and was bisected by the driveway, which was a bit less than half a mile long and unpaved. It passed our house and ended in front of the barn. The result was that our fort of three maple trees sat in a pocket at the edge of the lawn, looking down at the house and driveway, then across to the barn with its attached milk house. When I peeked up, I could see Dad, moving the tractor out from the barn with a hay rake hooked on back. Then I felt Kevin crouch down beside me.

"Look," he whispered, pointing down the driveway.

I looked, and saw four big trucks, kicking up dust, headed toward the big turn in our driveway that was between the house and the paved road. There was a stake truck with some men standing up in the back leading the convoy, then a box truck like moving companies have, followed by two dump trucks pulling trailers. The first one had a large round tank on wheels, and the last one towed a huge air compressor. With the lack of rainfall, the caravan kicked up a storm cloud of dust that rolled over everything, Kevin, me, the lawn and the trucks themselves as they rolled to a stop up by the barn. We forgot all about the Khyber Pass and the Bengal Lancers. This was good stuff, the real deal, and it was happening right here in front of us.

*   *   *

The dust was just beginning to settle as Dad walked back from the field, where he had parked the tractor and hay rake. He said something to the man driving the first truck and pointed toward the backside of the barn. We couldn't hear what was being said, but the man got out of his truck and followed Dad out of sight behind the barn. Everyone else, including me and Kevin, stayed where they were. Most of the men standing in the back of the stake truck were lighting cigarettes by then, talking and laughing like guys do. We counted six men in the back, plus at least three more drivers and the guy with our dad.

"What's going on?" Kevin asked.

"Don't know," I answered. "Looks like maybe they're here to get something?"

About then, Mr. Frank Mooney, the guy who'd showed up at suppertime the previous night, rolled up the driveway in his fancy pickup. We had been so intent on watching what was going on, Kevin and I hadn't heard him coming until he drove past us. We saw Frank Mooney get out of his pickup and walk toward the guys in the first stake truck. He said something to the men, they pointed, and he walked behind the barn where Dad and the first man had disappeared.

"Whaddaya think they're doing?" Kevin asked.

"Looking at something. Maybe the cows, or ... I don't know," I said. "Let's sneak up there and see."

"Daddy will yell at us."

"Not if he doesn't see us. We'll have to be slow and quiet, like Tonto. Come on, Kevin, we'll go around the top of the hill ..."

* * *

We were crouched over and running, almost to the silo attached to the back end of the barn when the bell started ringing. That's what Mom used when she wanted either one of us to come to the house. She had an antique handbell, like the teachers used in the old one-room schoolhouses. The thing was about a foot tall; the top half had a maple handle and the bottom was a thick brass bell with a heavy iron clapper. It had a beautiful deep ring when shook, and could be heard all over the farm, from the woods to the fields as it called us—like Pavlov's dogs—home to the house.

At the first ring, Kevin took off running as if Old Rex, the grouchy brown farm dog who lived next door, was trying to bite him in the butt. Truth be told, I wasn't far behind, but not before I saw Dad through a gap in the barn siding, counting money into the outstretched hand of Mr. Frank Mooney.

"What's going on Ma? Who are all these guys? What are they doing here? Why is Dad giving that guy money?" I asked in a gush as I took my turn washing up.

"They're here about the barn roof," Mom answered in kind of a flat tone of voice, like she used when you hadn't finished your schoolwork, but said you did, because you wanted to watch TV, and she knew you were lying.

"You come over here and eat your lunch now. And don't bother your father or those men, either. You stay away from them. Kevin too. I want you both to promise me."

"Okay, Mom," I said, and wondered what exactly was going on, as I worked my way through a peanut butter and jelly sandwich on white bread—there was no other kind as far as Kevin and I were concerned—and a cup of tomato soup with melted butter on top and shell macaroni waiting to be dug out below. It was absolutely positively my favorite lunch when taken with a big glass of milk and some oatmeal raisin cookies for dessert. Of course, chocolate chip was okay too . . .

*   *   *

We finished up and put our plates and empty bowls and stuff in the sink, where Mom said she'd take care of them. Kevin and I headed back outside to "recon the situation" just like Robert Ryan and John

147

Wayne did in the war movies. We decided to spy on things from behind the porch glider, where we could see the barn and the men working. I'd just stretched out next to the wall behind the glider, when Dad came down the driveway and up on the porch. I was looking up at the barn through my make-believe binoculars when he pointed his finger at me and said, "Jesse, you and Kevin stay out of the barn. Stay away from the crew and out from underfoot. I don't want to see you two around there. You understand?" Dad was a big man, and a strong one. When he talked like that, grown-ups paid attention. I realize now, as an adult, he didn't know how intimidating someone his size could be to someone my size, five six and ninety pounds soaking wet. Just the threat of corporal punishment from him was enough to make me nearly wet my pants. Believe me, you've never, ever had a spanking until you got one on your bare behind while bent over my dad's lap. He always hit us with his hand, but I promise you, neither you, nor your buttocks forgot it for a while.

"Yes, Dad. I understand. And I hear you," was all I said as he went in the house, leaving two scared boys and a rattling screen door behind. I felt the weight of his words for the rest of the afternoon. So did Kevin. There was no way for us to know then, that Dad and Mom were hanging on by their fingernails. It was almost impossible for them to make a living and pay the mortgage on a 160-acre dairy farm in 1957 in upstate New York with twenty four cows being milked by hand. I didn't know the price of milk barely exceeded, in some cases was less than, the cost of keeping the cows. All over the county, cows were being sold off or slaughtered. And I didn't know then, banks were foreclosing on some farms, while others were being sold to land developers. Around Sullivan County, where we lived, some farms were simply falling into disuse and general disrepair, the barn roofs spavined, the silos falling over and small trees growing in the barnyard where the cows used to gather morning and night at milking times. Any little setback, any sudden unexpected expense, accident or illness could be the fulcrum for the tipping point into personal disaster. Good-bye farm. Hello poorhouse.

* * *

But I didn't know any of those things in 1957. All I knew was my mother and dad were fussing at us, and at each other. Kevin and I retreated under the front porch, where it was cool and quiet, and where the wrath of adults was far away. We watched as Mr. Frank Mooney and his crew climbed ladders to the roof of the barn and worked with ropes and hoses and hammers up there, in the boiling hot sun.

* * *

We heard from the coolness of our redoubt, a loud BAARROOON as the big air compressor was started up. We saw a man up on the highest peak of the highest roof on the farm, and watched as he dangled from a rope, holding the end of an air hose while he cat-walked, back and forth, back and forth, back and forth, spraying the barn roof until it glistened, and shone like a polished silver dollar in the afternoon sun.

By late afternoon they were done and gathering up their tools and equipment. Mr. Frank Mooney pulled his pickup to the edge of the driveway, parked and came up to the porch door. The big trucks were pulling out and rumbling down the driveway, one by one, as he knocked on our porch door. We heard him talking to Dad.

"Stay off it for a few days while it sets up and gets hard."

We could hear Dad: "Looks good. You boys got done fast."

Frank Mooney: "I've got a professional and experienced crew. We use first-class materials and do a quality job."

Dad: "Guess I won't have to worry about rain ruining the hay anymore. If ever it rains again. I 'preciate the fast work, and the price."

Frank Mooney: "Yeah. I'll never do another job as cheap as I did this one. Hope you have a good summer."

Dad: "Yes—yes."

And then Mr. Frank Mooney got in his pickup truck and left, following in the cloud of dust that floated on the air like a dream, behind his last departing truck, the one pulling the big tank full of roofing stuff. Kevin and I turned our attention to road construction under the porch while Dad went up the driveway to admire the new barn roof. We never saw Mr. Frank Mooney or any of his men again.

*   *   *

The rains, usually prolific in May and June, were poor that year, and never came at all in July. By the first week in August, we had no water in the house as the artesian spring in our cellar had dried up, and Dad and I had to haul water in forty-quart milk cans. We carried six milk cans in the back of the old doodlebug, where Dad had taken the backseat out, and drove fifteen miles to the MacAllan spring to fill them each Saturday morning. The cows had to walk half a mile, down to the brook, now almost gone, for a drink. It was only a trickle, and barely met their needs. Then they would lie about, listless and morose in whatever shade they could find, slowly chewing their cuds and slapping their tails at the hordes of flies, so plentiful and persistent in the never-ending heat. The cows produced less and less milk as a result. Haying was just brutal. With the lack of rain the hay didn't grow much, and was full of milkweed, burdocks and thistles. We'd come up from the fields hot, sunburned, sweaty, thirsty no matter how much iced tea we drank, and covered in dust and hayseeds. The seeds itched and stuck to the sweat on your body like a bad debt on a credit report.

*   *   *

I didn't get much fishing done with Terry; his dad took the family to Cape Cod for the summer in an attempt to beat the heat. I didn't play much baseball either. It was too hot during the day, and even in the evening, so much heat was still radiating from the dry brown grass, not one of us kids had the energy for ball playing. The much-anticipated "Little World's Fair" wasn't too exciting either; it was just too hot to have much fun. Kevin and I didn't have any money anyway. Mom and Dad were always civil to each other when us boys were around, but even we could sense an unspoken tension between them.

Just when we thought it would never rain again, when we thought the whole county was going to turn into the Serengeti, the rains came. They came in the third week of August. It clouded up one afternoon, the wind freshened, leaves turned up on the trees, and it rained. It rained hard at first. It hit the dust in fat drops and made little craters that soon turned muddy.

After awhile, the hard rains slowed down and became a steady, gentle, drenching that continued for the next ten days. We went from nothing to too much, but it was okay, because the springs and ponds and wells were all filling up to the brim. Water filled the creek that ran below our lowest field until it ran hard and fast, and overflowed its banks. The pasture greened up almost immediately, and the tree leaves, washed of the dust, looked green and healthy for the first time all summer. The flies were down and the cows were up. Things were looking good. When the rain stopped we noticed it. The sun came out again, the last drops fell from the eaves of the barn, and we saw it. That's when Dad, Mom, Kevin and I saw that there was no shiny new roof on the barn. The roof, which had looked so new, that Dad had been so proud of, the roof he had borrowed at the bank to pay for, was lying in big ugly globs along the side of the barn. It was in a long windrow of gray gooey sludgelike stuff that looked like the entrails of some monster that had been gutted right there next to the barn. We couldn't believe it. The stuff, whatever it was, was nasty too. If you stuck your finger in it or got some on your shoes or pant leg, it burned and smelled like sewage and took kerosene or turpentine to remove it.

I thought Dad was gonna cry. His face got red, then turned purple. His arms and hands shook with rage. He was so angry, and clenched his teeth so hard that he bit the stem of the pipe he was smoking in half. As the still-smoking, hot bowl fell to the driveway in a shower of sparks, we all stood there with our mouths open in shock. We could not believe what we were seeing. "O-OOH NOO-OO!" Dad moaned out loud. "OH NO, NO, NOO-O." He walked toward the barn, never taking his eyes off of it, his big shoulders slumping, his hands clenched into fists. We all knew he was beside himself with anger, humiliated and shamed at being swindled. Without a word, Mom put her arms around Kevin and me, slowly walking us back to the house. Once we were inside, she spoke to us in her softest voice, one that was nearly a whisper . . .

"I think you boys should go up and play in your room. I'll be up after a while to tuck you in, but right now I want you both to go. And be quiet."

Kevin streaked up the stairs to our shared bedroom, with me right behind him. It was one of the few times in my young life that I had no rebuttal. It wasn't as if we were afraid of our father, we knew he loved and cared for us, would always be there for us, but we were very, very respectful and polite when he was angry about something. Mom, Kevin, and I all knew without being told, Dad was beyond anger over the situation; he was apoplectic.

For weeks after the drought broke, Dad was quiet, moody and prone to fly off the handle with the least provocation. He didn't know it, but I saw him pick up a two-by-four one day and hit a recalcitrant Holstein cow across her back with it. With one blow, he broke the board into pieces and put the poor cow flat on the ground, where she moaned and struggled to regain her feet. I think Dad scared himself that day, and I'm certain he felt guilty about it. He treated that particular cow as gently as he could thereafter, always petting and talking quietly to her, giving her extra feed and more straw for a softer bed. I think that, in his own way, Dad was apologizing to her, over and over. Suffice it to say without belaboring, the whole family went on tiptoe for a few weeks while Dad worked his anger out. The cow recovered, but she never gave the same volume of milk.

Like I said, we never saw Mr. Frank Mooney or any of his crew again. Dad always thought they were gypsies, and in a way they were; although not Roma, as the eastern European Gypsies call themselves. It took me fifty-plus years to find out about them, but I finally did. Frank Mooney and his crew were Travellers; nomadic clans of Scottish and Irish descent, who travel the country posing as legitimate contractors and builders, soliciting jobs and cheating people out of their money. Their most common scams involve roofing, painting and paving, but they come to town with a full bag of tricks and confidence schemes—always for cash, always for less than what a legitimate builder would charge. They are real. They are still operating in the twenty first century. They are seldom prosecuted, as they're usually gone before the victim realizes he's been swindled. They travel throughout the nation preying on those gullible enough, and larcenous enough, to buy the malarkey they are selling. When the Traveller shows up, with "leftover materials" from another job, the victim cons himself into getting what he perceives as a bargain price.

* * *

As for our family back in 1957, we survived and kept the homestead. Dad sold off the cows that fall and gave up his dream of farming. He took a job as a Sandhog, working in DeBruce, New York, on the West Delaware Tunnel project, part of the city of New York's upstate water system. At first he was a laborer, later became the foreman on a mucking crew . . . working 780 feet underground in shaft number six. The muckers followed the drillers and blasters, shoveling out the mud and rocks and debris, pushing the tunnel through solid rock, a few feet at a time until it was finished in 1960. Kevin started the third grade, I started the sixth, the Russians started the space age and we all dreamed of being astronauts. The big dams filled up from the mountain streams, the tunnels were completed and the water flowed down to New York City. There's hundreds more stories to be told about the Neversink, the two dams there, the farms and the sparkling pure Catskill waters where I spent my childhood . . . but they'll have to wait for another time, another place and another day to be told.

*   *   *

LAST THOUGHTS:

There were a lot of talks behind Mom and Dad's closed bedroom door that year, quite a few slammed pots, slammed doors and loud words, but I guess everything worked out okay, because the following summer, our little brother, Billy, was born. Billy was a surprise baby and a surprising man. He grew up, went to college, and became a respected builder and contractor. He built houses, churches, schools and office buildings all over the country. He turned out to be the biggest, handsomest and physically strongest of the Flynn brothers. Maybe it was all the MacAllan spring water Dad and I hauled in those milk cans. Who knows? Maybe it was.

Mom and Dad were married for 38 years. Dad died in the spring of 1983, a victim of lung cancer; he was 59 years old. Mom lived alone at the farm until she passed in the summer of 1999 at age 72. The farm was sold in 2000 and is still there, up in Neversink, amidst the shining, cold mountain waters that tumble down to the big dams where it's captured and impounded for the benefit of New York City, 90 miles to the south. Billy finally put a new steel roof on the barn in 1987. It looks great.

When the Empire was Bloodied

1963

When the Empire Was Bloodied

Late in the 1950's, Neversink was infected with a stock car racing craze . . . it was as sudden and virulent as an outbreak of Ebola virus, as irrational, widespread and exuberant as the tulip mania in seventeenth-century Holland, as incomprehensible as the attempts to turn lead into gold by the alchemists of the Middle Ages. The racing mania sprang up lemming-like as small, oval dirt racetracks of one-quarter to one-half mile in length sprouted up at county fairgrounds all over the northeast states like mushrooms after an overnight rain, and Oliver Varley was gob-smack in the middle of it all. In an instant, his old farm became the most popular place in town as supplicants trekked up Rhyolite Mountain, seeking an audience with Oliver, the accidental king of an empire of automobiles.

Oliver was in his element. The just-printed rule books of the new stock car racing associations stated that "only American automobiles, coupe or sedan bodies, manufactured in the USA between 1932 and 1948, with original drive-trains (motor-transmission-rear end) would be allowed in competition," and he had thousands of them, all lined up in neat rows, sitting on wood blocks, just waiting to be found and turned into stock cars.

At first, Oliver enjoyed the limelight, because all at once, he was every wannabe racer's new best friend . . . until they got the stock car body they wanted. Then they didn't pay attention to Oliver anymore. He wasn't angry, didn't get mad when he figured out he was being used. Instead he raised his prices, all of them . . . on everything . . .

no exceptions for new best friends either.

Oliver was making a fortune before he doubled his prices. Now, as the racing virus spread and sojourners from other states made their way to Rhyolite Mountain, he was on the verge of becoming wealthy, and he began changing. It was a gradual change, more a becoming than a metamorphosis, and was barely noticed at first even by his children.

Oliver, never a detail person, began wanting explanations and accountings.

"Daddy," one of his daughters, the oldest one at home usually, the one who was the surrogate mother in nominal charge of the household, would say, "Daddy, I need three hundred dollars."

"Why?"

"We need food."

"Why?"

"I haven't been to the store for two weeks, we're out of stuff."

"Here's two fifty. Will that do?"

"I was stretching to get everything for three hundred. Four hundred would be best, if you want to have enough to eat."

"Okay. Here's another hundred. That'll have to do."

"The beer truck will come on Wednesday. Don't forget to leave money for him, or you'll have to go to Liberty and pay full price at the liquor store."

"How much?"

"Another hundred. You've been going through a lot of beer. That's why the truck delivers all the way up here. You're a better customer than some of the bars."

"How d'you know?" Oliver said.

"Tommy told me."

"Who's that?"

"Tommy drives the beer truck."

"Oh."

Oliver was making more money than he'd ever even dreamed of. He was accumulating more cash than he could carry, which was how he'd always done it before. He didn't change outwardly, still wore denim overalls, and heavy steel-toed work shoes, still wore white T-shirts all summer and flannel shirts in winter, and he still favored the brown canvas barn coat with the gray, green and blue flannel lining he'd always worn. But as the money poured in, Oliver was morphing into something else, changed by all the cash like Dobbs was changed by the Sierra Madre.

Oliver didn't trust hospitals, banks or the U.S. Post Office. He'd never had a bank account, didn't mail anything and all of his children, except one, had been born at home. This proved to Oliver that he was absolutely right: seventeen of his kids, the ones born at home, were accounted for and okay; the exception was Studebaker, hospital-born, and disappeared seventeen years ago.

Letters get lost, banks fail and take your money, everything not under direct control could disappear. *No by God,* Oliver believed, *I ain't gonna trust none of those bastards.*

Oliver always carried a couple of thousand dollars in his overall pockets, so he could make change for the buyer and accommodate any sellers who might happen along. Everyone in the county with a wrecked or junk car knew they had two choices: leave the thing out back of the house somewhere, or call Oliver and get paid a few dollars for it. Sooner or later, almost all of the old cars in the county made it to Oliver Varley's place, up on Rhyolite Mountain. What no one knew was that in addition to his "change-money," as he called it, he always had ten or fifteen thousand dollars secreted in the bib of his omnipresent overalls, and a small J-Frame Smith & Wesson .38 caliber pistol he'd found between the rear seat cushions of a '53 Pontiac sedan. The pistol was a five-shot model called a "safety hammerless" because there wasn't an external hammer to catch on a pocket when it was pulled out. Oliver liked the pistol a lot, its only drawback being that he had a hard time getting his hand around the walnut grip while in his pocket . . . a problem he solved by tearing the top of his right pants pocket about an inch so his huge hand could reach in and get his "pet," as he called the pistol.

Oliver's problem was too much money. He only transacted in cash on the barrelhead, and it was accumulating faster and faster with everyone in four states wanting to build stock cars. When things got too complicated Oliver's brain couldn't process information fast enough, so it just stopped working and he'd go into a complete funk.

Oliver's funk would start with frustration, then turn to aggravation and irritation that culminated in anger. The anger stage was as frightening as a big budget horror movie because Oliver would destroy anything close at hand in a berserk rage. At six foot seven inches and 260 pounds he could overturn a small car as if it were a child's toy. His rages were the stuff of legend, and like a hurricane or forest fire, to be avoided at all cost until they'd burned themselves out. But he was never known to harm any living thing, only property, generally his own.

* * *

Tillis and Schneiter were on the road by six o'clock in the morning.

They'd gassed up Schneiter's '49 Ford pickup the night before, hooked up the tandem-axle car trailer and checked the running lights. They stopped and filled a thermos with coffee at the trucker's diner on their way out of town, hoping to make it from Danbury, Connecticut, to Beacon, New York, to catch the ferry to Newburgh before seven thirty. Then they'd drive straight up Route 52 to Liberty and on down to meet a guy named Oliver Varley, at some place called Rhyolite Mountain. They'd heard about it through the racer's grapevine. Tillis and Schneiter were a pair of track hoodlums, looking to buy, or steal if the opportunity presented itself, a stock car body and chassis.

Tillis settled on the seat and flipped open the wing window with his right hand and fished out a pack of Winstons with his left. He shook one out and lit it from a matchbook he carried in the same shirt pocket.

"Want one?" he said to Schneiter.

"Yeah."

"You know where we're going?"

"Sure. Stay on this road 'til we get to Patterson, then take 292 right on to Fishkill and Beacon."

"Yeah. We'll get the ferry there."

Schneiter swerved the truck, trying to hit an orange house cat who darted across the road. A thump from the front axle indicated he'd succeeded.

"Gotcha, you little bastard."

Tillis, the one who thought he was the brains of the pair said, "You dumb fuck. Whatsa matter with you? Maybe it was some little girl's kitty. Whad'ja do that for?"

"I hate cats."

"Don't fuckin' do that again."

"Sure," Schneiter said as he tossed the cigarette butt out the window and watched it hit the shoulder in a shower of sparks. He could just see the orange fur body on the asphalt as he crested a rise in the road, one paw lifted in the air as if trying to fend off the steel monster that had just taken its life. Schneiter smirked at the rear view mirror and started whistling to himself as he drove on. *Its gonna be a good trip with a start like this,* he thought.

Tillis turned the radio on and found a station playing Top 40 tunes, watched out the window, lost in thoughts of his own, as Schneiter drove them on toward Fishkill, the Newburgh-Beacon ferry and their rendezvous with Oliver Varley at Rhyolite Mountain. They made the seven thirty ferry from Beacon and were on Route 52 North by eight o'clock in the morning.

Schneiter's pickup was a three-quarter ton model, which meant it had larger heavy-duty wheels and tires, a truck four-speed transmission and bigger springs than a regular half-ton truck. He'd also installed a big Cadillac V-8 engine under the hood, so it had plenty of power to pull a car trailer, and they were making good time, although Tillis had kept up a steady stream of complaints.

"Why'd they charge us double-price for the ferry?"

"Because," Schneiter said, "we took up two spaces."

"Well, we only had one vehicle."

"One space for the truck, one for the trailer. Two spaces."

"Yeah, but . . ." Tillis said.

"Yeah but my ass," Schneiter said. "Why don't you shut up about it?"

Tillis sulked for a bit, then said, "What's with these friggin' stop lights. Every damn one is red."

Schneiter turned and looked at him without a word until Tillis busied himself lighting another cigarette. Schneiter reached over and took it, stuck it in his mouth and popped the clutch as the light turned green and they headed out of Walden, towards Pine Bush, Walker Valley and the crooked, winding trail that led through the Shawangunk Mountains and down to Ellenville.

They passed through Walker Valley and were in Cragsmoor, crossing the granite Shawangunks when Schneiter said,

"So, what ya know about this guy Oliver Varley?"

"He lives up on a mountain of cars, where a lotta the guys are getting race car stuff."

"Fuck, I know that. Anything else?"

Tillis gave it some thought while he dug under his right ear for a bit, then popped a ripe pimple with his thumb and forefinger. He examined the goo on his fingers, then wiped the mess on his pants leg before he answered.

"I heard he beat 'is wife to death because she left their baby outside and bears, or something, got him and ate 'im."

"Really."

"That's what I heard."

"Where?"

"Oh, around. Here and there."

"No shit, he beat his wife to death?"

"What I heard."

"He didn't go to prison?"

"Don't think so."

"Why not?"

"Dunno. Prob'ly some problem with the law, a technicality of some kind or other'd be my guess."

"How'd he get all them cars?"

"Prob'ly stole 'em or something."

"Yeah. Know how that works, don't we?" Schneiter said as he lit another cigarette.

They continued their fallacious conversation all the way through Ellenville, and on up Route 52 through Woodbourne and into Liberty where they stopped at a place called the Triangle Diner for some more coffee and breakfast.

Despite his bulk, Tillis waddled up to the door and inside, while Schneiter was locking the truck. He walked in and found Tillis in a booth by the front windows.

"I didn't know you could move so fast."

"Can when I'm hungry," Tillis said. "Right now, my stomach thinks my throat's been cut."

"Too many of those chili dogs you've been wolfin' at the race track. Those things are poisonous."

"They're good, though."

Nancy, the waitress, came and took their order, left coffees and put their order on a clip attached to a stainless steel wheel over the counter by the kitchen. The cook spun the wheel around, looked at it, and started cooking. Schneiter surveyed the other patrons over the rim of his cup, eyes fixing on each person for a second or two, then moving on to the next, as if he were assessing something only he could see. Tillis flipped through the selections on the wall-mounted jukebox in the booth, but didn't play anything.

Probably too cheap. He won't want to part with a quarter, thought

Schneiter.

When Nancy came back with their breakfast, Schneiter asked her if she knew where a man named Oliver Varley lived.

"No, but I'll ask Willie, the cook, for youse, he grew up here." Nancy said. She came back with the check and topped off their coffees, then said, "Willie says turn right on fifty-five, about a mile north of here by the lumberyard. When you get to Bradley's Corners turn left. You can see it from there, looks like a mountain of glitter. That's the place. He said you can't miss it."

"Thanks," Schneiter said, and watched her friendly-looking ass wig-wag and jiggle away from him for the third or fourth time before turning to his plate of pancakes and bacon. He noticed Tillis had both arms wrapped around his plate and was facedown, shoveling food like it was his first meal in three days.

They finished breakfast and Schneiter left Nancy a nice fifty-cent tip on the six forty tab. Tillis stiffed her. Schneiter paid the check and they gassed up next door at the Cities-Service Gasoline Station, then headed for Rhyolite Mountain.

When they made the turn at the lumberyard on to state Route 55, a sign indicated "Bradley 4 mi." and "Neversink 12 mi." underneath.

"Lissen a me," Schneiter said to Tillis. "Here's how we're gonna play it."

"Okay, m'listening."

"We get there, I'll talk to him. You look around, see what's what, where he keeps shit, while I keep him busy. I'll make a deal with 'im and go get the car, you get what you can. Don't worry if you can't, we'll come back at night, or when he ain't home. You hear?"

"Sure. I hear."

Tillis lit another cigarette, and Schneiter took it away from him. Anger flared in Tillis's face but he said nothing, lit himself a second one from an almost-empty pack.

The fucker. Tillis thought. *"He's gonna smoke all of mine, then make me beg for his all the way home . . . the dirty bastard.*

They could see Rhyolite Mountain from just outside the Liberty town limits, sticking out from the surrounding hills like a miniature Kilamanjaro dipped in diamond dust.

"Christ, will ya lookit that," Tillis said as they drove on, drawn towards Rhyolite Mountain like bears to a honey tree. They turned on Rhyolite Mountain Road when they got to Bradley and drove through a forest of sugar maples, white birches and hemlocks for a couple of miles before breaking out of the woods into a rolling meadow that was overshadowed by the looming presence of Rhyolite Mountain and Oliver Varley's empire of automobiles. They could see the Neversink Reservoir sparkling in the morning sunlight, down the road past the mountain.

"There's a dirt road, looks like it goes right up to it," Tillis said, pointing.

"Yeah."

Schneiter swung the pickup and trailer onto the dirt drive that led a half-mile up the side of Rhyolite Mountain to Oliver Varley's farmhouse, perched at the upper end of a hayfield with a large barn and several outbuildings on the flats beyond. Behind the two-story farmhouse and disappearing up the mountain, stood row . . . after row . . . after row of cars.

"Looks like we come to the right place," Tillis said.

"No shit, Sherlock. What gave you the first clue?"

Tillis looked out his window and said nothing.

Schneiter pulled up past the house and side yard with the car trailer hopping up and down and rattling over the rutted dirt and gravel road. He parked among several other trucks and cars that were scattered around haphazardly.

"Keep your eyes open," Schneiter said as he shut the motor off and got out, pulling his leather bomber jacket on. He was chewing on a toothpick as he started up the flagstone path to the front steps and porch with Tillis in tow behind.

The front door opened before Schneiter could knock, and he was met by a young woman with a baby on her hip.

"Hi there, Missus. My name's Schneiter and this here's Tillis. We're looking for Oliver Varley."

"That's my father, but he ain't here. You just missed him."

"When's he coming back?"

"Prob'ly this afternoon, he went to fetch a car."

The baby looked up at Schneiter, stuck its thumb in its mouth, and clutched at the woman's shoulder with its other hand, never taking its eyes off Schneiter.

"That's a pretty baby, boy or girl?"

"Boy," the young woman said as she hitched the baby higher on her hip, "and he's a handful."

"I can see he is," Schneiter said as he stared at the woman's breasts with undisguised lechery. His tongue made a surreptitious circle past his lips. "I came over here from Connecticut to buy a car from your daddy."

"Well he ain't here," the woman said, bouncing the baby again, her cheeks flushing.

"How's about we just have a look around, beings we've come so far and all," Schneiter said.

"You can't do that."

"Because . . ."

"Because Daddy don't allow nobody up among his cars 'less he's with them."

"Well he ain't here is he?"

"He's pretty particular about it. You can't go up there."

"Honey, I'm a grown man. I don't take orders from no goddamn woman and I'm going on up there."

"Don't call me 'honey,' don't swear at me and don't go up there without Daddy," she said. The baby was screwing his face up, starting to cry as she added, "I'm going to call my grampa."

"Well honey, you go right on ahead and call whoever you want but I'm going on up there to look around. I come a long way and I ain't taking no fucking orders from a half-grown girl," Schneiter said as he turned and left the porch and headed toward Oliver Varley's collection of automobiles. He heard the baby screaming and Mercer Varley saying, "You got no idea how much you're gonna regret this," as she slammed the door shut.

"Damn, Schneiter, I don't think that was a good idea, she's just a kid. You should'na talked to her like that."

Schneiter stopped at the truck to retrieve an old 1911A .45 caliber Colt automatic pistol from under the seat. He pulled the slide, which chambered a round, set the trigger at half-cock and stuck it behind his back. He pulled his jacket down, lit a cigarette and puffed on it before squinting at Tillis through the smoke, and said, "I don't give a shit what you think. Besides, it's our word against hers. We'll just deny it."

"Whadda ya need the gun for?"

Schneiter just smirked at him, making Tillis more uneasy than he was before he'd asked.

*   *   *

Oliver was almost to White Sulpher Springs when he blew a tire on the old Diamond T flatbed truck. *It's the kind of day when nothing seems to go right,* he thought, *dead battery, no gasoline, no Kaiser or Lincoln, the boys were off somewhere, now a flat on the inside dual, and no frigging spare either. What else can go wrong?*

An old screw jack and a two-piece truck lug wrench were all he had to work with, so it took a half hour to remove the outer, and then the flat inner-wheel and tire. He replaced the good one and tightened the lugs; he'd have to limp it back home for a replacement. There was no way he could haul a car on one wheel. *Shit. Shit. Shit and Shit,* he thought as he started back to Rhyolite Mountain, wiping the sweat from his face with the tail of his flannel shirt. *This is one frigged-over day.*

Oliver pulled into his driveway and turned around in front of the barn about two hours after he'd first left the place, noticing a nice-looking three-quarter ton Ford pickup truck with a tandem-axle car-hauling trailer hooked on back. He didn't see anyone in it, but stopped to admire the rig for a half-minute before heading on to his house.

Mercer met him halfway up the steps.

"They're up in the cars, Daddy. I told them not to, but the taller one told me he didn't take orders from no fukken' wimmen."

"Don't talk like that, Mercer."

"I'm not, Daddy. I'm just telling you what he said."

"How many are there and how long have they been up there?"

"There's two of 'em, a tall one an' a fat one. The tall one did all the talking. They went up there a little more'n an hour ago."

"You and the lil' one okay?"

"Yes, Daddy. I would of killed them if they touched Roger."

"Alright, child. Stay in the house and call Grampa and Uncle Howard. Tell them to wait down here for me."

"I already did. They're coming."

Oliver got back in the big Diamond T truck he'd bought from the onion farmers down in Orange County, and moved it alongside the strangers' pickup and trailer, blocking it in. It couldn't move unless Oliver moved first. Then he walked to the access road and peered up into his salvage yard, looking for the intruders.

He didn't think about being calm, keeping himself in control, or the consequences of his actions; Oliver just reacted. His reaction to anyone violating his sacred space, profaning his creation, the sacrosanct place he'd created and built with his own love, his labor and his sacrifices . . . was an overwhelming, all-consuming rage. A rage so total it infused every cell in his body. Answering some primordial urge, he became as a *berserker,* one of the barbarians come up the shore from a longboat with a dragon's head carved on either end, come to sack the monestary, to slaughter, kill, slay, pillage, rape, loot, burn and reave his way to exhaustion . . . or oblivion. His rage transformed him as it consumed him, and he became otherworldly, not able to rein himself in, not able to reckon, not able to control the events he was about to set in motion.

Oliver went to a shed next to his barn and got into an old electric golf cart he used for getting around in his junkyard. He backed out and started up the access road for the second time, his oversized body sticking out at odd angles, his ridiculous appearance masking the seriousness of his intentions; the mayhem in his heart, and the blood, pounding in his ears.

Tillis saw him first.

"Schneiter, get out here, somebody's coming. Big sonofabitch too."

Schneiter climbed out of the 1939 Cadillac sedan he'd been ransacking and saw Oliver headed toward them. He emptied his pockets and said, "Here. Put these in your pockets and let me do the talking." He handed Tillis several gearshift knobs and porcelain nameplates he'd been pilfering.

"Why I have to hold them?"

"Just shut up and do it."

Tillis put the half-dozen items in his pockets, looking unhappy.

"Go back there, like you stepped away to take a piss."

Schneiter turned to face Oliver, who'd just turned his golf cart down the row. He waited, hands behind his back in a casual pose that was anything but casual.

Oliver saw the two trespassers up by the last rows of cars, one had been inside his '39 Cadillac but now was standing in front of it. The other one, porky, had gone out of sight, into the next row. Oliver floored the golf cart, and turned down the row to confront both of them, never lifting his foot from the throttle and never taking his eyes off Schneiter. He drove down the row of cars at top speed, braking only at the last instant, sliding to a stop sideways in front of Schneiter. Oliver yanked the handbrake, jumped out before the cart stopped and grabbed a very surprised Schneiter by the lapels of his leather coat in a smooth-fluid motion that should have been impossible for a man of his size and age.

Schneiter was a man of about six feet in height and 185 pounds, but found himself lifted in the air by an enraged giant. A giant whose angry red face was three inches from his and seemed to be nothing but jaws and big square teeth, spewing flecks of spittle that covered Schneiter's face in a fine mist, like a heavy fog. A giant who was screaming at him with a voice that seemed to come from the depths of the earth, propelled by supernatural forces.

"WHO D'YOU THINK YOU ARE TO COME UP HERE? WHO?"

"I . . . uh . . . no . . ." was all Schneiter managed to get out. He was afraid he might bite the tip of his tongue off if he tried to speak because Oliver was shaking him with such violence his teeth were clacking like Spanish castanets.

Schneiter tried to pull the Colt pistol from his waistband, managed to pull the hammer into the fully cocked position, but then it slipped from his hand and fell on the ground. He started fighting, kicking and punching. He landed solid kicks but the giant seemed oblivious to them; it was as if he were impervious to pain, as if he reveled in it.

Tillis was crouched next to the left front fender of a '47 Chevrolet, watching in fear as the giant manhandled and screamed at Schneiter, the pair of them locked in a grotesque-looking embrace, staggering around in the next row of cars.

When he saw Schneiter reach for the pistol, Tillis felt a shiver of fear that traveled down his spine and lodged in his prostate, tightening his sphincter and drawing up his testicles. When he saw the gun hit the ground, he made his move, scurrying from his hiding place like a fat woodchuck heading for a stone wall.

He grabbed the pistol in a shaky right hand and pointed it toward the combatants.

"HEY!" was all he said.

Oliver Varley, who was seeing his adversary through a red haze, sensed movement alongside him and turned in that direction, keeping his iron grip on Schneiter's leather jacket, swinging him around as if he were made of straw, and sending him into Tillis, still pointing the automatic pistol.

When Oliver swung Schneiter into Tillis, Tillis pulled the trigger, discharging a 225 grain hollow point that bored into Schneiter's back, severing his spinal cord and destroying his heart before exiting his sternum in an explosion of blood, bone and muscle tissue, splattering Oliver's face and clothes, covering him in gore from his head to his knees. The flattened-out .45 caliber slug hit Oliver in the chest like a nine-pound hammer, and sent him over backwards in the dirt. Schneiter's lifeless body fell on top of Tillis's and pinned him momentarily as it spasmed in death, its legs quivering for a few seconds while the nerves and muscles died. Tillis, the only one not injured, was making a mewing sound, like a baby kitten, over and over again.

Old Solomon Varley was just turning off the blacktop county road when Oliver left the driveway in his golf cart. Solomon, the spriest seventy-two year old in Neversink, was driving his '58 Volkswagen. He had a cut-down thirty-inch double-barreled ten-gauge scatter gun and his son Howard with him. Howard was a badge-carrying deputy sheriff, and Solomon an elected justice of the peace, which he had been for the last thirty-five years.

"I see him, Pop. He's headed up the mountain."

"Okay."

Solomon was only two minutes behind Oliver. When he stopped next to the golf cart and they got out, the smell of cordite was hanging in the air. Oliver, covered in blood, was lying on his back. Another man, also blood soaked, who looked dead, his open eyes staring into the great unknown, was lying next to the golf cart. There was a third man, bloody and making strange noises, who was pushing the dead man off to the side. He had a pistol in his hand, waving it around as he tried to disentangle himself and stand up.

Howard pulled both hammers back on the ten-gauge and put it to his shoulder, aiming at the man with the pistol.

"Drop the gun and freeze, you sorry bastard."

Tillis, now babbling and crying, complied.

Howard moved over and picked up the .45, never taking his eyes off Tillis.

"Are you hurt?" Howard said.

Tillis shook his head, no.

Howard put Tillis behind the golf cart and rummaged around for something to secure him with. He found several pieces of baling twine, and tied Tillis's arms behind him.

"Sit here where I can see you, legs out in front."

Tillis complied.

"How's Oliver?"

"He's okay," Solomon said. "He's alive."

Oliver was dazed from the bullet. It had passed through Schneiter and struck him in the chest, penetrating his overalls and, as luck would have it, buried itself in his hoard of cash. He was carrying a bit over fifteen thousand dollars that day, about half of which was in fifty-dollar bills. It made a cushion that saved him from dying.

Howard went down to the house and called the sheriff, who was named Mike Edwards, but whom everyone in the county knew as "Curley" because he was bald as an egg, and within the hour Oliver Varley's empire was full of people. There were three sheriffs deputies, two New York State Troopers from Liberty Barracks, a Board of Water Supply patrolman, a coroner and two morgue attendants, Sheriff Edwards, three Varleys and Tillis, handcuffed in the backseat of a patrol car.

Somehow, word got passed along as it always does in small towns, and gawkers started showing up. This aggravated everyone, most especially Oliver, who was getting too agitated to give a statement. Finally Sheriff Edwards called for more help and two more state trooper cars came in to handle the crowds. A deputy blocked off Oliver's driveway but people were still parking along the blacktop highway, waiting to see whatever might happen.

By midnight everyone had left except for a sheriff's car down at the end of the driveway. Oliver had given a statement, and was backed up by his father and brother, so no charges were brought against him. The trauma, however, left him a different person, a person who was afraid of himself, afraid of his capabilities, afraid of setting loose the demon berserker he knew resided inside, and Oliver became more introverted than ever, although he continued buying and selling salvage automobiles until his death.

Tillis eventually pled guilty to involuntary manslaughter, and was sentenced to three to five years in the penitentiary. In a bureaucratic screwup of historic proportions, he was mistakenly sent to the

Clinton Correctional Facility at Dannemora, New York ... probably the toughest maximum-security penitentiary in the entire system, where he was beaten, robbed and repeatedly sodomized during his first two weeks there. On the third week, he jumped or was pushed to his death from the third tier of cell block B. On the afternoon of his death, his three cellmates spent the afternoon gambling for his blanket and change of clothing.

Schneiter, it turned out, had no living relatives. Oliver Varley bought his Ford pickup with the Cadillac engine and car-hauling trailer from the state. When he paid for it at the courthouse, Oliver made sure to give the clerk brown and stained bills ... the ones with holes in them from a .45 caliber dum-dum. Oliver was still driving the truck when he died of a heart attack ten years later. It was a good truck that he enjoyed driving, and he seldom thought of Schneiter, Tillis or the day the empire was bloodied.

The Paddy Farrell Narrative

The Paddy Farrell Narrative

Most of this story is true, but not all of it. It's about hard times, good times and past times . . . it's about friendship, common sense and practicality . . . it's about a father passing knowledge on to his son in his own unforgettable way.

Forty-some years ago when I was in high school, my best friend was Mickey Burke, and we, like many young guys, were infatuated with automobiles. We ate, slept and dreamed about cars, and could hardly wait to get driver's licenses and our own rides. Then, after what seemed like forever, I had finally saved enough and bought a '55 Chevy from one of our neighbors. My buddy Mickey bought a '40 Ford coupe with dual exhausts, bucket seats and a 300-horsepower Corvette motor. While my car was well-used, all straight lines and angles, his was cherry, and had more curves than Miss America. I thought it was the sexiest car in the world.

Anytime Mickey and I weren't in school or working odd jobs, we'd be at his house, out in the two-bay garage, working on our cars . . . washing, cleaning and polishing on them, or installing whatever few accessories we could afford to buy. Since our jobs usually paid a dollar an hour or less, we were pretty judicious about our purchases because we still had to buy gasoline, insurance, tires and all the other incidentals that car ownership entails.

We worked because we had to if we wanted spending money. In the 1960's, in the Catskill Mountains where Mickey and I were raised, there was no such thing as an "allowance" doled out every week by a generous and uninvolved parent.

Our lives weren't harder back then; our problems were different, as were our attitudes. Our parents knew all about hard times; they were children of the Depression, annealed in the furnace of World War II, and they made sure their kids were self-sufficient. My father, a plain speaker, put everything in focus when he said, "You want a car? Get a job. Want two cars? Get two jobs."

So that's what we did. We got jobs and bought cars, bought our own clothes and paid our own way through college. We stood on our own two feet as the old saying goes.

But in those golden years, 1962, '63 and '64, when we were high school hot-rodders, our world seemed safer, our horizons seeable, our outlook unencumbered and our ambitions unlimited; we always took for granted that our lives would be better than our parents' lives were. Our world turned on a golden axis that we were the center of, and our most pressing problem was if we had enough gas to drive twenty miles to the movies. Meanwhile, our parents were struggling to feed a family of five on twenty-five dollars a week, with enough left over for a couple of cartons of cigarettes.

In our world there was no gray, no in between; it was black or white, good or bad. We learned to make choices and had to live with the results . . . we knew exactly what personal responsibility was . . . and where the line was drawn, demarcating right from wrong. We obeyed our parents and respected our teachers, and knew the consequences of not doing so.

So we studied, we worked and we hung out, Mickey Burke and I, over at his place where we fiddled with our cars, learned to drink beer, and smoked our first cigarettes . . . which brings me to the

Paddy Farrell.

The Paddy Farrell was an outhouse. It was about one hundred feet off the backdoor of the Burkes' house, where Mickey's pop built it in the spring of 1951 when he'd started digging the foundation hole, so he could move the house he'd bought up to its new location.

"Pop", as we called Mickey's father, was an Irish immigrant cop who worked for the City of New York, Board of Water Supply, or BWS. He knew all about hard times, having left Ireland in 1923, right after the Irish Civil War and the Easter Rising of 1916, in which he'd taken part.

During the late 1940's, after World War II, the city of New York was completing a pair of water projects in upstate New York, at Neversink and Lackawack. They were building dams and reservoirs, connected by underground tunnels, to supply fresh water to their ten million residents one hundred miles south. By the early 1950's, the projects were nearing completion, so the last few buildings were being demolished or moved, including the house Mickey and his family were renting.

The city had quietly surveyed Neversink and surrounding parts of east Sullivan County in the 1930's. Then, when the Great Depression was in full bloom, New York City, by right of adverse possession, claimed all the real estate in Old Neversink, Bittersweet, Lackawack, Montela and Eureka, in order to build dams at Neversink and Lackawack. It was called the "time of the taking" by the locals, and feelings ran deep.

When completed and filled, the reservoirs would contain fresh drinking water for the city. They were so successful the city didn't even bother to install water usage meters until sometime in the 1990's.

Back in 1951, when Mickey and I were five years old and didn't know each other yet, Pop Burke bought a house he'd been renting from the city ... one of the city's adversely possessed properties ... for fifty dollars, after talking it down from two hundred fifty dollars. I can picture it in my mind:

"Hi Bill, how're you?"

"Fine, thanks, Reilly, just fine. I come ta talk t'you about the house me 'n Mary and the kids are livin' in ... I wanta pay youse for it."

"Sure. Been expectin' you. Got the sale bill right here, it's all typed out. It's got to be moved by the end of October."

"Sure, and I will."

"Ah, found it. Here you are."

Pop would've read the one-page document for a moment before the outburst ...

"Well for cryin' out loud, Reilly, what's this then, TWO HUNDRED FIFTY DOLLARS?"

"It's what they all sold for, Bill."

"Hey man, I ain't made a money ... didn't I dig the foundation with me own hands then? Didn't I lay the foundation, block by block, then? Goodness' sakes man, have a heart, will ya?"

"Don't get sore, Bill ..."

"Aw I ain't, but I'm here an' wanna pay ya, but I ain't payin' nothin' like that. Here. Here's fifty dollars. Take that and be done with it then."

"Okay, Bill, sure."

Years later, when Mickey was cleaning out some old files, he found the original house bill of sale, and sure enough, the typed amount was crossed out, "Fifty Dollars" written in cursive script above it. We both got some chuckles out of it, but the best was still to come.

Time passed and life moved on. We graduated high school and went away to college, got degrees and went in the service. Mickey made a career out of the air force and traveled all over the world; I moved out west and went into business for myself. The years rolled on . . . jobs, houses, cars and wives all came and went, but Mickey and I stayed friends, and through the years we carried on a lively correspondence or got together for drinks and dinner whenever we had the chance. Inevitably, we'd reminisce about our teen years, hot rods and the Paddy Farrell, the locus of some of our adventures. Then, in 2007, Mickey went to Ireland.

He went, taking his wife, Ellie, who'd never been out of the country, to visit his cousins Donal and Liam, both of whom lived in Dublin, and his ninety-three year-old Aunt Catherine, still living in Ballycumber on the family homestead up in County Offaly. She was his father's youngest and last living sister, and it was she who put a twist in the Paddy Farrell narrative.

The way Mickey told me, he and Ellie were having lunch with his Aunt Catherine when he mentioned something or other about the Paddy Farrell.

"Who's that?" Catherine said.

"Not who, what," Mickey said to her. "You know, the outhouse"

"Outhouse?" she said. "You mean the privy?"

"Yeah." Mickey said. "That's what Pop called it. I always thought Paddy Farrell was an Irish name for it, a euphemism, um, an expression."

Mickey told me when he got back home that his Aunt Catherine thought for a few moments, then she giggled like a young girl and

185

said, "No-oo, Michael, there's no such expression I know of. I'd guess 'Paddy Farrell' was someone William didn't like very much, or someone he had a dispute with."

We, Mickey and I, discussed this new wrinkle in our old adventures, and that afternoon, when I got on my computer and Googled "Paddy Farrell," up came the name, "James T. Farrell," a Chicago native, and a writer, who "purported to speak" for all Irish immigrants through his Studs Lonigan trilogy. In it, young Lonigan, an impoverished Irish lad, evolves from delinquency to criminal thugdom and ultimately, a bad end. Farrell claimed his writings were based on his personal experiences as a working-class Irishman from Chicago's South Side, and his books are considered to be classics of American literature. But, Farrell was also an outspoken communist, a Trotskyite and card-carrying member of the Socialist Worker's Party, writing and supporting communist causes during the '30's and '40's. I think that's what drew Pop Burke's ire.

Pop was a proud Irish American and a lifelong cop, who stood for law and order. I think he was offended by Farrell, and decided to name his outhouse in honor of the guy Pop figured was full of . . . well . . . you know what.

Mickey disagreed when I told him what I'd found, what I thought.

"Pop never knew anyone famous like that," he said.

"Yeah, but can't cha just see him doing something like that, with his wicked, dry-as-a-bone sense of humor?" I said. "Remember how he'd chide and tease us, how we wouldn't always get what he said until days later?"

When Mickey didn't say anything else, I decided to write the story, and the most extraordinary thing happened.

I was sitting at my desk in Colorado Springs, late on a snowy evening in March, putting the final touches on this story when I nodded off, right there in my chair. I don't know how long I was asleep, but I dreamt about Neversink. It was a summer evening and I was at Mickey's house, out in his garage, working on his '40 Ford coupe with him.

We were doing something under the hood, one of us on each side when we heard the BWS patrol car drive up. It was a '61 Chevrolet Biscayne, a six-cylinder with a three-speed shift on the column. It was black, the cheapest model General Motors had to offer, with a single "bubble gum" roof mount emergency flasher, a fender-mounted chrome siren and the letters "B.W.S. Police" neatly stenciled in white paint on both front doors. It made a distinct kind of whining noise too, followed by a pair of clicks when the motor was turned off.

Pop walked in, wearing his uniform, cop hat and utility belt. He put his right foot up on the front bumper, pushed his hat back and leaned over the grille, forearm on his knee, watching us. Then, he fished a pack of Chesterfields out of his pocket and lit one with a kitchen match he struck on the edge of his thumbnail. Turning his head to the side to keep the smoke out of his eyes, he looked at us and said, "Dummies. The pair a' ya. And what took yez so long then?"

I remember, his eyes were smiling, and I knew what he meant as I woke up.

Just Another Day

1968

Just Another Day

If you chose to believe what was in *Stars & Stripes*, the U.S. Armed Forces newspaper, after the Tet Offensive, our counterpunches "hurt the enemy bad" and there was a lull in major combat. But that was *Stars & Stripes*. That was there . . . and this was here. Here, the days were hot and muggy, while at night the air was chilly, and damp with the high mountain mist that was so prevalent in the west Central Highlands. We were about twenty five klicks east of the Laos-Cambodia border, at a little place called Plei Do Lim . . . up in Indian Country, II Corps of the Republic of South Vietnam. It was December 14, 1968, I'd been in country for eight months, but it seemed like my whole lifetime. I felt the war was using me up, and I was becoming an old man at the age of twenty five years, three months and 11 days.

The day had started out just like all the other days there, hot and muggy, interminably long, full of the sights and sounds and smells I'd come to associate with Vietnam: bright green triple-canopy jungle, rugged mountains, cook-fires, pigs, chickens, dogs, kids, momma and poppa-sans, ancient elders and grunts with weapons, all under a sky so clear and a sun so hot it felt like hell's own pottery kiln. But when the sun went down, the temperature dropped, the air got cool and fresh, and made me think of autumnal nights back in Neversink, up in the Catskill Mountains of New York, where I'd been born and raised. Where on fall nights like this, we'd be carving jack-o'-lanterns, drinking apple cider and eating doughnuts made from mashed potatoes. Instead, I was out here, halfway around the world, one of a five-man recon and resettlement team—not quite designated as special forces, but not too damn far from it either. Our company consisted of three sergeants first class, E-7's, named Booker, Sauceda and McCullough, our commanding officer, First Lieutenant Green, and me, Second Lieutenant Hayden Battle. For Sergeant Booker and Sergeant McCullough, this was their third war. Sergeant Sauceda had fought in Korea, and now Vietnam. All three were hardened combat veterans who had my attention and respect, who knew what they were doing, who'd better my odds of surviving the war, so I just stayed out of their way and let them run things. We were tasked with resettling, training and equipping the Montagnards, the indigenous tribal hill people of Vietnam, into a consolidated village that would be able to defend itself from the depredations and forced conscriptions of the Viet Cong and their North Vietnamese Army allies.

Our unit had been in Plei Do Lim for about eight weeks and I'd made friends with the villagers and knew their families . . . oldsters to babies, and aunties to in-laws . . . because most of them were wearing my clothes. I'd arrived at the hilltop with six boxes full of winter coats, sweaters, flannel shirts and such that I'd arranged for through donations by the Methodist, Dutch Reformed and Catholic Churches back in Neversink. The Central Highlands were cold at night, and most of the villagers lacked any type of warm clothes. Bringing some helped folks out and made them regard us in a friendlier fashion. Then too, there was a bit of comic relief. Nothing made me smile more than seeing old "Auntie Em," a tiny Montagnard woman whose eyes looked old as trouble itself; whose face was seamed with heartache, wearing her hot pink sweatshirt that boldly proclaimed:

KUM TO KRUMS

You can whip our cream

But you can't beat our meat!

FRESH GROCERIES MEAT MILK & SUNDRIES

Est. 1857   Neversink, New York

The settlement had grown up to nearly 300 souls, living in tents and hooches scattered around the hilltop. We'd selected the place because it was easy to defend—with the exception of two ravines that ran down from the hilltop—we had a great view of the surrounding countryside. We put foxholes with gun emplacements around the perimeter and both ravines were bracketed with artillery that was zeroed in. We didn't have concertina wire out yet, but I felt secure with the Montagnards in gun towers at the perimeter. We'd had peace and quiet so far, but for the last five days we'd been getting intelligence that an attempt would be made to overtake our position. We were on guard, but we were always on guard.

Lieutenant Green and the three Noncommissioned officers were out on a ten-day recon. I was minding the radio and relaying messages from the guys on patrol back to division HQ, a duty we all had in rotation. I'd been assigned a temporary medic, Specialist 4th Class Picard, to fill in for the absent sergeants who were our usual Docs, but Picard was a problem . . . a juicer and a doper, who'd managed to stay loaded for the entire four days we'd been on the hill together.

I was looking forward to the team's return in six days, when Picard would be gone.

With the full dark, Picard and I'd been alternating one-hour watches through the night and it was my turn again. As I pulled the radio over my right shoulder and an M-16 rifle on my left, I saw him take a long pull on his canteen.

"Anything happening Picard?" I asked.

"No, sir," he replied. "It's quiet. Haven't heard a thing."

Picard disappeared like a great green woodchuck, under a groundcover four feet down the foxhole we shared.

Helluva operations area. I thought to myself as I climbed over some sandbags and stood up. *Almost as nice as an office at the Pentagon.* Yeah. Right.

I was on the second circuit of my patrol route when I stepped away a few meters to answer the call of nature. I was taking a long, satisfying piss when the whole perimeter lit up. I heard a click, a whoosh, and an rocket-propelled grenade passed over my left shoulder and blew the number-three gun tower up with a stunning blast and sonic boom. I hit the dirt next to my steaming urine as small-arms fire and RPGs erupted around me. Concussion followed concussion as the grenades, rifle and machine-gun fire and Sixty-millimeter mortars kept shrieking in, while green tracer rounds buzzed over my head like radioactive hornets. I keyed the radio and started screaming call signs.

"Jericho! Jericho! Jericho! This is Sawhorse. This is Sawhorse. We are being overrun! I say again, Sawhorse. We are being overrun. We need air support. Now!"

After waiting for what seemed longer than the last week of school, the radio squawked: "Sawhorse. This is Jericho, the birds have left the nest."

" I need you now! I need you now!"

"Roger that."

Sappers had breached our defense. They were advancing and firing, fighting their way in the camp and multiplying like piranhas in a feeding frenzy as I pulled my M-16 and shot at the perimeter, drawing enemy bullets laced with tracers for the trouble. There was nowhere to go, no place to hide. All around me was mayhem, the village was aflame; bodies and parts of bodies flew through the air as the NVA and Vietcong were pouring out of a ground fog and up the ravines into the village. The Montagnards were putting up a good scrap but were giving way to the bigger numbers of enemy fighters. I tried to crawl toward the foxhole, drawing AK-47 fire. I cranked up the radio while lying on the ground on my belly . . .

"Where the fuck are you guys?" I screamed. "We're being overrun! We're being overrun! Goddamn it!"

Then the radio crackled.

"Sawhorse, Cobra One. Three minutes out. Need you to send up a flare marking your position."

"Roger! Get here quick!"

Crouched, and tucked into as small a ball as I could make myself, I ran about ten meters to the sandbagged pit where we stowed the small arms ammo and grabbed a hand flare. I crawled out a few meters, held it in my left hand and punched it off with my right. It climbed for altitude while I flopped over, changed clips in my M-16 and fired toward the perimeter at anything that even looked like it was moving. The perimeter was collapsing as I rekeyed the mike.

"Cobra, Cobra come on, we need you NOW!" I screamed.

"This is Cobra. We lost visual on your flare. Can you send another?"

"Jesus Fucking Christ!! What's the matter with you guys? This whole fucking place is a firefight!"

I crawled under continuous fire and got a second flare, pumping it off from the side of the pit. As I watched it shoot to the sky, I wondered if I'd live to see the dawn. And then the sky lit up like God's own Roman candle. Three AH-1G helicopter gunships popped into view with all weapons hot, firing rockets and grenades and .30 caliber miniguns simultaneously. It was like every fireworks display I'd ever seen in my life going off at the same time. The choppers raked back and forth, back and forth, then up and down like airborne Grim Reapers, scything everything in their path. The ground vibrated with exploding ordnance, while the miniguns buzzed, spitting out tracer rounds in a bright red stream, and smoking hot shell casings that rained down on me.

Then it was over, as suddenly as it started. Quiet came back, to a world run amok, where chaos ruled and the insane were in charge. The village was destroyed. What wasn't knocked down was on fire. What wasn't on fire was bathed in gore. Bodies and parts of bodies were everywhere, blood was pooling on pathways and in doorways where yesterday women fetched water and carried babies, where children laughed and chased each other, where the elders held councils of one. As my hearing returned, I could hear anguished wails, the shrieks and moans of the despairing, and pleas for help from the wounded and dying. The enemy troops were decimated. Those who were still alive had either fled, or were being dispatched by the Montagnards with savage efficiency.

Still on my belly, I thanked the chopper pilots; they told me medevacs were on the way. I was unhurt, but shaken, as I climbed to my feet and made my way back to the operations foxhole, where I found Picard at the bottom of it. He'd been there the whole time, hugging the dirt. When he stood up, I saw that he was drunk and had lost bladder control.

"Picard, get out of there and start doing your job, we've got beaucoup casualties. Start with the Montagnards at the perimeter. MOVE, you sorry son-of-a-bitch."

I was full of adrenaline and a case of combat jitters, but things were starting to come back to normal speed in my brain as Picard gathered his kit and headed for the perimeter. I could see all four gun towers were destroyed . . . knocked down and on fire, the lookouts dead. The radio squawked, and I knelt behind a pile of sandbags to answer it.

"Sawhorse, this is *Top Hat*. We are incoming for evacuation, ETA five minutes."

"Roger. Do you need flares?"

"Shit no. The whole ville is on fire. We see you just fine."

I got to my feet and made for the perimeter, where I gathered the surviving Montagnards who were still ambulatory and started triage among the casualties. Triage is pretty simple: you separate the dead and the soon-to-be-dead from the living, and start basic first aid. It was ghastly work I turned over to the senior-most Montagnard as soon as I heard the whop-whop-whop of the inbound slicks, the ubiquitous Huey transport choppers, coming in high and hard, wary of sniper and RPG fire in the hot landing zone.

I was in touch with *Top Hat One* and we had visual. He came in fast, and I was backing up, guiding him in for touchdown when

I backed into a foxhole and went ass over tin teacup in the dark, looking like a clown. If the chopper driver was laughing, he was gracious enough to keep it off the air. He asked if I was okay, then touched down while I climbed out of the hole, and the medics began tending the wounded, and just like that, I was out of a job.

Still twitching with unexpended adrenaline, I found a place to make myself small, and shake off the nerves that always came after a firefight. I sipped some warm water from my canteen and watched the first crack of dawn . . . I was drained . . . running on fumes, but unable to unwind. It was the jittery feeling you get from too much adrenaline and too little sleep; the shakes that come when combat is over, and you're still alive. I tried, and failed, to put the sight of Auntie Em's body out of my mind. I'd seen her torso, minus both legs and most of her left arm, lying in the pathway outside what remained of her hooch, where an NVA mortar scored a direct hit. She was still wearing her pink KRUMS sweatshirt.

As I watched the sun rising, with its promise of a new beginning, another chance at life, I thought, *just one day*. Yesterday and last night was just one day I survived, still in one piece, another precious pearl to slide on my personal string of days, hoping, praying, to get to the magical 365th one and a ticket home.

I was alive. Behind me, the whole village was devastated. Why? What for? Does anyone know what's going on over here . . . does anyone care? I had seen death before. I wasn't a stranger to it, nor it to me. In the eight months I'd been in country, I had been in many firefights, seen many deaths. It held no mystery, but this was different. This was personal. Death had reached out and tried to put his hand on me, he was close, impersonal, unprejudicial and unrepentant. He had taken others less deserving and spared me. It was just another day in Vietnam. Yesterday was over, today just started, and I still had four more months to go. I thought about the green hills and peaceful valleys back in Neversink, full of cold tumbling waters, and I thought of home. As I sat there sipping water, watching the sunrise, I couldn't stop crying.

Stoners

1972

Stoners

Fifteen miles northeast of Rhyolite Mountain, Slapper McSorley was trying to clip a hot roach onto a surgical hemostat in moving darkness, while his cousin Jimmy Dunnahay drove them down a dirt road that wound around the northeast corner of an unnamed precipice somewhere in the middle of the Catskill Park Wilderness. It was a little before midnight, two days before Halloween. They were on their way home to Neversink after spending the day visiting Jimmy's father, Slapper's uncle Steve, at the Albany VA hospital, where he was dying of lung cancer.

"This is some badass shit," Slapper said, passing the roach.

"Oh yeah," Jimmy agreed. He took a hit and steered the '72 El Camino around a curve, passed the roach back to Slapper. "One-a my army buddies mailed it to me from 'Nam; I sent him some windowpane on the back of some stamps."

"Windowpane?"

"Acid, my man. Acid. LSD. You never tried it?"

"Naw. I'll stick to pot," Slapper said as he tried to take another toke off the dead roach. He relit it with a butane lighter, making a seed pop as it exploded.

"Ow! Oh, fuck man! Burned my nose on a fuckin' seed."

"Lotta seed, but far-out dope," Jimmy said.

Slapper pulled the ashtray out and was putting the roach clip in it when Jimmy said, "What the . . ." and swerved the El Camino hard left and then right. Slapper looked up in time to see what he thought was a child, but then his fog-bound brain registered, *No, not a child. Some . . . something short, two-legged, two arms, strange head, long fingers, big black eyes, but . . . but sort of grayish. No, green, greenish,* all impacted on his consciousness in less than a second as the thing flashed by, and out of the headlights glare.

"DID YOU SEE THAT?" Jimmy said.

"Yeah . . . but what was it? Just what the hell was it?"

"Damned if I know. You wanna go back?"

Slapper almost said, "No, it's just a prank." Instead, always the inquiring mind, and to his everlasting regret, he said, "Yeah. Let's see what's doing."

He wished afterward that his lips had been sewed together with steel wire.

Jimmy hit the brakes and flicked the steering wheel, sending the El Camino into a long, gut-lurching slide that left Slapper's stomach back there, somewhere on the side of the road, and Slapper himself holding the armrest and seat back in a death grip. Jimmy hit the gas, spinning the rear wheels, throwing twin rooster tails of dirt and gravel . . . and executed a perfect 180-degree turn at speed. They were headed back to find the thing on the road, whatever it was.

"Kee-rist, Jimmy."

"Just keep your eyes open. I think it was right along here somewhere."

They drove back up the road a quarter mile and slowed to a crawl. They were going at a walking pace when Slapper spotted it again.

"Turn the lights out, Jimmy. See, over there, the flickering light?"

It was off the road, down in the woods about fifty feet or so. It kept appearing and disappearing in the dark, as if it were passing behind some invisible object or was only a reflection in a revolving magician's mirror. The green thing, whatever it was, kept appearing and disappearing like a conjurer's trick.

"Yeah," Jimmy said, "it's him."

"How'd it get so far down the bank?"

"Who knows? C'mon."

"What're we gonna do, Jimmy?"

"Go see," was all he said.

*   *   *

Jimmy pointed the truck toward the woods and slapped it in park. He left the engine running, and we left the doors open, just in case we had to get out of there in a hurry. Personally, I was scared shitless. Sounds easy enough to do, hearing about it in the daylight, but you just try sneaking up on the unknown in the dead of night, alone, way the fuck out in the woods. No lights, no help and no phone for fifteen miles. You'll find out what you're made of. Yes. You will.

"Wait a minute," Jimmy hissed as he went behind the seat for his briefcase and a flashlight he kept there, "let me get Mr. Smith." He laid the briefcase on the seat and opened it up and took out "Mr. Smith," a blued steel .357 magnum Smith & Wesson revolver with a four-inch barrel. He checked the load, and handed me the flashlite and we started into the woods together.

I was about to crap my pants. Up ahead, this thing is going flick, flick, flick. Now you see 'um, now you don't. Each step was scarier than the last, and harder to take. I was pointing Jimmy's flashlight but it wasn't a lot of help because the friggin' thing had been rolling around behind the car seat since Grant took Vicksburg and the light was pretty dim. My hands were shaking so bad the flashlight was flickering on and off. I think Jimmy was scared too, but he wasn't saying a word. He just kept moving, step by step, toward the little spaceman thing with Mr. Smith in his outstretched right hand. As we got closer, we could feel and smell something in the air . . . electricity or ozone. It made the hair on my neck and arms stand up on end. I was covered in goose bumps and I could feel my scrotum sucked right up to my navel, I was so, so scared.

We got about ten feet from the creature and it was apparent this wasn't like anything we'd ever seen—even in the movies. It was kind of a bluish-greenish color, shaped like a four-foot human with a head like an upside-down teardrop, long arms and only four fingers, large black eyes and no ears we could see, no nose, no hair. But it was covered with fuzzy looking stuff—sorta' like on the stalk of a tomato plant, but coarser.

Okay, so there we were, middle of nowhere, walking up on God knows what in the dark, when all of a sudden the thing must've heard or seen us because it turned and started to raise its arms and move forward.

That's when Jimmy did it. He took a two-hand combat grip on the .357, and crouching in a shooter's stance, cranked off two rounds in quick succession, Wham! Wham! hitting the thing center mass. Then came the big one. KER-WHAAM! as the green being exploded. It was like the world turned inside out; sorta like a movie special effect, but for real. You ever see the pictures of the atomic bomb blasts . . . it was like that, only worse. Shit was flying everywhere. A bright light flashed and there was a huge boom, like a sonic boom from a jet plane or being close by a lightning strike. Yeah, that's better—it was like being right there when lightning hits. Along with the gunshots and explosions, a bunch of other stuff was happening too. First was the smell. It was like when you tear the leaves off a geranium or tomato plant—you know how you get that peculiar smell that aggravates your nose? Yeah, like that only at least a thousand times stronger. I went down in a heap, the flashlight went flying and Jimmy went ass over elbows on his face, right into the exploded watermelon mess where the creature had stood.

"Awwww, fuck!" he shouted.

"Take it easy," I said. "Are you hurt?"

"Naw," he said. "I just got this slimy green crap all over me. It stinks something awful."

I retrieved the flashlight, which was a few feet away, glowing with a feeble light next to a big rock. Jimmy stood up and seemed okay, except for this gooey wet green stuff on his shirt, hands and arms, and on his knees and shoes.

"You okay?" he said.

"Yeah, skinned my hand though," I said. "Whaddya think that thing was?"

"Beats the shit outta me. Aw fuck," he said for the second time in less than a minute.

"What now?" I said.

"I can't find my Blue Meanie," he said.

Jimmy had this little round tin with an enameled picture of the Blue Meanie on it from *The Yellow Submarine* movie, the size and shape of a snuff can; it was where he kept his dope. You know, his pot . . . Mary Jane, marijuana, wacky-tobacky.

I came over with the flashlight and we found the Blue Meanie in the middle of the green mess that used to be whatever the hell it was. The lid had come off and the contents were scattered in the gook. We retrieved the tin top and bottom and wiped them out with some dry leaves from the forest floor.

"Damn," Jimmy said. "I really hate wasting that dope. It was some Southeast Asian ass-thumper I just got. I've got a little more at home but it's really expensive, lotsa blossoms."

"Yeah," I said. "Sure toasted me."

I recovered Mr. Smith from the leaves and put him back in his briefcase. We made it home to Neversink about an hour later and never mentioned the incident again.

My cousin Jimmy Dunnahay was killed a week before Christmas in a one-car smashup on Route 55. He was coming back from the Downstream Bar where he'd been playing pool and drinking depth charges—a mug of beer with a shot glass of bourbon dropped in—all afternoon and evening. Route 55 down below the Lackawack Dam runs along the river and is full of turns, switchbacks and hills. It's a great place to practice your race-car act on a snow-packed road, 'specially with a blood alcohol level of .17, twice the legal limit. "Go early, die young and make a great looking corpse." That's what they say in my family anyway.

But really, Doctor Blade, what I wanted to tell you is this.

A couple weeks ago, I was coming back from Albany and took the same exact shortcut for the first time in nine or ten months. It was just before July 4 weekend, so nine months I guess, since that time with Jimmy. Well, I stopped at the place where we saw the green space-thing and got out to look around, see if I could see anything, you know. So I walked through the woods to where it happened and there was just a ton of pot growing there. The stalks were at least ten or twelve feet high, and really bushy. Lots of leaves and buds with zillions of seeds. I've seen dope growing before, I even grew some myself on the horseshit pile over at my mother's barn, but I tell you Doc, I ain't ever, I mean, ever, seen anything like this dope that's growing up there in the woods. Awesome doesn't begin to do it justice. The plant stems were three inches thick!

I know I shouldn't have, but what the hell, that stuff was just begging to be smoked so I cut a few stems with my Swiss Army pocketknife and dragged 'em back to the car.

Yeah, dragged. They were pretty big. Took a while to cut 'em down too.

So I stuffed those giant-assed pot plants in my car trunk and took out for home. When I got there I noticed that a bunch of the seeds had fallen off and were lying on the floor. My car's an old Plymouth Valiant; it's sort of rusted and anyway, there's a bunch of holes in the trunk where it's rotted out. My point is, a bunch of those seeds must've fallen out on the way home because a few days later there was pot plants coming up all over the place. But I'm getting ahead of myself.

When I smoked some of that dope it was un-fucking believable. I've done some great shit before but this was the best. One or two hits and you were gone away, tripping, seeing Lucy with kaleidoscope eyes dripping with diamonds. It was the best, just the best high I've ever been on, and it lasted until the next evening! About thirty hours. I went to sleep stoned and I had the most lurid, most intense dreams of my life and when I woke up I WAS STILL STONED! I was like, concussed, man. Simply concussed.

Man! I gave some to my pals, Denny, Mike, Sandra and Kathie, Dougie and a few others, I forget their names. We partied the whole weekend and on, until we ran out of dope. "No problem," I said. "I know where there's a ton of it, free for the taking." So, well, we all set out—three or four carloads—headed up fifteen miles past Rhyolite Mountain. Everyone intent on a share of the illicit goodies.

We got up there about two hours after we started out; I remember it was still a couple hours till dark. When I got there I could hardly believe it. Where I'd dragged out the pot plants weeks ago was just covered with new-growth plants about eight feet tall! The seeds must have fallen off as I was hauling the plants to the car. Not only that, the first-growth plants were now about thirty or forty feet tall —the stems probably a foot in diameter—just incredible growth. It was like kudzu on steroids. All the plants must'a been, I dunno, several hundred, had huge, bushlike leaves and super big seed buds. My companions all thought they'd died and gone to heaven.

So naturally, they all started acting like jerks. First thing, Bill Garcia and Eddie Black tore up a couple of three-footers and were fighting with them. One would swing his bush and the other would retaliate with a backhand riposte like they were swordsmen or something. Others were laughing and chewing on leaves, ripping up bushes and stuffing pieces of them in their clothes. The entire group, myself included, degenerated into bacchanalian mayhem for an hour or two. One couple was last seen playing nymph and satyr, no clothing, out in the woods. They finally came back a little after dark but we never did find all of their clothes. There were pot plants lying all over the area, stalks bent, leaves torn off and scattered in random fashion over grounds several times bigger than the original area.

Well, guess what? The pot patch got bigger by the day. Before the week was out, more friends of friends and their friends were all trekking up to get a little grass. I have no idea how many harvesters have been up there but I'd estimate at least four or five dozen. Several things have happened simultaneously as well, Doc.

First, the stuff, pot, has been sent out all over the place. Those who've been up there have sold or given away many, many bags of it. What do I mean by all over the place? Boston, Montreal, Florida, Oregon, St. Louis, Dallas, Texas, and Colorado Springs, Colorado. And that's just where I know of. Which brings me to the next point.

Secondly, you see, this cannabis grows like hell just about anywhere. Throw a roach out the car window and you'll find a pot plant two feet tall a coupla days later. Throw seeds out, multiply the effect. If it's wet or raining, stuff grows even faster and thicker. And speaking of it spreading, it's all uphill of the Neversink reservoir. It's going to grow right into the water supply, and soon. Real soon. It's a stoner's dream.

That's the last thing—see, we're all starting to have side effects, if that's the right words. I've smoked dope a long time. Since I was twelve years old. Every day. Probably five, six, seven joints every day. See my point is, I know how to handle it. It's like Willie Nelson said one time, "I smoked a bale of that shit and it ain't done nuthin' to me."

So, like, I can handle it except, except now I stay loaded way longer, days instead of hours and my memory is just for shit. I can't remember things when I wake up and I have really intense dreams when asleep. Things chasing me. Always chasing, ever closer. Closer and closer. When I finally wake up I'm covered in sweat, and it smells bad. Really stinks. It smells like a mixture of tomato and geranium plants. Only worse. It's got a kind of green oily sheen to it, and my skin does too. But Doc, that's not all. That's not the worst. The worst is I don't eat much anymore. I crave water. I drink quart after quart of it and suck on copper pennies all day. That's not good I know, but it doesn't scare me. What scares me, scares me a lot, is this, Doc. The day before yesterday, Tuesday of this week, I started to piss bright green . . .

Starfall on the Neversink

1973

Starfall on the Neversink

It was a warm summer evening and the bar had half a dozen drinkers, two pool players and Oliver Varley, sitting by himself drinking shots of Canadian Club with Coors Light chasers. He was a big man who handled his liquor well enough, but he carried a burden that, along with his years, was wearing him down. He looked eighty, was shy of seventy, and tired of the sadness he carried inside. So he drank. He drank to ease the pain, and he drank to forget. But it never worked; he always remembered and it always hurt ... before, during and after he drank.

He had felt like that for more than twenty-five. *Why Hell*, he thought, *its damn near thirty years now. Thirty years since the day Irma died and baby Studebaker disappeared.* He tossed the shot back with a practiced motion, swallowed the whiskey, then drank the beer in the draft glass. He stared at the bar, looking but not seeing, lost in his private universe and its personal world of anguish. He brooded for a time, but eventually signaled the bartender for another CC and beer back.

The bartender's name was Jeep. She was the tenth child born to Oliver and Irma Varley, named for the all-purpose army vehicle that helped win the war. She, like all her brothers and sisters, had been born at the Varley homestead, up on Rhyolite Mountain. The exception was Studebaker, born in a hospital, disappeared at age eighteen months, never seen again.

Like all the Varleys, Jeep was tall, big-boned and strong as a quarter-sawed oak plank. They weren't pretty children, but they were all tough and self-reliant, able to take care of themselves. They'd had to. After Irma died, the kids, from Auburn down to Reo, the youngest, had had to take care of each other.

Jeep was on the phone talking to her brother Oshkosh.

"He's been here all afternoon and evening."

She held the phone with her head and shoulder as she opened two bottles of beer, set them on the bar in front of Kenny and Tom Swink, took a ten and made change as she listened, then said, "No. Not yet. But I'm afraid he might. You know how he can get."

She looked at Mr. Yamashita, the physics teacher at Neversink High School, sitting alone at one end of the bar. She rolled her eyes and grinned at him, made a "quack-quack" motion with her right hand. He smiled back and pointed at his empty draft glass. She nodded, raised her right index finger in the "one second" sign. She took the phone in her left hand.

"I gotta go, Osh. I'm getting backed up at the bar. I just think it's a good idea if you would. 'Kay? Okay. I gotta go. Bye."

She drew a glass of tap beer, put it in front of Mr. Yamashita.

"This one's on the house, Yamashta-san. I'm sorry you were kept waiting." He nodded his head in a silent "thank you." Jeep went back to her station, poured a shot of CC and drew a glass of Coors Light for her father, carried it over to him.

"You doing okay, Daddy?"

"Yes, Child. Just thinking."

"That's why I asked if you're okay. You've been here a long time today."

"I can handle it."

"I know you can, Daddy. I just worry about you is all. We all do. You seem like you're lonesome all the time."

"Its okay to be lonely."

"Just not too lonely."

"Yes, child."

Jeep collected five dollars from him and went back to the bar. Oliver watched her go, sat twirling the full shot glass. Thinking. Remembering.

The bar was three and a half miles below the spillway of the Neversink Dam and Reservoir, and sat in a meadow at the intersection of White Birch Road and Hardrock Street. It was just a good stone's throw from what was left of the Neversink River after the City of New York got done with it. The city was forced by law to release a certain percentage of water from its reservoirs, but a loophole allowed it to calculate and release the water based on the total of all the reservoirs rather than a percentage of each one individually. The law, called the Delaware River Compact, allowed New York City to release water when and how it saw fit. As a result, the Neversink, once a crown jewel of trout streams, was starved of water downstream from the dam. The city passed it off as "flood control," but the result was a shallow, dull stream full of warm water. It was unfit for trout, a cold water species, but great for junk fish like carp, suckers and chubs.

The bar was named the Ten Eel Tavern because back in the nineteenth century, when the Neversink was still wild and free, an eel fisherman struck fishy gold one afternoon when he speared ten eels just off the tavern's front steps. Try saying "Ten-Eel-Tavern" when you've had a couple of snorts, and you'll know why all the local folks called the place Dingman's or Brownie's, after the owner Brownie Dingman.

Someone fired up the jukebox and an old Jim Reeves tearjerker came on. He was singing about "Four Walls" when there was a thud, followed by a flash of light and a concussive boom, like a cherry bomb in a phone booth. A hole appeared in the ceiling, then smoke, the stink of charred wood and dust mixed in with particles of insulation, sheetrock and false ceiling panel. As if by sorcery, a meteorite spattered down on the oak dance floor with a clunk and lay there . . . burning a hole in the parquet.

It was about the size of a man's fist, as it lay there glowing, giving off an odor like rotten eggs and dead skunk. A moment of stunned silence, then a cacophony of sound as everyone spoke at once.

"Jumpin' Jesus, what was that?"

"Beats the hell outta me."

"Shit. Looks like a rock or something."

"It's a meteorite," Yamashita said from the end of the bar. "Don't touch it, it's probably a thousand degrees or more."

Rickey Santangelo and Tony Garza, the guys playing pool up on the raised area where the stage used to be, didn't hear or ignored his warning because Rickey walked over and stepped on it to put the fire out.

There was a sound like a can of whipped cream being emptied, a flash of fire, smoke, more stink and a scream as Rickey realized his light summer moccasin was on fire. The sole had melted. His shoe, sock and a little bit of his pant leg were burning, and his foot smelled like burnt pork as it sizzled and cooked.

Rickey was on his back holding his right knee as he writhed on the floor screaming in pain, trying to get his shoe off. Kenny Swink went over and tried to help. He said, "Hold still," as he poured his beer on Rickey's burning foot.

"Careful," Yamashita said, "don't get liquid on the meteorite."

"Who cares?"

Yamashita said, "You will if the son-of-a-bitch explodes."

"What should we do?" Jeep said.

"Give me those stainless steel forceps. The ones you fish the pickled eggs out with."

"The tongs. We call them tongs."

"Whatever. If you've got a large bowl, go get it," Yamashita said as he took the forceps from her and stepped over to the dance floor where Rickey Santangelo was sitting on the floor holding his injured right leg, which he had crossed over his left. All the bar patrons except Oliver gathered around, looking at Rickey or the meteorite, still burning and spitting on the floor. The smell was almost overpowering.

Yamashita took a red Swiss Army knife out of his pocket and opened a screwdriver blade. He pried the meteorite out of the socket it had burned in the floor, lifted it with the forceps and deposited it in the bowl Jeep brought from the kitchen.

He said, "You guys need to pack Rickey's foot in ice and a clean towel and take him to the hospital. He's probably got third-degree burns on his foot. If he doesn't get medical attention it could get infected."

Jeep brought ice and towels and several of his friends carried Rickey out to his car.

"Somebody call my wife," he said, "tell her where I am."

"I will," Jeep said, "don't worry. Harris Hospital?"

"Yeah," Tony said as he drove away with his injured pal.

Oliver Varley had not moved, nor had he spoken as the meteorite drama was unfolding. He watched but was uninvolved, as if he were seeing events on television. He was disinterested in another man's problems.

I wonder, he thought. *I wonder if this is the sign . . . my sign that it's time to move on. Time to cash in my chips and find a new game?*

He drank some beer and stared at the neon pink and green "Cerveza dos Equis" sign on the wall.

Yamashita carried the bowl containing the still-hot meteorite back to the galley kitchen and put it on an unlit stove burner to cool. He looked around, and found a nail in a drawerful of junk. He touched the nail to the meteorite, where it stuck . . . it was magnetic.

Yamashita went back out to the bar, motioned to Jeep.

"I need to talk to you."

"It'll be a little while. I'm cleaning up out here."

"I'll wait."

Oliver watched as his daughter got a broom and dustpan, cleaned up the debris the meteorite had spread around. He downed the shot of whiskey, felt it slide down his throat and set fire to his gut. He extinguished it with the rest of his beer, set the glass on the table with care. *Funny,* he thought. *I've been at it for six, seven hours now and I'm as sober as I was when I came in here this afternoon. Wonder why . . . no matter. Maybe I'll figure it out sometime.*

Jeep came by with her broom, sweeping. She said, "How'ya doing, Daddy? You okay back here?"

"I'm fine, child. Bring me another."

"You sure, Daddy?"

He looked at her, said nothing.

She said, "How about something to eat? I'll cook you a nice hamburger . . ."

"Sure," he said. "Bring another whiskey and a beer too."

She put the broom away, went to the bar and got beer and drinks, and made change before she went back in the galley to cook. She got a frying pan and two hamburger patties. Before she could light the stove she had to move the bowl with the meteorite. *Not quite cool enough to touch. But it looks like a regular old burnt rock to me.* The hamburgers were just starting to cook when Yamashita came in. He stood in the doorway with a beer glass in his left hand. He leaned against the door frame with his right shoulder, watching her cook. He said, "You know anything about meteorites?"

"Nope."

"Would you like to learn?"

"Sure."

"Okay. Here's the short course. Every August the earth passes through the debris left by a comet named Swift-Tuttle and we get a meteor shower. Its called the Perseid shower because it appears to come from the constellation Perseus, but it really is pieces of the comet's tail."

He watched her toasting a hamburger bun, said, "Nearly all the meteorites burn up in the atmosphere."

"Falling stars."

"Or shooting stars. That's right. So it's very rare to have one hit the ground, and it's much, much, much more rare to have one cause property damage."

"Hit the building, you mean."

"Yeah."

She got a serving platter out, put potato chips, pickle slices, lettuce and a pair of tomato slices on it that she got from the refrigerator. She put the bun halves on the plate and turned the burgers in the frying pan. They were almost cooked. She said, "Why are you telling me all this?"

"Because it's valuable."

"The meteorite?"

"Yeah."

"How valuable?" she said as she put the burgers on the bun and shut the gas off on the stove.

"About thirty-five or forty thousand dollars."

Jeep stopped what she was doing and stood dead still for several moments.

She turned to him and said, "Are you serious?"

"As a five-alarm fire."

"You're not joking."

"Not in the least."

"Why?"

"Why what . . . ?

"Why are they so valuable?"

She was holding the platter.

"Why don't you go serve that and come back and I'll explain it."

"Good. I'll be right back."

Jeep went to the back booth, put the steaming plate in front of her father. He reached for the ketchup bottle Jeep put on the table, and said, "Thanks. It looks good."

"You're welcome, Daddy. I'll go get your drinks too."

Jeep got her father's beer and shot, made change and waited on several other customers as if she was sleepwalking. It was several minutes before she got back to the galley and Yamashita. He was examining the meteorite, which had cooled enough to be touched without getting burned. He was so intent he didn't notice Jeep until she spoke.

"Yamashta-san, would you like another beer?"

"Two is my limit. But tonight's so extraordinary . . . why, yes. Yes, I believe I'd like another."

Jeep was back with a fresh one in less than a minute.

"Here you go. Would you tell me about the meteorite now?"

"Sure."

Jeep stood in the doorway to the galley so she could watch the bar. Yamashita said, "Meteorites are hard to find. Most of them fall in the ocean or burn up in the atmosphere before they get to the surface of the earth, and they're small. About the size of pea gravel."

Yamashita took a sip of beer, then continued.

"Meteorites are old. Billions of years old. They're made up of the leftover stuff of the universe, from the formation of the stars and planets, so they're important objects of study by scientists looking for clues to the origins of the universe."

Jeep said, "When was the universe formed?"

"About fourteen billion years ago. It started with the big bang."

"Big bang? What's that?"

"The big bang is what we science-types postulate started the universe . . . a big explosion."

"Oh."

It was apparent to Yamashita that he was losing his audience. Jeep didn't seem to be following along. He leaned against the sink and sipped his beer. He thought for a moment, said, "Don't worry about all of it right now. It's the meteorite you need to know about."

Jeep went to the bar and got a beer for one of the guys sitting there. She checked the rest, came back to the doorway, waited for Yamashita to speak.

He cleared his throat and said, "There's two basic types of meteorites. Stony and metallic. This one," he pointed with his right index finger, the one holding the glass of beer, "is metallic. It's magnetic too. Only about five percent of all meteorites are in that category. That fact, plus its size, plus the fact several of us observed its fall and property damage, make it highly desirable and valuable."

Jeep took the used frying pan from the stove to the sink and began washing it. She was quiet, thinking, turning over in her mind all Yamashita had told her.

In the last booth, sitting by himself, Oliver Varley was thinking too. He picked up the hamburger and bit into it without enthusiasm, chewed and swallowed, washed it down with some beer. *Thirty years.* he thought. *I can't believe thirty years has gone by. It seems like the blink of an eye at the same time it seems like a hundred years ago. Life hasn't been the same without Irma, and I wonder what became of Studebaker. Still have nightmares about him. Couldn't save him. Should have saved him. I should of seen him grown to a man, like his brothers.*

Oliver put the hamburger down. He didn't feel like eating. He could see the other drinkers out at the bar, still talking about that damned meteorite . . . damndest thing any of them had ever seen, that's for sure. *Wonder what Jeep and old Yamashita are up to in the kitchen back there. Oh well, she's a grown woman. Her own business I guess. Time for me to go anyways . . .*

Oliver Varley left his daughter a twenty-dollar tip and went out the backdoor. No one saw him leave. His exit that night was as humble and unpretentious as his whole life had been. He stood in the dirt parking lot looking at the stars, still thinking about his dead wife and lost son. *Maybe they're both up there, among the stars,* he thought. *Maybe each star up there is a lost soul, looking down at us here on earth, shining their starlight for us to see and remember them by.* The thought comforted him as he got in his truck and started for Rhyolite Mountain, the Varley homestead and his empire of automobiles. When he got in the pickup and started it, the big Cadillac engine responded with a throaty roar, like a hungry lion, that settled to a steady purr as Oliver Varley pulled out on Hardrock Street, heading up toward the Neversink Dam spillway. His red taillights looked like the eyes of a great jungle beast as they disappeared into the night.

When Oshkosh Varley came in Brownie's place a half hour later, it was nearly eleven o'clock. The drinking crowd, most of whom had to be at work the next morning, had thinned down to the Swink brothers, Tony Garza, who'd brought Rickey's wife, Marcia, so she could get their car, and Mr. Yamashita. Jeep was behind the bar, leaned back against the cash register with her arms crossed. They were all listening to Tony.

" . . . so the doc says to Rickey, 'how'd you burn your foot?' and Rickey says, 'I stepped on a meteorite.' And the Doc says, 'No. Seriously, how'd you do it?' Rickey tells him again, 'I stepped on a goddamned meteorite.' The Doc turns and asks me, 'What kind'a drugs you boys been taking tonight?' I tell him. 'No, Doc. He really did. He stepped on a meteorite.' Doc says, 'Don't bullshit me. I'm not in the mood. Meteorites don't just drop in and they're not hot.'

We finally told him we had a bonfire."

Yamashita said, "The doctor was both right and wrong. Stone meteorites aren't hot when they land. That's what nearly all of them are. This one was rarer. It was metallic. They land hot, as we can all attest."

"Well," Tony said, "he put bonfire mishap on the chart. But I told him he could drop in here and see the hole in the roof."

"He could see the meteorite," Jeep said.

Yamashita looked at her, made a slight shake of his head.

Jeep said, "Hey, Osh. Thanks for coming down. You want a beer or something?"

"No thanks. I gotta work tomorrow. Where's Pop?"

Jeep came around the end of the bar and motioned with her head. Osh followed her to the last booth.

"Daddy was sitting right here. I made him a double hamburger like he likes, but it got real crazy around here for a while." She told him about the meteorite, Rickey's foot and most of her talk with Mr. Yamashita. "And then when I had a chance to look up, he was gone. I don't know when he left, but he didn't eat hardly none of his hamburger, and he left me a twenty-dollar tip."

"He ever do that before?"

"What?"

"Leave you a big tip like that?"

"You kidding? No. He generally eats every bite of his hamburger too. He loves those things."

Oshkosh Varley was an uncommon man. He was not only uncommon large in size, he was uncommon smart, as if all the Varley intelligence and size genes were concentrated in him. He was a straight-A student in high school and a *summa cum laude* graduate of the State University of New York at Binghamton. And while he was book smart, Osh Varley didn't lack for common sense either. He possessed all his father's reasoning ability, as well as a strong sense of deductive reasoning, or "street smarts." It's what made him such a good cop. He was a sergeant with the state BCI, the Bureau of Criminal Investigation ... an arm of the New York State Police. Osh didn't like the direction his thoughts were taking him in. He said, "Okay. Tell you what. I'll drive on up to the farm and check on him. I'll call you from there."

"Sounds good. Thank you, Osh."

"It's okay, sis. I want to make sure he's safe and sound too."

Osh left through the front door, almost touching the frame with his head and shoulders.

Jeep wiped the table top in the booth out of habit more than anything else, and almost collided with Yamashita when she turned around to go back to the bar.

"Oh. Yamashta-san, I didn't see you."

"I didn't mean to startle you, my wife says I walk like a cat."

"You want another beer?"

"No. Thank you. I want to give you more meteorite information."

She looked at the bar, where the three other patrons were talking.

"Sure. Looks like everybody at the bar is all right for now."

Yamashita sat in the booth where Oliver Varley had been drinking. He said, "You need to know about the meteorite hunters."

"Hunters?" Jeep said as she sat down opposite Yamashita.

"Yeah. Maybe tomorrow, but most definitely by the day after, the meteorite hunters will descend on you like sharks after blood. They'll all be wanting to see the meteorite and they'll all try to buy it."

"Why? And who are these people?"

Yamashita thought for a moment, pulled the cuffs of his blue button down shirt and said, "Money, prestige, science would be my best guesses. The people involved are collectors, broker-dealers, enthusiasts and representatives of museums and universities. They're all interested in meteorites. The meteorites themselves are incredibly old and are some of our best opportunities to learn about the makeup of the universe."

Jeep looked around at the bar and the hole in the roof that needed to be fixed. She was making wages for herself and keeping current with her mortgage payments to Brownie Dingman, but there never was any extra money. She felt like she was treading water, more often than not. She sighed, and said, "Were you honest, when you told me how much those things are worth?"

"I'm always honest," he said. "The brokers will be here first and offer the least. At first anyway. But they'll up the ante as soon as they see some competition appear. The universities and museums will not be able to match what a rich broker or collector will. On the other hand though, the museums and universities have a more noble purpose, which is to further human knowledge."

"How come you know so much about this, Yamashta-san?"

Yamashita looked uncomfortable. He said, "Because my undergraduate degree is from The University of Texas. I studied astronomy at the McDonald Observatory."

"So were you involved with meteorites there?"

"Yes."

Jeep looked up front at the bar. They were still talking, had most of their drinks left in front of them. She said, "So, did you try to get meteorites for them?"

"As a grad student, yes. But as an undergraduate, no."

Jeep said, "It sure would be nice to get a chunk of money, then I could pay Brownie off and fix the place up a little. But I'd like to further science too." Then she said, "Hey. How are all those people going to know about it? The meteorite, I mean."

Yamashita looked at her face, into her eyes, then said, "They track them with telescopes and plot the descent trajectories. There are amateur astronomers all over the world. They notify each other by telephone. I'm sure there's trackers on the way here already."

The Swinks and Tony Garza all stood up and waved at Jeep.

"We're outta here," one of them said.

"'Kay. Thanks," Jeep said. "Come back soon."

"We will."

"I'd better go too," Yamashita said. He took a card out of his coat pocket and scribbled on the back of it.

"Here's my phone number. Call if I can help in some way."

"Thank you, Yamashta-san. I will."

"Don't forget to put it away somewhere safe."

"I will. Thanks and g'night."

Jeep locked the doors and turned the outside lights off, turned the "Closed" sign on in the front window. She thought hard as she cleaned the bar, about tomorrow. When she finished she totaled the cash register, pulled the tape out and put it and the cash into a vinyl bank bag, then put the bag in the safe in the office. She locked the safe and wrapped the meteorite in a pair of white bar towels. She cut the lights and was just about out the backdoor when the phone started ringing. She stepped back in behind the bar, picked up the phone . . . and her life changed forever as soon as she said,

"Hullo. Brownies Tavern."

"Jeep. It's Osh."

"I know that. You at the farm?"

"No. I'm not."

"Where . . ."

"I'm up at the stone bridge, down below the spillway. I'm patched through on my car radio. I . . ."

"What's the matter, Osh? I'm tired, I wanna go home. Daddy's okay?"

"No. No he's not. He's dead. His truck was upside down in the river. I got here about the same time as the volunteer ambulance crew. They've got him out. The troopers and Board of Water Supply cop are doing the accident report."

A great wracking sob escaped from deep inside Jeep and she dropped the phone, both hands covering her face, tears coursing out from her fingers.

"Jeep? Sis, you there? Are you all right? HEY! JEEP . . . say something. Please . . ."

She got control of herself, picked up the phone and said, "I'm okay. I'm all right now. I'm okay, Osh." She sniffed and wiped her face with a clean bar towel she ran under cold water in the sink.

She isn't really okay, he thought, *she's just holding herself together.* He said, "Would you make some coffee please? I'm coming back down there as soon as they get Pop in the ambulance. They'll take him over to Monticello for an autopsy."

"Not now, Osh. Not yet. I'm not ready. I can't believe Daddy's gone."

"I'm sorry, sis. Not thinking good either."

"You want me to call anyone . . ."

"Not yet. I'll be there in fifteen, twenty minutes."

Jeep set up a big sixty-cup commercial coffeemaker, filled it with water from a black six-foot rubber hose attached to the kitchen faucet, added two pounds of coffee and started it up. She took out a small percolator and made a pot for her and her brother. Then she got the meteorite from her purse and locked it in the safe. As she respun the dial to lock it, someone started rattling the front doors. She looked at the clock in the office, the one with the correct time. It said 3:45 a.m. She'd been working for eighteen straight hours.

When she got to the door, it was quivering on its latches from the force hammering on it.

"Alright already," Jeep yelled as she began undoing the deadbolts, "don't knock the damn doors off. I've got enough to fix around here."

She thought, *And don't forget to call Billy Flynn first thing tomorrow. Tomorrow, hell. In a couple of hours. Get him over here to fix the hole in the roof.*

She slid the last deadbolt back and opened the door for her brother.

"Jeez, Osh. You always beat on people's doors like that?"

"Guess I got carried away, sis. Didn't mean to."

"C'mon back, I started coffee. You call Susie?"

"Not yet. I'll call in a couple hours when she and the kids are up."

Jeep poured two mugs of coffee, put one in front of her brother.

"That smells good, we'll probably need a bunch of it."

"I've got it covered. You want something to eat . . . I can fix you some breakfast."

"Sure."

As an experienced investigator, Osh Varley knew enough to eat whenever he could. No telling when or where the next meal might be. He sipped his coffee, watched his sister.

Jeep started frying potatos, eggs and ham. She said, "Tell me about Daddy."

Osh shifted his seat, his broad back almost disappearing the chair. He said, "There's not a whole lot to tell at this point. I started for the farm and ran into a BWS cop putting flares on the road, by the stone bridge. They were in the middle of the turn, before you see the bridge. I stopped, and rolled the window down, it was Willy Burley. I asked him what was going on and he said, 'Better brace yourself lad. It's your pa.'

"I thanked him and eased on around the turn to the bridge. Two Staties were there, Eddie Ryan and Frank Monday. I know 'em both, good troopers. I pulled over and parked. Pop was lying on the bank down below the bridge with a blanket over his face. He was thrown from the vehicle after it went over the side. His neck was broken. The pickup was in the middle of the Neversink, on its roof with the headlights still on. The cab and roof were crushed down near flat when Lil' Mout, the black guy from Liberty, pulled it out with his wrecker. He towed it over to Liberty. The Neversink Volunteer Ambulance took Pop to Monticello, to the coroner's. He'll do an autopsy next week. Eddie Ryan told me he and Frank looked hard, but couldn't find any skid marks. Not one. It looked like he ran off the road, doing about fifty or sixty miles per hour, sailed seventy-five or eighty feet in the air, then hit and flipped over several times."

As he talked in a low monotone, giving his report in a professional manner, Osh's voice caught as he finished and he found it necessary to blow his nose. Jeep wept openly as she dished up a breakfast platter for her brother and a dinner plate for herself. She wiped her eyes with the bar towel draped over her left shoulder before she put four slices of toast on a saucer and delivered it all to the small table where her brother was sitting. She refilled their coffees while Osh got them silverware and condiments, and they ate without speaking, the ring of knife and fork on china and the clink of coffee mugs on Formica taking the place of small talk or questions, asked and answered.

At a quarter past five, the galley was cleaned, the dishes were being washed in the dishwasher, the big coffeemaker was almost ready and Jeep and Oshkosh Varley were formulating their action plan for the day.

Osh notified the trooper barracks and his captain that he was taking a week of personal leave because of his father's death. Then they started notifying their brothers, sisters, aunts, uncles, nieces and nephews. By ten o'clock in the morning, Brownie's Ten Eel Tavern was filling with all shapes and sizes, all ages and both sexes of Varleys. They came from near and far, by car, truck, camper and motor home. Over the next few days the parking lot at the tavern had all the color and drama of the infield on a race weekend at Talladega Superspeedway. There were even a couple of NASCAR flags being flown.

Just before lunch, the crowd had grown so much, Jeep announced she couldn't afford an open bar; kinfolks or not, everyone had to pay for their own drinks. It met a mixed reaction at first, but everyone complied after a little while.

It was exactly four o'clock when the first meteorite hunter came. Like a shark circling a baby seal, he didn't attack at first, getting a sense of the place before making his move.

Billy Flynn, after issuing his condolences, sent a crew of three men at eight a.m. They repaired the roof, inside and out, replacing insulation, sheetrock and false ceiling tile, and were done before lunchtime.

The first meteorite hunter, whom Jeep named "One," hung around the end of the bar for twenty minutes before he approached Jeep. After pleasantries and a few platitudes, he got to the point. "I heard you had a meteorite hit last night."

Jeep didn't say a word. Nearly dead on her feet after being up for thirty-two hours, she had no patience for a line of BS. She wiped the bar and tidied up, waiting for One's next move.

He said, "Did I hear right? Because I'm a collector. I'd pay a thousand dollars for something like that."

"I'll bet," Jeep said. "No."

"What would it take?"

"More than that. A lot more."

"What's a lot more?"

"You know. I'm busy. Leave me alone."

The second meteorite hunter, who was now in the bar, watched as Jeep walked away from his competitor.

Must of low-balled her, he thought, as he deliberated his opening move.

Soon there were four of them. Two were broker-dealers, one represented an Ivy League university and the fourth represented himself. They all knew each other from previous meteorite encounters, but remained a respectful distance apart. Not because they wanted to avoid the appearance of collusion, but because they didn't like each other. Not one bit. They were all disappointed on that day, however; Jeep was so exhausted she was hallucinating. At six o'clock she called Otto Dunker the relief bartender and went home to her trailer and collapsed into bed, sleeping for almost fourteen hours.

Oliver Varley died on a Tuesday evening. Sergeant Oshkosh Varley and his older brother Hudson, who was the Neversink justice of the peace, used all the influence and built-up favors they both possessed to get the autopsy completed and Oliver's body released on Thursday afternoon and sent over to the Neversink Funeral Home for embalming and a plain, gray metal coffin. They planned for the viewing and wake at seven o'clock Friday evening at Brownie's Ten Eel Tavern, and the burial on Saturday morning at the Neversink Cemetery.

Jeep closed the tavern at two o'clock on Friday afternoon, in preparation for the wake. Her brothers, Lincoln, Kaiser and Reo, all pitched in and helped get the place ready, moving tables and chairs, cleaning and setting up a huge barbecue pit by the backdoor. It was eight feet long and three feet wide, normally used by the firemen for their yearly clambake. The barbecue was for Saturday, after the funeral, when the Varley clan and all the mourners would gather together for mutual comfort . . . and to swap stories about the deceased.

By Friday all four meteorite hunters were getting antsy. None of them had as yet seen the meteorite, although they had all heard plenty about it. It was, after all, a most unique event and the talk of the town. Thing was however, the story changed with each retelling.

It's not that anyone lied or twisted the hunters on purpose, but each teller and reteller had to add their own little details, as they recalled the story. After awhile the meteorite hunters, all strangers to Neversink, must have assumed half the town had been there when the Perseid meteorite struck Brownie's Tavern three nights ago. All four of the hunters were afraid to cede to the others, lest the competition gain the meteorite at their expense . . . so they all stuck around, waiting to make their pitches to Jeep Varley, bartender and proprietress of Brownie's Ten Eel Tavern, down on the Neversink, three and a half miles below the Neversink Dam and spillway.

On Friday morning, a collection was made for barbecue supplies, and the four meteorite hunters were good sports about it, kicking in one hundred dollars each, thereby ensuring plenty of chicken to grill. The place was taking on a carnival atmosphere: dogs and small children running helter-skelter through the parking lot and splashing around in the warm shallow water of the Neversink River, throwing stones or sticks for the dogs to chase. Portable grills popped up here and there, and a few hardy Varleys were camped out in tents on both sides of Hardrock Street along the water.

At four in the afternoon, a hearse pulled in from the Neversink Funeral Home and a team of Varley brothers carried the mortal remains of their father into the tavern and stood the coffin in his favorite booth at the back where the table had been removed.

The coffin was upright, leaned back on the wall, and Reo nailed a small wood cleat on the floor to keep it from slipping. Baskets of flowers were sitting all around him, brought in by the funeral home personnel. Votive candles were placed with care, and the top half of the coffin was unlatched so Oliver's upper body, hands and arms crossed holding a small wood cross, could be seen.

Lincoln Varley said, "Ain't he a bit crooked in there?"

"We had to make some allowances . . . for his size," Mr. Poundstone, the funeral director said, "and make some adjustments."

"What adjustments?"

"You have to understand," Poundstone said.

"Understand . . ."

"How big he was. This is the largest casket we had in stock."

"Didn't quite fit in there?" Lincoln said.

"No, not quite. We had to wedge him in. That's why he's a bit crooked. It couldn't be helped."

"Don't worry about it. You did the best you could," Lincoln said "Besides, Dad was different all his life. No reason he shouldn't be so in death as well."

The turnout at seven in the evening was huge. It seemed like every person in Neversink came to show their respects and give condolences to the Varley family. At nine o'clock that night, out-of-town folks were still coming in and the formal part of the viewing was extended for another hour to accommodate them, as one by one the friends, family and business acquaintances filed past Oliver Varley lying in his coffin like a fallen president in the capitol rotunda.

Jeep managed to get the building cleared by midnight. As she said her good nights she told each of the meteorite hunters she would have a private viewing and auction at noon on Sunday. Whoever was the high bidder would go home with the meteorite. Bring cash and be ready to buy were the only requirements.

Oliver Varley's funeral was held at ten a.m. on Saturday. The service was short but eloquent and was attended by an estimated fifteen hundred people, according to the two BWS patrolmen who directed traffic for the event. It seemed as if every person in the county turned out to pay their respects and say good-bye to Oliver Varley, who was large in life, and destined to be legendary in death.

After the graveside service at the Neversink Cemetery, where Oliver was laid to rest alongside Irma, everyone was invited back to Brownie's for refreshments. It turned out to be a wingding fitting for a man of Oliver's stature.

The tavern was closed. Outside on the parking lot, the barbecue was set up, five kegs of beer were iced, ready to tap, the grill was lit and the coals glowing as a team of four Neversink firemen started cooking the first thirty pounds of chickens lathered in a special barbecue sauce. By tradition, every family attending brought some kind of homemade dish: there were cakes, pies, noodle salads of every description, potato salads, deviled eggs, baked bean casseroles, pitchers of lemonade, iced tea and every color of Kool-Aid ever made.

The Oliver stories started making the rounds right after the first keg was tapped.

"I heard he could pull a car engine out with his bare hands."

" ... drink twenty-five beers every day ..."

" ... strongest man ever lived ..."

" ... made a fortune ..."

" ... up on Rhyolite Mountain ..."

" ... buried probably ..."

The rumors grew with each telling and the conjecture increased to the point that for years amateur treasure hunters snuck around at night, digging holes all over Rhyolite Mountain.

The gathering after the funeral continued until all the food was eaten and the empty dishes and bowls reclaimed by their owners, the ice was all melted and five kegs of beer were done away with, and darkness came. That's when they saw it.

The Perseid meteor shower was particularly intense that year. Meteorites had been falling all day and were at their most intense on Saturday night. As darkness fell, the sky came alive with fire as hundreds of meteorites flashed through the atmosphere for several hours in a display of Mother Nature's power and beauty.

As promised, Jeep Varley held the private auction for her meteorite on Sunday at noon. When the four meteorite hunters arrived, they found a crew of firemen and Varley brothers cleaning up after the barbecue outside Brownie's Tavern. Inside, they found Jeep and her brother Osh, a table set up on the stage area with four chairs and Hiro Yamashita. He was sitting on a fifth chair next to the table, at the edge of the stage. Oshkosh Varley, all six-foot eight inches and 275 pounds of him, was standing at parade rest in front and to the side of the burn hole in the floor.

Jeep greeted each man as he came in the door, thanked him for attending and indicated the stage, then locked the door.

When they were all seated, she said, "Thanks again for coming today. You are here to bid on a magnetic, metallic meteorite of approximately three and a half kilograms. I'm going to present it for your inspection as soon as I finish with the auction terms, which are these: You will have ten minutes to examine the item. Its authenticity is guaranteed. You see for yourselves the burnt area in the dance floor. I witnessed the event and will provide a notarized affidavit for the winning bidder and I have the ceiling panel it fell through as well. I will provide each of you with a white three-by-

five index card and a golf pencil. Please write your name and phone
number on the first two lines and your bid amount underneath. This
is your only chance to make an offer, so make it your very best. After
you have written your offer, you will give the card to Osh and retire
to the bar where I will be serving free consolation cocktails for the
losers. The terms are cash, payable immediately. The winner will
leave with the meteorite while the others stay here for a half hour or
so. Are there any questions?"

Number Three said, "Who are these two guys?"

"The man on the dance floor is my brother, Oshkosh. He's a
detective sergeant with the New York State Police Bureau of Criminal
Investigation. He's here to make sure all of us are safe and sound."

Yamashita stood and gave a slight bow, spoke for himself, "Hiro
Yamashita for The University of Texas, McDonald Observatory."

Jeep said, "Any other questions? Is everyone agreed as to the
auction terms?"

When all had given their assent, Jeep nodded to Osh, who handed
each man an index card and a small golf pencil.

It was over in a matter of minutes. Jeep produced the meteorite
from a green Boy Scout knapsack, and with all the flair of a female P.
T. Barnum, she laid a white towel in the center of the table and put
the silver-gray and black meteorite on center, with Yamashita's test
nail still stuck to it.

There was an intake of breath all around as the hunters tried to be
casual in the presence of such a magnificent example. It lay on the
table like a talisman, silently calling "take me" to each and every one
of them. They stared, hypnotized by it, lusting for it in their heart of
hearts. Each one saying to himself . . . "It's mine."

"Time," Jeep called. She picked up the meteorite and wrapped it in its white towel, placed it back in her knapsack. Osh gathered the five bid cards and handed them to her. Jeep took the cards and the knapsack and went behind the bar. She read them and said, "Number Three, south seat, come with me." She led him into the galley and closed the door, putting them in close quarters.

Be prepared. she thought. *If anything's going to happen, now is the time.* She could feel the five-shot Smith & Wesson in her waistband just under her left breast. She felt a trickle of sweat roll down her side. *Stay calm, be strong,* echoed in her head.

"Okay," She said, "show me the money."

"Now?"

"Yes, now."

The man pulled a money belt off his torso and counted out stacks of cash as she watched.

"It's all there," he said.

"I see."

She do-si-doed with him, picked up the cash and put it in a paper bag. She pointed to the knapsack with her chin, her right arm under her blouse as if she had an itch, the gun close to hand.

He took the towel out, checked the meteorite and put it in a ubiquitous blue and white Pan-Am flight bag.

"The backdoor is there, to your left."

Without another word, the man she'd tagged as "Three" went out the door and disappeared.

As soon as the door closed, Jeep locked it and turned the deadbolt. On legs that quivered as she walked, Jeep went to the big Dieboldt safe and put the cash, less five thousand she put in her jeans, into a vinyl bank bag, then locked the safe. She took a moment to check her makeup, then stepped back into the bar.

"Sorry, boys. Can I buy you a drink?"

They declined and after the stated few minutes, disappeared out the door in the same quiet way they'd shown up.

Jeep poured a Coca-Cola for herself and her brother and a glass of draft beer for Yamashita. She said, "Thank you both for your help. I couldn't have managed without you."

Yamashita said, "I think they all raised their bids some when I mentioned UT and the McDonald Observatory."

"I'm sure of it," Osh said. "I saw some jaw clenching as you introduced yourself."

Yamashita chuckled. "Guess they didn't know it was my alma mater."

"Well anyways," Jeep said, "it worked."

She handed each of them twenty-five one-hundred-dollar bills. "Thanks."

"That's twice what we agreed," Osh said.

"I included a bonus for both of you. It turned out better than I hoped."

"You're happy with the results?" Yamashita said.

"Yes," Jeep said. "I'm very happy."

Jeep never disclosed the sale price to anyone. She did however, renegotiate her deal with Brownie Dingman and paid him off with cash on the barrelhead. She made some gradual improvements to the place and had Otto Dunker or his wife Cheryl tending bar a little more often. The folks at the Neversink Library came in one morning and found a generous cash donation in the slot for mail and returned books.

The fortune seekers up on Rhyolite Mountain continued searching that first summer, but were always disappointed, finally quitting in frustration. Still, the legend of buried cash grew, and new holes kept appearing every spring when the weather got warm. The stories of Oliver Varley's feats of strength and unconventional life grew to legendary status as the years passed and they were told and retold. The tragedy of Oliver Varley, the loss of his youngest child and his wife Irma's death by her own hand the same day has been repeated countless times . . . it is still told today . . . and the legend grows even more in August when the Perseids fall and the people of Neversink remember the night Oliver Varley died . . . when stars were falling on the Neversink.

The empire of automobiles stayed up on Rhyolite Mountain for years, like a glittering, shiny monument to a man who was larger than life. Oliver Varley's sons sold a few cars here and there over the years, but the bulk of them were still up on the mountain when the town, in a burst of civic pride and an attempt to capture the Renaissance Prize for sprucing up, passed an ordinance outlawing automobile graveyards. Heavy equipment was brought up to the Varley homestead, and one by one the remaining cars, almost 9,500 of them, were crushed and sold for scrap metal.

Somewhere, Oliver Varley still grieves.

The Crawfish Incident

2003

The Crawfish Incident

According to Buck and John, times were hard and there wasn't any work worth having in the county: Route 17 and the 17K bypass were finished, the Rondout, Neversink and Downsville Dams were finished, and so were the water diversion tunnels.

"Oh sure," they said, "there's a few suck-ass jobs at the prisons and on the state, county or town road crews, but you pretty much had to be related to somebody to get hired there. A guy could always go down to the city, but you were forced to buy a union book and button from the Mob and put up with all the horseshit."

Nope. Things were just plain hard, according to them. That's when Buck and John decided to go in to the crawfish business and that's when the shit hit the fan around here.

Buck and John had grown up together and were lifelong friends. They went to grade school, middle school and high school together, got drafted together and got in trouble together. They got the drinking habit together, although John was worse about it than Buck. Buck took pills in addition to his drinking jones. Prescription or street, it didn't matter to him . . . just as long as they made him high. Having addictive personalities, they hit full stride in Vietnam, where the bars and pharmacopoeias were always readily accessible, cheap, fully stocked and open twenty four/seven. It was a drunkard's dream and an addict's paradise over there.

When they came home from Fort Sill, Oklahoma, after they were discharged from the army, all of the big construction jobs were pretty well over, although they did get a good year in on the Route 17 project when it was building out past Roscoe, on its way up to Binghamton. Winters, and the rest of the time when they were laid off, they drew rocking chair money . . . as unemployment insurance was known . . . which gave the pair of them plenty of time to drink, hunt, fish, chase pussy and work at about any kind of odd job to be had: cutting brush and timber, digging holes or ditches, wrecking buildings, trimming trees or what have you, they were your boys. "We'll work," they said, "for money paid under the table. So as not to mess up our rocking chair money. You understand?"

No, sir, Buck and John weren't lazy. No way. They had both a work ethic and an independent American-born spirit. They weren't just a couple of country woodchucks. They'd rather die than go on the dole or take food stamps, rocking chair money excepted. However, to be honest about it, those two weren't always what you'd call dependable. They might work eight or ten days straight, go home of an evening, tell you good night and "see ya in the morning" . . . get thirsty that night . . . and you wouldn't see hide nor hair of them for three weeks, until they ran out of beer, or money, or both, and decided to sober up and come back to work. You couldn't expect too much work out of them for a couple of days while they got back to eating once in a while and got over the jitters. They were damn hard workers though, when they were there. Worked cheap too, as long as you paid them in cash and weren't bothered by periodic unexplained absences.

Anyway, the time I'm telling you about, during one of their bouts of temporary unemployment, Buck was sitting in John's trailer with him, drinking beer. It was a Sunday so they were probably watching baseball or preseason football, because it was the middle of August.

They were finishing up the first six-pack, not even drunk yet. John, who possessed the brains of the two, says, "Did you know that crawfish is worth four dollars a pound?"

"Crawdads? No shit?"

"Yeah. I seen it on the news. They're selling 'em at the Fulton Fish Market in the City. Four dollars a pound."

"Damn. That's a lot."

"True. That's true . . . and they ain't hard to catch neither."

"What do you mean?" Buck said as he popped the next-to-last beer and took a long swallow.

"Well, if I built some traps outta that half-inch galvanized screen wire, we could catch and sell 'um."

"You got wire?"

"Some. Not enough."

"I know where there's some . . ."

"Get it. And all the clean five-gallon buckets you can find. Can you get all that stuff here . . . when . . . how soon?"

"First thing tomorrow. I need the truck."

"Don't fuck up. I can't lose it."

"I won't."

And just about that fast, Buck and John were in the "crawfish bidness."

By the next evening John had rigged up three-dozen crawfish traps. They were round, about two feet long and twelve inches in diameter. One end was a funnel, with an inch-and-a-half hole. The other end was flat and removable, tied together with waxed cord. The traps were tied together with a yellow nylon clothesline, four to a string, about twenty feet long.

"Okay, Buck. Start loading these here in the truck. Try not to get 'em tangled up."

"Yas'sah boss. Yas'sah." Buck grinned as he started picking up the sets of traps and heading out to the truck, a powder blue '66 Chevy Suburban. The thing had been painted by the two of 'em, one hot afternoon a couple years ago, using four-inch paintbrushes and two gallons of Glidden house paint Buck had salvaged from a garage cleaning job. It didn't look too bad at first, as long as you were fifteen or twenty feet away. But gradually, the stuff blistered and flaked off where water got under the blue paint, and it showed some of the original white paint underneath. After awhile the whole thing took on a mottled look, like a big speckled egg. The red spray-painted wheels with the big white "X" through the center . . . John's idea of old-fashioned spinner hubcaps . . . set the whole thing off in a jaunty kind of way.

Buck and John set out for the Rondout Reservoir, about a mile outside of Neversink Village. They set the traps, baited with food scraps they'd dumpster-dived at various restaurants around town. It took about three-five gallon buckets full of rotting meat scraps to bait everything, and the boys were pretty odoriferous by the time they finished. They used a neighbor's boat with Buck rowing while John baited and threw the traps overboard. He'd attached ten feet of line to the last trap, with a white Clorox bottle tied on the end. That was the float, which enabled them to retrieve the traps. They stuck to the shallows, so they wouldn't interfere with the fisherman who rowed back and forth pulling trolling lines.

Three days later they pulled the traps. Each one had about forty or fifty crawfish, roughly three pounds, in them. Buck rowed and pulled traps out of the water while John emptied the critters into an ice chest, rebaited the traps and threw them back in. By the time they were halfway through the trap line, the ice chest was full of two-to-three inch crawfish, some of which were locking claws and fighting one other.

"Feisty little sum-bitches, ain't they?" Buck said.

"Oh yeah. That's 'cause they're fresh. We're gonna have to get more ice and another ice chest. Head for the truck, we'll get the rest of 'em later."

Buck swung the boat around, headed for shallow water and the Chevy Suburban. He was putting his back into it, making the oars squeak in the locks and leaving an ever-widening ripple in their wake. Old Buck wasn't much good when it came to tying knots or tatting lace, doing any kind of fine work, because he only had nine fingers . . . his right index finger having been surgically removed following a misunderstanding involving a twelve-gauge Mossberg shotgun and a fairly plump married woman's disgruntled husband, but he was lean and sinewy, all hard muscle, built for strength and stamina, so he was just plain hell on wheels when it came to fetching or carrying heavy loads, rowing boats and such. Yessir. Buck was your man for hard labor.

Now . . . it's been repeated countless times . . . God looks out for drunks, fools and little children. I'd like to amend that old saw to say "souses and stump-jumpers." Because wouldn't you know, as Buck and John started back to John's trailer over on the Sundown Road, the truck broke down right in front of the Town Line Tavern. The transmission linkage fell off, and it wouldn't stay in gear. The old truck had done it before and John kept a box of washers and cotter keys under the seat to fix it with.

"We gotta push her outta the road, Buck. I can fix it soon's it cools down some. The frigging linkage is alongside the exhaust pipe and it burns the shit outta my arm. She'll cool off in a bit an' I'll take care of it."

They managed to push the Suburban over onto the Tavern parking lot.

"The ice is pretty near gone in the chest," Buck said.

"I know it," John replied. "C'mon up to the bar."

When the pair stepped into the taproom, it was cool and quiet; in the dimness the lights flickering on the jukebox sent a neon welcome, beckoning them in. They sat at the bar, the only ones in the place.

"Yo. Jerry. Where you at? Halloo, anybody home?" John yelled.

"Better get out here 'fore we hep ourselves," Buck added, slapping the bar.

The way the place was laid out the patrons entered from a side door, stepping in at the end of the bar with booths and a dance floor on the left, the bar itself on the right. All the way down at the other end was a double door that led to a kitchen, storeroom and back entrance. Jerry Smith, the owner and bartender, came through the door, carrying two cases of Ballantine Ale.

"Hey John. Hey Buck. You boys aiming for an early start on the festivities?" Jerry said as he put the beer on the counter, started loading them in the cooler.

"Naw. My truck broke out front," John said, then added, "What festivities?"

"It's Wednesday. Fish fry night. All you can eat for five bucks. You oughta try it. Starts at four thirty or so."

"Can we get a couple buckets a ice from you?"

"Ice? What for?" Jerry said as he straightened up and dried his hands with a bar towel.

"We got about fifty pounds a fresh crawdads in a cooler an' our ice's just about gone."

"No shit . . . whatcha gonna do with all them?"

"Oh we're gonna sell 'em. They bring four bucks a pound at the Fulton Fish Market in the city."

"I know, Buck. The city's ninety-five miles away. You going in that old speckled truck? Think she'll make it?"

"Well, yeah, " John said, puffing on his cigarette.

"You can have the ice. Let's go look at them crawdads."

When they got to the truck, the crawfish were just as lively and fresh as they'd been a couple of hours ago, most of them having locked claws with one or two of their neighbors. The ice was melted, but the water was still cold and there weren't any dead ones at the bottom.

Jerry Smith was a good businessman as well as a good cook, and he knew opportunity when it came knocking.

"Tell ya what, John. I'll buy your crawdads for two fifty a pound, save ya goin' to the city."

They haggled for awhile, finally agreed on three dollars a pound, one ice chest full for a hundred and fifty bucks.

Jerry agreed to take one hundred pounds that very day. Buck got him to throw in a case of ale as part of the deal. When the boys left, Jerry had a washtub half full of ice, crawfish and running water out back of the bar. Buck and John fixed the truck and hurried back to pull the rest of the traps. Jerry went back in the bar to dig out his big

253

cook pots and make some new signs, raising his prices. American ingenuity had just met American entrepreneurism and a whole new "bidness" was a-borning.

The Town Line Tavern was strategically located right at the town line, which was also the county line. Neversink was a one hundred percent dry town, "and we got the drunks to prove it," as the local wags put it, so Jerry's place was the only watering hole for miles around in any direction. He sold cold beer at fair prices and was always busy. The place was popular with tourists passing through, fishermen on the Rondout Reservoir as well as the always thirsty local crowd of prison guards, loggers and the increasingly hard-to-find farmers. In addition to all the adult drinkers, just about every one of Neversink's teenagers who had the urge to try, had their first drinking experience at Jerry Smith's Town Line Tavern. The drinking age in New York State is eighteen and Jerry had a liberal interpretation of who did, or didn't, look to be of legal drinking age. In other words, he never carded anyone, never checked IDs, so he was popular with the kids too ... real popular.

The first fish fry and crawfish boil was a howling success. Seemed like half the people in town were there, eating North Atlantic haddock, which Jerry bought frozen from the wholesalers then dipped in pancake batter, deep fat fried and served with corn on the cob, corn muffins and cole slaw he mixed up in seventy-five-pound tubs. The crawfish were boiled in water that had been doused with cumin, chili and curry, then heaped steaming hot onto serving platters and sprinkled with hot sauce. The result was that folks sat around tearing crawfish heads off and sucking the innards out, dipping it in sauce made from equal parts ketchup and ground horseradish, to their heart's content, then drinking beer to cool off with when the spice aftershock hit them like the heat wave from an atomic bomb blast.

Jerry had raised the dinner price from five to ten dollars for the crawfish boil and doubled his investment with Buck and John. Plus, he damn near sold out of beer and had to restock the following day. It was his best sales day ever, and he'd run the place for thirty years. Buck and John were $300 to the good . . . with more coming. They started their partying by going through the case of ale within a few hours of leaving Jerry Smith's with their money. Things were looking great for everybody the first week, and they were all making plans for their expected windfall.

By Monday evening, Buck and John were broke and dead drunk from five straight days and nights of nonstop partying. The inside and outside of John's 1947 Zimmer trailer home looked like something you'd see after a few sticks of seventy percent dynamite had been exploded in the world's biggest trash heap. There was shit, crap and corruption everywhere. John was passed out in the front yard next to a log he'd been sitting on after he fell in the campfire they'd had going all week. He didn't quite fall in; he'd slipped on his takeoff while trying to broad jump it. Afterward, he was sitting on the log, pouring beer on himself to take care of a few hot spots, when he passed out and fell off. The party was breaking up by that time anyway because there was no more beer, no more potato chips, Oreo cookies, hot dogs or chili con carne they'd been feasting on. Buck was on his back . . . snoring on the living room floor, behind what was left of John's green vinyl couch . . . his pants down around his knees and raw scrapes on both of his knees from fornicating on the floor back there with a fat woman no one knew.

Empty cans, bottles, food wrappers, sticks, wheels, tires, car seats, paper plates, Styrofoam chunks from disposable picnic coolers, a busted-up wooden cable spool that the revelers used as a picnic table and dance floor were strewn about the driveway and around the front door. Two of the five steps and most of the wood railing that had been the entrance to John's place were broken ... torn off and burnt in the campfire when the partygoers had run low on firewood. The screen door had been kicked in, torn off and thrown underneath the front porch.

Inside, the house was just as bad as the outside, because that's where the fight started. There were still about thirty people in various states of inebriation at the party when Raymond McHenry, the self proclaimed "Missouri Hillbilly" who lived in another trailer a quarter mile down the road, got into an argument with Claude Thibadeux, a big angry Canuck who was staying at his nephew's place over in Kerhonkson. Neither one of the fools could recall what started the ruckus, but before it was over they were tearing the doors off of the kitchen cabinets and beating each other with pans, pots, kitchen utensils and various articles of furniture. By the time Raymond's brother, Albert, along with four other revelers, were able to get them separated, Raymond had lost two teeth, his left eye was swollen shut and bleeding, and he had a big gash on his forehead. Claude Thibadeux had a broken nose, badly sprained right wrist and the top third of his right ear had been bitten off. The good news was that no knives or guns were involved. Although "some sumbitch" demonstrating with a Taurus .357 Magnum did manage to put a couple of thumb-sized holes in the left-rear quarter panel of John's old Chevy Suburban.

John woke just before dark, as it was starting to rain. He was still wearing the same faded carpenter's pants, caked with dirt and grease, and a short sleeve polo shirt that looked as if it would be better to throw out than try to wash, crusted as it was with food, smoke, grease, body fluids, little holes and round yellow stains under both armpits. He reeked of burnt cloth, body odor, urine and vomit as he staggered through the wreckage of his abode and, weaving gently, pissed on a laurel bush as he surveyed the damage.

John heard Buck's snoring before he found him on the floor, behind the couch.

"Yo, Buck! Wake it and shake it," John said as he lit a half-smoked cigarette he'd found on the kitchen drain board.

"Buck, get'cher ass up! Buck! Yo." John lobbed a couple of empty beer cans off the wall behind the couch. He heard a rustle of clothing, the snores stopped and Buck's feet, with his old Red Wing lace-ups clunked against the wall.

"Quit throwing shit. I'm awake." Buck was tall, about six foot two, and his head appeared from behind the couch as he sat up. Then he stood, pulling on his boxers and black jeans. His brown eyes were grave as he took in the scene around him.

"Jesus—Jesus—Jesus, hoss. That was some party. I feel like snakes are crawling inside my head."

John had his head under the cold water tap in the kitchen. He was trying to control the dry heaves, and keep from puking in the sink. When he could stand, with water streaming down his face and tangled beard, he said, "Do you know what day it is, what time?"

"I'm pretty sure it's Monday night. Why?"

"What time?"

"I dunno, prob'ly about nine or ten o'clock."

"You sure?"

"Pretty sure."

Buck stepped over the couch and came into the small kitchen.

"Really ripped the place up."

"Tell me something I don't know."

"You ain't got no shoes on."

"Damn," John said. "I don't." He started to look around.

"Don't bother," Buck said as he bent over the sink to cup his hands and drink from the faucet. "You threw 'em in the campfire last evening. Socks too. You was getting ready for your second jump. That's when you passed out and fell off the log. We couldn't wake you up so we just let ya sleep."

"Sweet Christ on a crutch," John said. "I'm gonna shower up, see if I can find some clothes and shoes. You okay to work? We need to go check our trotlines first thing."

"Yeah, I'm okay," Buck answered. He started to upright the overturned furniture. "You got somethin' to put trash in?"

By the next morning, they had things sort of put back together around the place. The trash was burned, the garbage ready to go to the dump, and the aluminum cans were collected in plastic garbage sacks in preparation to go to the scrap dealers. The doors for the kitchen cabinets looked pretty fixable but they were going to need gluing and clamping, along with new hinges and screws. John set them on the small workbench out in the lean-to he'd built on the side of the trailer. He figured he'd fix them when he got a little spare time. There wasn't anything that could be done for the screen door. Buck chopped it up with an axe and they put the pieces in with the aluminum cans.

About eight thirty on Tuesday morning the place was looking as good as it ever did. That's when they ran out of Pepsi-Cola.

"Hey John, there ain't no more Pepsis in the icebox."

"Look in the ice chest."

"You got any money?"

"Just a few coins, no bills."

"Aw shit. Me neither."

Even with the proceeds of John's commemorative quarter collection, they could only come up with $2.36, not nearly enough to buy Pepsi and ice for the crawfish cooler.

The Pepsis were vital. Hard beer drinkers like John upset the pH of their bodies drinking brew instead of eating. They are more likely to suffer from gout as well. Some crave sugar and suffer from insomnia. That's where the Pepsi-Cola comes in . . . it's sweet and has a high concentration of sugar, and guys like John substitute it for food. He often drank a dozen Pepsis a day. He had to have it.

"Buck, gather up the bags of cans, wouldya? I'm going to take my scrap in. Just put them in the truck." John disappeared into the shed and came out with several bucketfuls of bits and pieces of copper, brass and stainless steel that he'd picked up on his odd jobs.

"Just like money in the bank."

"Oh yeah," Buck replied as they headed out to the junkyard.

Two and a half hours later, they were "back in bidness," $42.88 to the good. They were up in Liberty, New York . . . where the scrap metal dealer, a Russian Jew named Osnicove was located . . . which meant they had to go right by the package store on their way back to Neversink. Just as if it were locked on to radar and guided by a laser beam, the old truck turned right in, where Buck and John fueled up with four cases of Old Bohemian and still had eleven dollars and some change left. They went across the street to the convenience store for five bucks worth of gasoline, a pack of cigarettes, some Pepsi-Cola, canned pork and beans, hot dogs and bread. They were down to a few coins in the net worth department when they came out.

"Don't worry, Buck. We'll be back in the chips when we empty out the traps in the morning." John was steering with his knees as he lit a cigarette with both hands.

"Shit. I wish I'd a built more traps though."

"Let's just get this week's haul first," Buck said, "get some money . . ."

"I hear you there," John replied as Buck passed him a beer.

They were back at John's trailer by four o'clock. Buck cooked hot dogs and beans, while John got materials together for more crawfish traps.

They ate supper outside at the cable spool table, sitting on overturned five-gallon plastic buckets, listening to shitkicker music on WVOS radio, the "Voice of Sullivan County," sipping Old Bohemian beer, at peace with themselves and the rest of the world . . . for the time being.

They sat out there at the edge of the clearing, and they were relaxed, drinking slow, smoking the last of John's cigarettes and talking about their "crawfish bidness" and what they would do when the money started rolling in. When the rain began around dark, they were back inside, rigging up more traps, and making more plans to expand their nascent empire.

By five thirty on Wednesday morning, fueled up on rock-and-roll music, old Bohemian beer and a couple of hits of crank that Buck had secreted in tinfoil in his shirt pocket, courtesy of some outlaw bikers he knew . . . the two pals and "bidness" partners had a pretty good buzz going and another thirty crawfish traps built. It was time to run the trotlines, down on the Rondout Reservoir.

"Man!" Buck said. "That shit has got me tuned like Dale, Jr. at Daytona. My motor is racing. Just a-racing I tell ya."

"Well race these ice blocks and the cooler out to the truck," John said. "While I fetch the oars from the back bedroom." John had the jittery feeling that comes from too much booze and dope, not enough food or sleep. They piled the supplies and two six-packs in the truck, headed for the Rondout Reservoir. The early morning mist was rising like smoke from a Civil War cannonade, while dawn was turning the sky into a rose-colored commotion, with wisps of gray and white clouds that drifted high and far. Just as they launched the borrowed rowboat into the black and featureless water, a pair of wild ducks lifted off from the far shore . . . the air so still and quiet that their flapping, splashing and quacking sounded plainly, all the way across the water.

"Damn, that's pretty," said John from the stern. "See them?"

"Uh-huh. Too bad we ain't got no shotguns," Buck said, pulling hard on the oars. "Mebbe we'd have duck dinner." Buck's face was flushed, with beads of sweat on his forehead and neck, his pupils the size of pinpricks.

"Like we ain't got enough shit to carry already. Head thataway," pointing toward the shallow bay where the first sets of traps were laid a week ago.

Fishing was good, the traps were bursting with plump, gray

crawfish. They were so full, Buck was using all his strength to pull the strings of four traps up to the boat. They were halfway through the first set of traps and had the cooler full to the top. There was still more than half of their traps . . . damn near three-quarters of them in fact . . . yet to be pulled up and emptied. If this kept up, John figured, they'd have four coolers-full today. Thinking of a huge haul, he had a smile on his face a fire axe couldn't have knocked off.

"This keeps up we're in the chips."

"Yeah. We'll need a wheelbarrow to carry it all home," Buck said. He started to beat a drum riff tattoo on the cooler in his enthusiasm.

Buck and John were flying on the beer and crank.

"Head yonder, Buck," John said, pointing with his chin at the other shore where the next sets of traps were waiting. "Let's see if our luck's still as good."

Halfway across, the water was black . . . smooth and mysterious as polished obsidian.

The sun came up over the horizon, bright and yellow as the Walmart smiley-face. That was the moment, the near-perfect moment, when they saw the black Zodiac inflatable boat with a sixty-horsepower high-performance four-cycle outboard coming at high speed, on an intercept vector, straight at them. There were two men in the Navy Seal–type boat, both wore dark navy blue uniforms, badges, dark-lensed aviator glasses and had nine-millimeter Glock pistols strapped to both right legs.

"Be cool, Buck. Be cool, for fuck sakes," John said, in a low voice. "Let me talk."

One of the cops had a bullhorn. "Ahoy, you in the rowboat. Stop where you are."

"Buck, ship your oars," John said, as he waved at the slowing Zodiac. "Morning officers."

"Keep your hands where I can see them."

The Zodiac was alongside now, and the officer threw a line to John.

"Tie on to us."

John did as told. Buck sat still, his eyes never leaving the two cops. The driver shut off his motor and stayed behind the wheel, silent, watching Buck and John, his eyes invisible behind the dark sunglasses.

The round cloth insignia on the ball caps the officers were wearing read, "NY CITY—DEPT. OF ENVIRONMENTAL PROTECTION." The silver shield-type badges pinned over the left pocket of their uniform shirts read, "POLICE—NYC BOARD OF WATER SUPLY," with a number inscribed in the center. Squinting, John could make out TAD W. SMOOT engraved on the silver nametag over the second cop's right shirt pocket. He was the one doing the talking. He was the hard-ass. The one who took himself so, so seriously.

Most of the DEP/BWS cops were "good ole boys." They'd grown up in the area, knew most everybody, and were just marking the days, putting in their time until retirement, not making waves, avoiding confrontation. They looked on their job with amusement, seeing it as a low-stress source of a steady paycheck in an economically depressed area.

Since the terror attacks of 9/11, however, the Department of Homeland Security had been ramping up manpower in the DEP/BWS. Money flowed in and the bureaucrats quickly expanded their empires. They built buildings, bought expensive, exotic equipment and hired more help. A lot of new help came from outside the area. Most of them were quick to adapt to the old routine . . . put in their time until retirement, take the steady paycheck, make no waves . . . same as always.

There were a few, however, who thought their newly granted authority with badge and gun gave them the power to dictate, the ability to bully others as perhaps they'd been bullied or the right to get even with anyone who'd had the misfortune to cross paths with them. They were bullies with badges who saw every situation they were involved in as another chance to even their personal score with the world. Tad W. Smoot was such an officer.

On city property, the DEP/BWS police had near-total authority over any and all persons, including the right of arrest and detention. The offset was, any tickets they gave out were adjudicated by the local justices of the peace . . . elected officials who'd grown up in the area and were friendly with all of the Bucks and Johns in town. Advantage, homeboys. Everyone knew this, except the few hard-asses, who saw themselves as the reincarnation of Marshall Matt Dillon, as bringers of truth, justice and the American way. Officer Smoot was proud of himself that morning . . . he had apprehended two perpetrators . . . in the act. He began speaking in his VOICE OF COMMAND, the one of "don't fuck with me" authority.

"I am Officer Smoot of the New York City Department of Environmental Police. I need to see some ID and fishing licenses and boat permits. I'm going to ticket you for failing to have your boat registration number affixed." *That's for starters*, he thought.

John knew enough to keep his mouth shut. He'd learned that the hard way when, as an army private 1st class he'd gotten drunk and lipped off to a big military cop with a bad attitude, got his ass kicked and spent three days in the stockade. He was worried about Buck. Buck's jaws were clenched, and John could see the muscles flexing in his neck and cheeks. He looked at Buck and shook his head, almost imperceptibly. He said to Officer Smoot in his meekest voice, hoping for clemency, "Sir, I confess I don't have a fishing license, but I didn't think I needed one. I'm catching crawdads," as he produced and handed over his driver's license. "My friend here is kinda retarded. He's just rowing the boat. He ain't fishing. He don't have a license. He can't drive."

"I've been watching you two with binoculars. Me and Officer Bates have observed you pulling up a line of traps. That's a trotline. That's illegal. Crawdads are crawfish. That's fishing."

"I thought that it was okay to catch bait."

"Nice try. Sit down. I'm going to start writing. Fishing is fishing. Gonna fish . . . get a license."

"To catch bait? Jeezus Keerist."

Officer Smoot glared in John's direction, then sat down in the bow of the Zodiac and began writing furiously on a metal clipboard with John's driver's license attached to the top. Neither Officer Bates, driving the speedboat, nor Buck, rowing the rowboat, had said a word. They continued their glaring contest with no end in sight. John waited for whatever was coming with the resignation of a condemned prisoner, waiting for the executioner. He watched the water, rippling with the morning breeze, and stared at the far shore, keeping his own counsel. He lit a cigarette, cupping his hands around it, put the burnt match in his shirt pocket and took a puff, waiting.

After what seemed like an eternity, Officer Smoot finished writing and moved to the side of the boat, next to John. Pointing with his pen, he said, "I'm citing you for failure to register and inspect your boat, I'm citing you for not having a valid fishing license and for jug fishing or running a trotline. I'm not going to cite your retarded associate here, and I'm not going to impound your boat and equipment, which I can legally do. Sign right here, saying you agree to appear Tuesday after next, that would be the twenty seventh, before the town justice of the peace, which I've indicated here on line ten." He handed the clipboard to John, who thought for a moment of fumbling the handover, and dropping the whole thing into a hundred feet of water. He decided at the last instant not to do it, kept playing it straight. He signed and handed it back to Officer Smoot, who tore out the third copy, which was marked "DEFENDANT" in red block letters at the bottom. As he passed the ticket back to John, Smoot said, "Oh, one other thing, you'll have to bring your boat into the DEP Headquarters downtown for a safety inspection and registration number. Call first for an appointment, ask for Mr. Mehoff, he does the inspections. You understand?"

"Oh, yes sir, Officer, yes I do."

"Okay, get outta here. And don't let me catch you again like this. Have a nice day."

"I won't, officer. I surely won't," John said to the pair of DEP/BWS cops, who couldn't hear him as they'd cranked their high-powered boat up and cast off from Buck and John in a show of power and authority, leaving the rowboat rocking in their wake. They sped away toward the gatehouse at the far end of the reservoir.

John coughed and hawked up a mouthful of phlegm, which

he spat into the water in the direction of the departed speedboat. Buck was already working his anger off, pulling lustily for the shore, cursing with every stroke.

"At least them sumbitches didn't take our crawdads," John said. "Or all the other traps we got still soaking."

"Fuckem, fuckem, fuckem," was Buck's only comment, with each sweep of the oars.

The fact of the matter was, Officer Smoot was so pleased with himself, and so excited by his first big bust, that he'd plain forgotten to confiscate their catch, or their illegal traps. He was beside himself with anger when his partner pointed it out. He wasn't mad at himself ... he was mad at Paul Bates and Buck and John for not pointing the error out sooner, when it could be rectified.

Buck and John, meanwhile, had loaded up their illegal gear, unlicensed boat and contraband catch and lit out for John's 1947 Zimmer out in the woods, plotting revenge all the way home.

In the end though, not much ever happened. "The Crawfish Incident," as it came to be known in local legend, just faded away like last week's hangover.

Buck and John sold their half-catch to Jerry Smith, who'd laid preparations for an even bigger Fry 'n Boil on the second week. They successfully retrieved the rest of the traps after dark, making a huge haul of three hundred pounds of crawfish. Trouble was, not many people showed up at the Town Line Tavern, as the high school football season started that night, and Jerry had two hundred fifty pounds of crawfish that slowly died and started rotting on him. He wound up burying them in the field out back of the tavern. He never paid for the second delivery of crawfish, which was lucky for him, but not so good for Buck and John.

Buck and John had another drunk-a-thon with half of their catch money and barely sobered up enough for John to make it to court on the 27th. He went in front of Hudson Varley, Jr., justice of the peace for Neversink. He pled guilty and the fines totaled up to $475.00, of which $450.00 was suspended. Huddy and John went to school together and were teammates on the varsity wrestling squad. John paid the fine and had enough left over for cigarettes and a couple of cases of Old Bohemian.

Officer Tad W. Smoot was transferred down to the South Bronx where he walked a beat, checking for leaks in the water mains. He was disarmed, as the only tools needed on his new job were a flashlight and an iron crowbar to remove the manhole covers in order to shine his light inside, checking for leaks. He was beaten with aluminum baseball bats one afternoon by two prospects for Los Gatos Rojo after he tried to ticket the gang's warlord for some minor infraction.

Buck and John are the same good ole boys, stump-jumpers and woodchucks they've always been. They're still up there, someplace in Neversink, living close to the land and water, waiting for John's next big "bidness" idea.

Fictition

In the Near Future . . .

Fictition

On Tuesday, a clear, bright fall morning when the air was clean and crisp, with a snap to it that was as sharp as a broken heart, John Tweety felt a trembling in his feet as he walked down the driveway to get the newspaper.

It was only a tickle at first, so slight he almost didn't notice. Then it came again. This time it was stronger, and lasted a couple of seconds longer.

Almost like putting one of those electric back massager things on my feet, he thought. *Weird. Just one more weird-assed thing in a whole damn barrelful of 'em.* Like the lawn, always soggy. It was so wet that the kids couldn't play out there without coming in all wet and muddy. And there was the permanent mud puddle, a big one, behind the house where he parked his pickup. Betsy had sunk to her knees in it when it appeared like magic one afternoon. *Can't remember when it last dried up,* he thought. *And I don't think it's rained much lately. I'll check with Betsy when I get back to the house.*

At the end of the driveway, he hopped across a rivulet of water where the culvert was backed up because the drainage ditch that paralleled the main road was full.

He retrieved the *Times Herald-Record* from its delivery box underneath the mailbox and stuck it under his left arm. He glanced at the pair of three-inch hoses that ran down the other side of the lawn from the sump pumps in his basement, and saw they were running at full capacity. John walked back to the house with his newspaper, being careful not to splash mud on his shoes or uniform.

He went around Betsy's car and his pickup, and entered his three-bedroom Cape Cod through the backdoor where the mudroom was ... saw his wife Betsy moving gracefully around the kitchen. Betsy was what Mr. A.M.C. Smith referred to as "a traditionally built woman," and a blue-ribbon cook. John never ceased to be amazed by her talent in the kitchen. *Plenty of woman to hold on to in the bed,* he thought to himself. He got a mug from the cupboard and poured some coffee, took it to his place at the table.

Jeez, I should of put boots on. It's really wet out there. John frowned as he inspected the cuff of his light gray CO, corrections officer, uniform pants, found a few drops of mud and wiped them with a paper napkin.

"Have you checked the well-house in the last week?" Betsy said without turning from the stove where she was making pancakes. "Call the boys, this is ready."

John walked three steps to the stairway and called up: "Robert, Roger, get a move on. Your mother has breakfast ready. NOW."

He sat back down and helped himself to a cranberry muffin. He said, "Betsy, these are great," as he chewed and dabbed at a crumb in the corner of his mouth with his right thumb.

"Have you checked the well-house?"

"Yeah, honey. A few days ago."

"This week?"

"No."

"I think you'd better. It's really wet out there. I think it's overflowing again."

"Okay. I'll do it when I get off work tonight."

"Don't forget, okay?"

"'Kay. I won't."

Roger, Robert and Fearless, the boys' blond cocker spaniel, all came tumbling down the stairs, laughing, racing and barking, all determined to be the first.

John had a mouthful of muffin but swallowed the whole lump and said, "Take it easy, you two. Don't get the dog all riled up."

"He has to go to the groomer's," Betsy said. "I'm dropping him on the way to school."

"He does stink," John said.

"It's because he gets all wet whenever he goes outside."

"Roger, put Fearless in his run and make sure you latch the gate. Robert, help your mother set the table. Chop-chop boys, get a move on, I gotta go to work."

"And we gotta go to school," the twins said in unison as they went about their assigned tasks. Fearless Fosdick was at the door, wagging his stub tail so hard his whole body was quivering. He yipped twice while Roger got his yellow rubber boots on.

The Tweetys finished a breakfast of pancakes and bacon by 6:20 a.m., the same as any other weekday. The boys were out by the mailbox waiting for the school bus a few minutes later. John gathered his Department of Corrections utility belt and buckled it on. He was going on tower duty today, something he looked forward to as it got him away from the general population, or "genpop," in the argot of the Eastern Correctional Facility where he worked. It was a maximum-security penitentiary at Napanoch, New York, a short ten-minute commute from his house in Wawarsing, but he wanted to be there early today, so he could draw a rifle and relieve the other two COs in whichever tower he was assigned. He was hoping for the northwestern one because he could just make out the roof of his house with the binoculars.

Wish my feet would quit trembling and twitching. Maybe I'm going on a journey, he thought. *Yeah, that's it. I bet I'm going on a trip.*

Betsy was putting the last touches on her hair and makeup when John leaned in the bathroom door.

"I'm out of here, sweetheart."

"Bye, honey. Would you put Fearless in the car on your way out? I'll drop him off on my way to school."

"As you wish, my foxy beauty," John said as he nuzzled her neck, with his hands feeling her breasts.

"You fresh boy."

"Ever and always. Ever and always, m'dear," he said as he went out the door to retrieve Fearless and put him in the car. Neither one of them guessing that by six o'clock in the evening, they'd be separated and on the national news, or that they would be at the epicenter of the greatest man-made hydraulic disaster since the Johnstown flood killed 2,209 people in southwest Pennsylvania on May 31, 1889.

The flood occurred when heavy rains, poor engineering and lack of proper maintenance caused the failure of the South Fork Dam, fourteen miles upstream from Johnstown. The dam impounded the waters of the Conemaugh River, forming Lake Conemaugh, for the exclusive South Fork Fishing and Hunting Club, whose membership included Andrew Carnegie and Henry Clay Frick as well as other luminaries and local dignitaries. The lake was stocked with fish and was two miles long, more than a mile wide and sixty feet deep at the dam. When it failed, a "moving wall of water and debris forty feet high and half-a-mile wide swept downstream with an estimated force of Niagara Falls." The villages of South Fork, Mineral Point, Woodvale and East Conemaugh were totally destroyed, and Johnstown so heavily damaged, it took five years of concentrated effort to rebuild. The lawsuits, brought by the flood survivors against the South Fork Fishing and Hunting Club and its individual members, seeking damages and redress for death and suffering, was denied.

The disaster was deemed . . . "an act of God."

After the trial, Jerry O'Reilly, a bereaved coke shoveler, was heard to say, "act o' God my arse. 'T'wasn't God put that sodding bloody dam up there and 't'waren't God doin' the fishin' up there neither."

At 6:40 a.m. John Tweety turned south on Route 209 to make the three-mile commute to Eastern Correctional. By eight a.m. he was in the northwest tower, armed with a .270 caliber Winchester bolt action, model 70 rifle with a 12 x 20 Leupold scope, surveying his field of fire from behind dark aviator sunglasses, fully prepared to kill any rioters or escapees without hesitation.

At 8 a.m., Betsy Tweety had just dropped Fearless at Wendy's Grooming Service in Kerhonkson and was on her way to New Paltz, where she taught modern American literature. She was hurrying because her first class was at nine, and it was forty miles away. The twins were doing the pledge of allegiance in their second grade classroom at Ellenville Elementary with Mrs. Henderson and twenty-two other kids.

Other than the trembling in John's feet, it was an ordinary day in every respect so far . . . but it was about to change. Big time.

Six miles as the crow flies, to the northwest of Wawarsing is the dam and gatehouse of the Rondout Reservoir, one of the last links in a chain of reservoirs built by the city of New York in the 30s, 40s and 50s to supply fresh drinking water. The Rondout, which is seven and a half miles long and contains about fifty billion gallons, collects water from three streams and three other reservoirs, the Pepacton, Cannonsville and Neversink, then sends it ninety miles south to the city via the Rondout West Branch Tunnel. Sitting at the dam is the gatehouse. It controls and regulates the flow of water down the twelve-foot tunnel, which passes straight through Wawarsing, 650 feet below John and Betsy Tweety's house. It carries up to nine hundred million gallons of water per day; thirty-seven million per hour, and all of it under high pressure.

The tunnel, built from 1939 through '42, was last shut down completely in 1958. For the last fifty-some years it's been running near capacity, twenty-four hours a day, every day of the week, month and year, and with all the budgetary constraints and cutbacks, maintenance was first "deferred," then ignored. Consequently, the engineers couldn't guarantee the tunnel wouldn't collapse if the water was shut off.

The Department of Environmental Protection management was terrified. They knew the Wawarsing section of the tunnel was plagued with problems . . . problems lacking solutions. To begin with, this section of tunnel went through an area with excessive groundwater. Then there was all the shale: a type of rock the tunnel drivers and geologists called "rotten" because of its tendency to flake into small pieces at the slightest pressure. Folks living in Wawarsing had been complaining about water leaks to city officials for twenty years. The city had been denying and obfuscating the facts of the issue and ignoring the complaints for an equal amount of time.

Beau Shemwaller came to work that Tuesday morning groggy from lack of sleep, hungover from drinking like an escaped inmate, and pissed off because he'd lost three hundred dollars playing pool and liar's poker the night before.

His agitation increased as he approached the fence enclosing the Rondout gatehouse, it was open, the gate swung wide, which could only mean Glen Dillard, his co-worker had beat him to work, again. Beau knew he'd hear about it all morning. He gritted his teeth as he closed the ten-foot chain-link fence and locked it, his head thumping like a bass drum in a marching band. *I hope I don't ralph all over the place*, he thought to himself as he parked his Monte Carlo Super Sport alongside Glen's old green Land Cruiser with the monster tires. It was four thirty a.m., Tuesday morning. He popped three Tylenol and dry-swallowed them.

The gatehouse is square, about one hundred feet to a side, built of native New York State cut-granite blocks and finished in a 1930s no-nonsense government style. It has two huge banks of windows in front with a massive overhead door in the center and a four-sided beveled roof, and another bank of Palladian windows overlooking the ever-changing, blue-green and black waters. Inside, the building is mostly open space, dominated by a raised fourteen-foot diameter octagonal platform in the exact center, which is the tunnel access. It's covered by a thirteen-inch thick steel-reinforced concrete cover.

Beau fished out his keys, unlocked the small entry door and stepped inside just in time to see Glen moving the electric overhead crane into position over the hatch cover.

"Morning, Glen."

"Hey, Beau. Glad you could make it."

"Aw, bite me, Butt-head."

"Bring it over here Beavis, and I will."

Beau flipped him the bird and punched in at 4:33 a.m. *Close enough*, he thought. *Close enough.*

Beau saw the coffee was brewed, and poured two cups, took both of them out on the floor and handed one to Glen.

"Thanks for making coffee."

"No problem. You look like something the cat dragged in."

"Gee, thanks for caring, Glen."

Glen blew on his coffee, took a sip and said nothing for a change.

"You got any idea what time the divers are getting here?" Beau said.

"Probably around seven, depending on traffic. They're coming up from the city. They were supposed to leave at five, according to the powers that be."

"As of yesterday?"

"Yeah."

"Well, we ain't gotta bust our asses then," Beau said.

"Fine by me," Glen said. "I ain't eager to haul the crap that's stuck down there. Last time there was a dead deer full a maggots. You got your rubber gloves?"

"Yeah."

Although most periodic maintenance was deferred or ignored by the city, a semiannual clean-out of the trash rack was an absolute necessity. The trash rack was the filter that caught the debris: sticks, garbage, leaves and dead critters of all shapes and sizes which found their way into the reservoir. During the spring and summer, Glen, Beau and others used garden rakes and boat hooks to fish out what stuff they could, but each fall two scuba divers and a divemaster would come around to clean and inspect the giant one hundred foot inlet valves and the stop shutters that controlled the inlet of the Rondout West Branch Tunnel.

Glen moved the crane into position and lowered the pintle hook so Beau could insert it in the steel loop on the hatch cover. Moments later they had the cover slid over to the side, resting half on the hatch and half on four large jack stands. The tunnel access and inlet gaped open, they could see the water fifty feet below, and the access ladder and work platform too. Glen moved the crane back to the side and peered in the hatch.

"Damn. I'm glad I'm not going down there."

"You and me both," Beau said. "It's like crawling in a giant butthole."

"Jeez, Beau."

Beau sniggered and opened the overhead door so he could move the John Deere tractor they used for snowplowing in winter and grass cutting in summer. After it was outside, out of the way, Glen closed the overhead door.

"Nippy out there," Beau said as he came back in.

"There'll be frost on the pumpkins 'fore you know it," Glen said.

"Let's have coffee," Beau said. His stomach was doing the flip, flop and fly, he felt like he might puke any minute and his head was pounding like a five-ton trip hammer. He popped two more Tylenol. *Hope I make it through the day,* he thought. *I feel like I'd have to get better to die.* He sat in the gray metal side chair with the stuffing falling out of the holes in the arms, sipping his coffee. Glen sat at the desk, slowly going through the *TH-Record,* reading the comics.

They waited for the dive team to arrive so the clean-out could begin.

The divers showed up at quarter to eight, forty-five minutes late, bitching about morning traffic on the thruway and an excess of state troopers on Routes 17 and 209 slowing them down. The griping and whining began as soon as Glen unlocked the gate and let them on the property. They were in a dark blue one-ton Metro van, just like the ones used by the police SWAT units, except for the round decal with the "NY City" seal and "BWS Dept. of Environmental Protection" on the front doors.

The divemaster was a guy named Coleman Jenkins. The divers were Dimitry, a wiry little man who bounced on the balls of his feet when he walked, looking like he'd been around the Horn a couple of times, and a tall woman, a Latina named Feliciana, a woman who looked as hard as she was tall. She was lithe and moved with the grace and confidence of a world-class athlete, her eyes constantly in motion, ever alert for threats.

Beau opened the overhead door and they backed the van in, stopping twelve feet from the open access shaft. As soon as it stopped rolling, the woman was out of the truck.

"Where's the ladies room?" she said.

"Back there," Beau said, pointing. "One size fits all, everyone welcome."

She hustled in that direction with Beau admiring her backside through bloodshot eyes.

"Forget it, pal. There ain't no way. She'll cut your balls off."

Beau looked away, and his eyes met the divemaster's.

"Just wanna save you some pain, buddy. She's a known man-hater. She's busted balls all over the city. My name's Coleman. Coleman

Jenkins. "That guy," he pointed with his thumb at the man who'd jumped from the backdoor and was unloading dive equipment, "is Dimitry. The hottie in the crapper is Feliciana, the untouchable."

"I'm Beau Shemwaller. The guy who opened the gate is Glen Dillard."

"Rough night?" Coleman said.

"Kinda, sorta," Beau said.

"Kinda sorta looks that way. Youse got any coffee?"

"Yeah."

Glen came in the side door, rubbing and blowing on his hands to warm them.

Coleman said, "Hey, where youse got the coffee?"

"Oh sure," Glen said. "It's over here, in the office. Want some?"

"Naw. I just wand'a'know if youse had any," Coleman said as he strode over and helped himself, taking the big mug, the one with the "NYC-DEP" seal on it, usually reserved for the supervisors on periodic inspection tours. Coleman drained the pot, set it back on the hot plate, then helped himself to a generous amount of creamer and sugar.

"Make som'more," he said to Beau, then slapped the restroom door with the flat of his hand. "Lets go darlin', don't go camping in there."

Her reply was immediate, and muffled by the closed door but it didn't sound like "happy birthday" to Beau, and suggested a physically impossible act. He smiled and made a fresh pot of coffee. *This is gonna be one helluva day*, he thought, but had no idea how prophetic he was.

Dimitry and Feliciana, in wet suits and masks, with scuba tanks and communication gear, stepped into the wire basket Glen brought on the overhead crane. They did a commo check with Coleman, who would relay commands to Glen operating the crane. Beau's job was to operate the shutter valve, which closed the tunnel and shut off the water. It wasn't supposed to be totally shut; in fact, all the BWS employees had been warned: *Do not shut the valve 100 percent.* The water had to keep flowing so the deteriorating tunnel wouldn't collapse. The first fifteen miles of the Rondout West Branch Tunnel had been steel reinforced because it was driven through shale, a flaky, soft rock referred to as "rotten" by the tunnelers, who also had to deal with high concentrations of groundwater. Rotten shale, groundwater and lack of maintenance all add up to problems, but . . . when the concrete factor is added in . . . the tipping point for disaster is exceeded.

The concrete factor is simple, and sorry. The contractor building that section of the tunnel in 1939, '40 and '41 said he was having problems getting concrete, so he convinced the city engineers to let him manufacture his own concrete on-site. With costs rising due to shortages of men and material because of the impending world war, the temptation to cut corners must have crossed his mind . . .

In the seventy years since the tunnel was built, it was completely shut down only once, in 1958. During that time the concrete was developing trillions of microscopic cracks, which were undetected by the torpedo cameras sent down the tunnel by the city. The cracks allowed water molecules to migrate throughout the concrete, making it porous, which rusted and then rotted the reinforcing steel. So when Beau Shemwaller, through inattention, ignorance and ineptitude closed the shutter valve to the full OFF position at 9:18 a.m., he started in motion the chain of events, which later became known as the Rondout Blowout.

Around nine o'clock, John Tweety's feet trembled with such violence, he had to sit on the desk in the guard tower. They twitched and shuddered so much that Bob, the other guard noticed. He said,

"What's with your feet, John? Looks like you got the jake leg, the DTs or something."

"Dunno," John said, "they've been trembling since I got up."

"This bad?"

"No. More of a tickle at first. This is the worst it's been though."

"Maybe you oughta go to the infirmary, get checked."

"You mean what? Checked what?"

"I dunno. Maybe you're having a stroke or something."

"Nah. I ain't having a stroke. I'm not fat, don't smoke and my blood pressure's one twenty over eighty, same as it's been since tenth grade."

"Well, I'm just saying . . ."

"I'm fine. It'll pass. Probably slept the wrong way. Betsy thinks it's a premonition of some kind, like I'm going on a tr . . . what the hell . . ."

The desk, floor and walls, as well as the tower itself, shook slightly, the aftereffect of a small earthquake caused by 1,500 linear feet of the Rondout West Branch Tunnel collapsing after the water was shut off. The cave-in started at John's house and went toward the Shawangunk Mountains . . . the deepest part of the tunnel system. John Tweety looked at the clock on the tower's back wall, it was 9:48 a.m.

Back at Rondout, the water rippled for fifteen or twenty seconds, but no one even noticed. The divers were in the water, clearing the racks and inspecting each one of the stop shutters that controlled the inflow to the tunnel. Everything had to be in proper working order, maintenance or not, because the Rondout West Branch Tunnel supplies one-half of New York City's daily water. It was indispensable.

Coleman was on the radio to the divers, just before lunchtime. "Dimitry, how much longer? Over."

"Couple hours. Twenty minutes. Who knows. We'll finish when we finish. Over."

"I wanta get outta here ASAP. Over."

"Right."

"You've both been down about ninety minutes total dive time. We're pressing the safety envelope, over."

"We ain't that deep. Only just started on'r third tank. We dove this before y'know."

"Say "over" when you're done talking."

"Like you just did? Out."

Coleman was irritated and in a hurry to leave, so he could beat rush-hour traffic back to the city. He glared at Glen Dillard, who kept staring up at the crane, and didn't talk. Beau, the designated trash hauler, was semiconscious on the tractor seat, waiting for the next load from the shaft, doing his best to stay awake.

The next basketful of trash was the last one. Dimitry pronounced the divers were finished at 1:40 p.m. He and Feliciana opened their bouyancy valves and bobbed to the surface, moving their legs in a slow scissors motion in order to maintain their positions, waiting for the pickup basket to come down.

"Any problems?" Coleman said.

"The gearing for the stop shutters is worn out," Dimitry said. "It should be replaced."

"Copy that," Coleman said. "I'll note it in my after-action report. Anything else?"

"Yeah. But, wait until we're out of the water. We're tired and cold. There's more maintenance issues."

Beau emptied the basket. He drove the farm tractor and dump trailer outside and parked, went back inside and closed the big twenty-foot overhead door. His head was still concussing and he thought he was getting diarrhea, felt his stomach gurgle.

God, he thought. *I will never drink again. Oh, shit. I can't wait for today to be over, I gotta get some sleep.* He finished with the door, just as the divers were stepping on dry land. *They look done-in,* Beau thought. *Same as me.*

Feliciana headed for the restroom to dry off and change clothes. Dimitry sat on the lip of the access hatch peeling off his gear, shoulders slumped in exhaustion. He munched on an energy bar, drank water from a plastic bottle, debriefing with Coleman Jenkins.

"We need to step on it, if we're going to get back to the city at a decent time" Coleman said, as he started hauling diving gear back to the truck. "And we still have to get the water back on."

"One of the maintenance items is the stop shutters," Dimitry said, "there's something wrong with the seals. I think the gaskets around the edges are worn out. We kept getting chunks of rubber in the filters. It's one of the reasons we were down so long, we kept having those pieces to contend with."

"I'll note it in the after-action report. Anything else?"

"Everything is worn out, for starters."

"We all know that. You know as well as I do, the City won't fix a damn thing."

"They will sometime. They'll have to."

"Yeah, sure."

Beau called out from the control panel, "We ready to open up?"

Coleman looked at Dimitry, who shrugged, giving his assent of a sort as he jumped in the truck to change out of his wet suit.

"Open up," Coleman said. He had his right arm raised and twirled his finger in the air.

Beau pushed the button, activating the giant inlet valves, opening the stop shutters. His attention was diverted by the sight of Feliciana coming out of the bathroom, buttoning her blouse. He caught a glimpse of lacy white bra, taking his attention from the control panel, causing him to fully open the stop shutters, then pass full open, where they jammed and broke. To make matters worse, down below, the rubber and brass gaskets that lined the shutter frames had peeled off and wound through the shutter mechanisms, fouling them. The inlet was stuck wide open. Millions and millions of gallons of water poured into the Rondout West Branch Tunnel, pounding like hell's own hammers toward Wawarsing where its irresistible force was about to meet the immovable cave-in.

The RWB Tunnel drops approximately 950 feet in elevation during its six-mile journey from the dam site to Wawarsing. The weight of six miles of water, twelve feet in diameter, dropped from a height of almost a thousand feet is calculated in tens of trillions of foot-pounds of energy . . . the equivalent of several atomic bombs.

The water hit with stunning force, its impact felt and noted in science labs all over the world. It took the path of least resistance, up through the rotten shale and supersaturated ground and found an escape route, a pressure-releasing path that went directly through John and Betsy Tweety's house.

The ground shook for ten or twenty seconds, then came a hiss, a giant moan and a roar, as if a train were coming out of a tunnel at high speed, and the Tweety's two-story house exploded into fragments as a giant geyser of mud, rocks and water shot a hundred feet in the air.

At the Rondout gatehouse a water hammer, backpressure from air and water trapped in the tunnel by the sudden, violent surge from the wide-open inlet and shutter valve, blew back with such force that the three-ton hatch cover was blown partly through the roof of the building, thirty feet in the air, followed by a jet of water. The hatch cover came down on the roof of the dive van, flattening and destroying it, crushing Dimitry's right foot, then flipping it to the floor like a giant Frisbee, killing Glen Dillard. He was the first death from the disaster.

The gatehouse was filling with water. Dimitry was screaming in pain as his partially amputated, crushed foot spouted a fountain of blood. Feliciana and Beau both struggled through the rising water to help him.

"There's a medical kit in the office," Beau said.

"One in the van," Feliciana gasped, taking a mouthful of water as she half-walked, half-swam toward the van, Beau following behind.

The water was over waist-high, with no end in sight. Coleman made it to a window. He was screaming and beating on the wire-reinforced glass with a crescent wrench he'd snatched from somewhere, trying to break out. The glass broke after repeated blows by the frenzied divemaster. Terrified, he smashed at wire and glass, enlarging the hole to man-sized, screaming and shouting incomprehensible words, as he worked his way into the window frame, unaware of the many cuts on his arms, face and hands.

Beau saw what he was trying to do, yelled across, "No! Don't!"

Too late. Coleman was through the window. They could hear his scream as he fell forty feet into the water, cut short as he was sucked into the wide-open stop shutters and disappeared down the Rondout West Branch Tunnel.

Feliciana moaned.

"Don't," Beau said shoving her back, pushing her to the van. "We can't help him."

They got to the van and climbed in the passenger door to help the semiconscious man inside who was in danger of bleeding to death and who was slipping into shock.

Beau wormed his way into the crushed interior while Feliciana grabbed the medical kit from its place on the wall.

"Put a tourniquet on his leg," she said. "Use your belt. Hurry up, damnit." Seeing the sick look on Beau's face as he crawled through the gore, she said, "It's only blood, *pendejo*. It won't hurt you."

Beau, moving in a daze, managed to get past Dimitry's head and shoulders, inching himself along until his face was in line with the wounded man's knees. He pulled his belt off and wrapped it around Dimitry's leg, in the middle of his calf. Beau pulled it as tight as he could and held on, having no way to secure the end.

"Here. Use my shoelace," Feliciana said, passing it over and handing it to the blood-covered Beau.

"Got it," Beau said.

"Good. Now get out of the way, *cabron*."

Feliciana changed places, pulling the medical kit behind her. Dimitry was shivering, his teeth chattering, and he was turning gray with shock.

"Stay with us, Dimitry," she said. "I'm gonna take care of you. You're going to be fine, *hombre*. Relax."

Feliciana, now completely in charge, and applying first aid, said, "You, call for help."

Still covered in blood, Beau looked at the flooded gatehouse. The water was still waist-high and seemed stable; it wasn't rising or falling. It lapped at the walls like an indoor lagoon. He started toward the office, to see if the phone worked. It was a couple of minutes after two.

Six miles south, Wawarsing was being flooded as fifty billion gallons of water were pouring from the Rondout Reservoir out through the hole where John Tweety used to live.

The gusher came down in height as the size of the hole increased. The blowout, as the hole was named, started at about fifteen feet in diameter, with rocks, mud and water shooting up a hundred feet in the air, like the Bellagio Fountains in Las Vegas. It grew in size fast, and within minutes it was a half-mile across with water burbling up in the center. The hole now crossed Route 209 and was flooding Kerhonkson to the north and Napanoch to the south. The Walkill River was fifteen feet past flood stage and threatening every home and village all the way to Kingston, where it met the Hudson River. Alarms and civil defense alerts were going out all up and down the Hudson Valley as the disaster spread.

At ten minutes before two, John Tweety's feet stopped twitching. The tingling was gone too. He said, "Hey Bob, look there my feet have quit twitching."

The words were barely out of his mouth when they felt the ground rumble and shake. Bob Orr said, "Hey, look!" and pointed at the eruption of water, mud and debris.

John Tweety looked with the binoculars. Then said, "Noooo." It came out like a howl, a long drawn-out, lip-stretching howl and low moan that came from the lowest bottom of his heart.

"Ohhh-noooo. That's my house. Jesus H. Christ. That's my house."

Bob looked through the scope on his rifle, neither one of them watching the prison yard.

John's horror grew as they watched the disaster unfolding, watching the hole grow to immense size, cutting off the highway. John snapped back to reality when he saw a minivan plow into the spreading pool and disappear. He hit the button that set off every alarm in the prison compound and picked up the phone to the warden's office.

"We've got a situation," he said. "A bad situation."

His words were the most mild and understated of all the words spoken, printed, reported and analyzed over the next hours, days, weeks, months and years about the Rondout Blowout.

The water ran unabated for twenty-five days and nights while different temporary fixes were tried and which soon failed. The current was so strong that divers were unable to go in the water and fix the stop shutters. Electric power to the gatehouse was shut off for fear of electrocution. Temporary diesel construction generators were moved on-site but everything the engineers came up with was impeded by water. Water was flowing out of the reservoir at a rate of a billion gallons per day. The logistics of moving the kinds of huge construction equipment needed on such short notice was a nightmare. The water kept flowing day after day.

The village of Wawarsing was destroyed beyond repair. All the homes and businesses were lost. One hundred and seventy-two lives were lost in Warwarsing alone, close to four hundred deaths were attributed to the Rondout Blowout and property loss was 4.75 billion dollars.

New York City of course, denied all liability, calling it an "act of God" and fighting each and every claim, managing to drag the litigation on for decades. Plaintiffs in some cases died of old age without settlement, while law firms went broke trying, and failing, to sue the city of New York for Rondout Blowout claims.

The villages of Kerhonkson and Napanoch, and Ellenville to a lesser extent, all suffered damage and were forever changed by the Blowout. The prison at Napanoch, having been built in 1905, was abandoned. After much debate, argumentation and infighting the new higher security prison was built in neighboring Orange County. The rumors, unfounded of course, of bribery and political backstabbing went on for years.

In the aftermath of the Rondout Blowout, when Glen Dillard was buried at the Neversink Cemetery, most of the town was there. Coleman Jenkins's body was never recovered. Dimitry Androvich was given a seventy-percent pension, a prosthetic foot and retired in the Brighton Beach section of Brooklyn. Feliciana Morales is now a divemaster and an instructor at the New York City Police and Fire Academies. She is still available for dive teams in emergency situations, and is a highly regarded disaster lecturer.

Beau Shemwaller, for reasons known only to higher authorities somewhere in the city's vast and murky bureaucracy, was made a foreman at the DEP-NYC Department of Water Supply and appears to be on a fast track for higher management.

John and Betsy Tweety are living in a rented two-bedroom house in Ellenville. Their insurance company refuses to pay their claim for the total loss of their house and their personal property pending resolution of the city of New York's "act of God" claims. Their mortgage payment is still due on the fifth of every month and John is managing to keep it up-to-date by taking a part-time security guard job at the new Walmart superstore that was built in Monticello. His job at the NYS Department of Corrections continues, but he has to commute to Orange County, an eighty-five-mile daily round trip. Betsy continues teaching and working on her master's degree in New Paltz. They're hanging on as the litigation drags on, but just barely . . . and getting tired. Robert Tweety said at one of their now-rare family meals together, "Gee Dad, this is like a fiction of the 'magination. Like at the movies."

All John Tweety could do was smile and ruffle his son's hair.

The Destiny of Skyriders

Somewhere in Time . . .

The Destiny of Sky Riders

I was broke down on the shoulder of a two-lane state highway, somewhere close to the high desert out by the Colorado-Utah state line, near a place called Montela. It was "luck of the Irish" that things came apart two miles from town instead of out on the desert, because you could die in the desert.

"NO GAS - NO PHONE - NO FOOD - NO WATER - NO HOPE - NO FOOLING" was what the highway sign at the edge of town said. I believed it too.

Scouting for the University of Colorado, I was on my way to watch a high school football game and evaluate a potential scholarship candidate named Caleb MacMann. MacMann, on the films his high school coach had sent, appeared to have all the tools to be one of the great college tight ends. He had the hands, the moves and the speed of a wide receiver, in a body with the size and strength of an outside linebacker. Best of all he was "under the radar" of all the other Division 1 recruiters, as he played eight-man football in an obscure league. It helped that his coach was a Colorado alumnus who'd played on the championship teams of the late 80s and early 90s, and was still a Colorado Buffalo, heart and soul.

I had the hood up and was looking at the engine as if, with mental prestidigitation and high-energy brain focus, I could fix it.

The truth is, I know as much about auto mechanics as a Miller moth does about the stock market. I just knew that looking at the motor was what a guy was expected to do.

I had both arms draped over the grille, and my ass in the wind, when two men pulled up in a tan '56 Mercury two door hardtop and stopped on the other side of the road. The driver put the transmission in park and sat there, the engine idling with a menacing V-8 rumble and stinking of gasoline and exhaust fumes, watching me.

Oh, shit, I thought. *These two dudes look like they came straight out of Stephen King's* Hearts in Atlantis *or a crazy time warp of some kind.* The driver climbed out of his car and staggered toward me as I watched with increasing trepidation.

"Broke down?" he asked, pointing with his chin at my pickup.

"Yeah. It just quit, I don't have a clue why."

"Does it turn over?"

"Nope. Doesn't click. Nothing."

"Okay," he said. "My brother and I have a garage about a mile from here. We could tow it over there and fix it for you. Ain't nothing for miles around but us. We fix everybody's cars."

"Sure," I said. Thinking, *I don't have much choice.*

"C'mon, ride with us. We'll go over to the garage and get the tow truck. I'm Joe Cruz, but everybody calls me Loco."

"Mike Burke's my name," I said as we shook hands. His hands were cold, and he ticked when we touched, like the shock from leather shoes on a nylon carpet.

"Let me get my keys and briefcase."

I retrieved them and started across the road, wondering if these two were psychopaths or good Samaritans. I took a deep breath and climbed in the back seat of the Merc with my heart going about 120 beats per minute.

"Mike, this is my brother, Frank. Everybody calls him Lobo.

Loco and Lobo the Cruz brothers are cruising tonight!" he said and touched fists with his brother.

"Hi, Lobo. Nice to meet 'cha" I said.

"Pleased t'meet ya," he mumbled.

I noticed when I got in the car Lobo seemed to be looking elsewhere, somewhere just over the horizon, somewhere no one else could see. He got more animated when Loco dropped the transmission in drive and we started off for their place.

"We'd offer you a beer, but we drank 'em all," said Lobo.

"That's okay," I said. "I'm not much of a drinker anyway. You okay driving, Loco?"

"Hell yeah," he said. "I'm too drunk to walk."

He and Lobo had a laugh while I sat in the backseat, nervous as a blindfolded pledge on the first night of Hell Week.

"Is it very far to your place?"

"Naw, as a matter of fact, we're there."

He turned off the highway, onto a dirt road that wound through the sagebrush and cholla and cactus. A gray clapboard house stood a few hundred yards off the highway and a metal Quonset building stood next to it. The outside pole light was on and I could see a faded white sign with black letters outlined in red on the front of the Quonset that read "L and L Garage." Underneath, in smaller red script, it said "The Auto Wrecksperts." Cars and trucks were sitting everywhere, out back and on both sides of the building, making a huge and ever-expanding auto graveyard. Six or seven dogs of all colors, shapes and sizes, barking and running around like hell's own hounds on methamphetamines, finished the scene. My nerves cranked up another few notches as I wondered, *What, oh what, have*

I got myself into? I asked if they had a phone I could use.

"Them things don't work out here," Loco said just before he got out of the car and was surrounded by dogs. He was yelling and slapping at them as they all took turns jumping on their hind legs and putting their front paws on him, all the while barking, baying and howling.

"Don't worry," Lobo said to me. "They'll quiet down in a minute or two. They always act like this when we first get here. Gimme your keys and I'll go get your pickup."

I gave him the keys and we both got out of the car. Lobo disappeared, and in a few moments I saw an old white tow truck with the garage logo on its doors heading out toward the highway.

The dogs shut up then, and found other entertainment . . . giving me the sniff test. Loco called and herded them into a yellow school bus that was on blocks next to the house. He went up the steps and disappeared in the front door, reappearing a minute later with half a case of Old Milwaukee's finest that he left on the porch rail, then went back inside. He came out again with two five-gallon buckets, one filled with water and the other with dry dog food.

"Haveta feed the puppies."

The dogs set off another chorus of "BAAROOS" and yelps as he went in the yellow bus . . . Loco yelling to shut them up. When he came out he was engulfed in a hurricane of dog hairs and serenaded by a chorus of growling, gulping and slobbering.

"Jesus Christ-a-mighty," Loco said, brushing at dog hairs on his shirt and pants. "Them hounds will be the death a me."

"Good thing they weren't hungry."

"Sure enough," replied Loco, as he opened a beer can with an old-fashioned metal opener on his key ring. He sat on the porch steps and took a big swig, burped, then said, "Ahh. Like mother's milk. Want one?"

"No thanks," I said. "I appreciate it but I still have to work tonight."

"Whad'a you do?" Loco asked between slurps.

"I'm a football coach, for the University of Colorado. I'm headed for a game, to evaluate a young player."

"On a Thursday?"

"Yes. It's a small school, they play eight-man football. I'll go see the game, then head back up to Boulder. It's our bye week so we don't have a game this Saturday."

"I seen you on TV?"

"No. I'm an assistant coach. I'm usually up in the booth, watching and calling plays down to the guys on the field."

I saw the tow truck coming back up the highway, watched it make its way up the drive with my pickup truck hooked on behind. It made a 180-degree turn in front of the quonset while Loco opened the two big doors, and Lobo backed straight in the garage.

He got out, dropped my pickup off the boom and parked the tow truck outside in the driveway. While Lobo got a beer, his brother had the hood up and was doing something under there. I found a place to sit on one of the bench seats from the school bus that were stacked to one side and watched.

From what I could see, both of the Cruz brothers were competent mechanics but they were also drinking a lot. While I watched, they had two beers apiece, and I had no way of knowing how many they'd had before they picked me up on the road. I had plenty of experience with drunk young men. Even football players, the big men on campus, weren't immune to the party atmosphere on university campuses in today's permissive age. The coaches are always the "number to call in case of emergency" at the Boulder Police Department, as well as in each player's wallet. I had, in fact, more knowledge of the subject than I wanted to.

I noticed that Loco, the shorter one, seemed to be needling Lobo about something, and Lobo, more sober, was doing all the work. They were arguing and it was getting louder. Lobo was working under my pickup, lying on a cart with wheels called a creeper. Loco, now pulling on another fresh Old Milwaukee, was leaned over the fender watching. Loco said something I couldn't hear, and the fight started.

Lobo came out from under the pickup, and in one motion, stood and threw a wrench at his brother, screaming: "DAD SAID I WAS THE BEST MECHANIC!"

"No he didn't," said Loco.

The wrench clanged on the hood of my truck and bounced off the engine to the floor.

Lobo stormed out of the garage. He got in an old Chevy truck, started the engine and floored it, spraying dirt and gravel all over me, my pickup and his brother. I watched his taillights disappear down the state highway and my bad day just got worse. Loco looked at me and said, "Don't worry about him . . . he gets pissed off and lights out, but he'll be back later on if he's not too drunk."

"How do you know if he's not too drunk?"

"He won't come back," replied Loco with perfect drunk logic.

"Look," I said, "I've gotta get out of here. I've got a job to do and responsibilities. Could you loan or rent me a car?"

"Can't."

"Because..."

"The Merc won't make it through the desert. It's a hundred and sixty-five miles of bad roads and one hundred ten-degree heat. Ain't nothing else that runs, or has plates."

"The tow truck?" I asked, already knowing the answer.

"No way," Loco answered.

"Would you take me back to Montela? Maybe I can get a ride from there..."

Loco thought for a minute, reinforcing his thinking with the last of his beer. He threw the can back in a corner of the garage before he answered. "I better not. See, I'm supposed to go to prison tomorrow. Sheriff Curley said he'd come check on me tonight, make sure I was here. Told him I would be. Always keep my word. How my daddy raised us."

"Why?"

"Vehicular homicide," he answered. "I was drunk. Rolled the car I was driving right there at the driveway. Killed my wife."

I was dumbstruck. What could I say? I thought for a moment then said, "How long did you get, if you don't mind my asking."

"Naw, I don't mind. Kinda helps to talk about it . . . I got nine years . . . three on the DUI and six on the vehicular. The lawyer pled it out with the judge. He figures I'll get out in five years or so with good behavior. Won't never have a driver's license though, permanent lifetime suspension . . . make it hard to make a living." His conversation trailed off at that point and he got the same faraway look his brother had had earlier.

"Sorry for your troubles, Loco," I said.

"Brought 'em on myself."

I made my decision. I thanked Loco, told him I'd be back late tonight or tomorrow morning to get the pickup. I got my briefcase and started walking, back toward Montela, hoping to find a working telephone. I owed it to the MacMann kid and the university to watch as much of his game as I could. I set off for town at a fast clip, walking fifty paces then jogging five hundred, walk fifty, jog five hundred, into the growing darkness.

I was making good time, thought I'd covered more than half the distance back to town. It was late September and totally dark by seven thirty pm. I couldn't see my watch, so I guessed it was near eight o'clock and kickoff time, when I heard a car coming. I could see headlights in the distance, headed in my direction, on my side of the road. As it got closer the headlights dimmed from high to low beams, and I heard the pitch of the engine change as the driver slowed, then stopped beside me.

I gawked, not believing my eyes, at the Corvette Sting Ray coupe, because it looked like it had just come from the new car dealership. I could even smell the paint cooking off the engine. Cars like that are legendary, they're pricey and considered works of art. At the classic car auction every January down in Phoenix, Arizona, they sell for high five and six-figure price tags. I'm nuts for vintage cars and to see two in one night, both being driven, was just amazing to me.

There I was, standing on the side of the road at the back of the outback, sweaty and looking as if I'd just fallen out of the stupid tree and hit every limb on the way down, when the driver got out. He stood beside the car with his door open, and I could hear the radio playing "Up on the Roof" by the Drifters. He looked about eighteen years old, was muscular and tall. He had on a blue madras shirt, old-fashioned brown plastic-framed glasses and a crew cut.

"Need a ride?"

"Yeah, I sure do."

"Where're you going?"

"I'm headed for Eureka," I said, "to evaluate a football player named Caleb MacMann."

"Hop in. I'll take you."

"You sure?"

"Yeah, I've been looking for something to do."

"Thanks," I said, as I got in the car. It was silver on the outside and red on the inside and it smelled new. As I got in, I was having trouble with my briefcase, trying to hold it between my legs in the bucket seat.

"Here," my companion said, "you can put it behind the seats."

"That'll work," I said, twisting in the car's narrow confines to lay the briefcase in the space behind us. That's when I saw the rear windows ... there were two of them. On a night of surprises, seeing the back of the Corvette was one of the biggest. Nineteen sixty-three was the first year of the Corvette Sting Ray, the only year for two back windows. Car guys called it the "split window coupe," the most prized of all the Sting Rays, and rarest of the rare. Worth six figures plus, it was a treasure and sort of like finding an original Frederick Remington painting at a garage sale. The radio kicked right into "Walk Like a Man" by the Four Seasons as we started down the two-lane highway into the night. As the young man wound the Corvette up through the gears, I relaxed a bit ... I was still pretty keyed up from my stint with Loco and Lobo Cruz.

"Say," I said, "thanks for picking me up. Can't tell you how appreciative I am. It's pretty desolate out here."

"Yeah, it is."

"My name is Mike Burke, I'm an assistant coach at CU"

"Charlie Grey, Coach."

He seemed shy. I told myself it was his age. Trying to draw him out I said, "I gotta say, dude, this is an awesome ride. Who restored it?"

"Nobody," he said. "It's how I got it."

We rode in silence for a while, my senses distorted by the evening's events and the fact that I was riding in a brand-new classic car. I settled in the seat and watched the desolate landscape roll by, listening to Ray Charles singing "Take These Chains from my Heart," an old Hank Williams song I remembered my grandpa singing. It was then that I realized I was hearing an honest-to-God radio program, not a tape or CD, because I heard occasional bursts of static, as faraway lightning impeded the broadcast signal. Shivers ran down my neck and back when I heard Casey Kasem, the "curly-headed kid in the third row," announcing the songs.

Still trying to start a conversation I said, "You play sports, Charlie?"

"Yeah. Used to anyway."

"Football?"

"Yeah, I was an end. Offense and defense."

"Tight end or wide receiver?"

"What do you mean?"

I explained that a tight end was primarily a blocker who caught a pass once in a while. A wide receiver was a pass-catching specialist.

"When and where'd you play?" I asked, pleased he was opening up at last.

"Nineteen sixty-three. In upstate New York in high school, in a little town called Neversink. We played eight man football, didn't have tight or wide ends. Just ends."

"You're not serious…"

"Serious as can be," he said.

"But that would make you, what, *twice as old as me?* I can't believe … you don't look any older than eighteen or nineteen," I said.

When he turned to me, his eyes were as luminous as a moth's wings in the dashboard lights.

"I was seventeen when I died in September of 1963."

His words, so matter-of-fact, had the hard metal of truth in them and turned my insides to ice. I felt as if I'd been flash-frozen. I was deaf, frozen and speechless. I thought … *Charlie Grey is a ghost. If he's a ghost* … MY GOD, WHAT AM I?

As if he could hear my thoughts, Charlie said in a calm voice,

"Easy Coach, easy. I know how hard it is when you first realize …"

"That I'm dead? Am I dead? You mean I have died?" I said.

"Yes."

"How …"

"Car wreck. Same as me."

My brain flipped over into warp drive, but still wasn't fast enough to process the images and thoughts going through my head faster than light-speed. I felt like a steer in the slaughterhouse chute that's been whacked but hasn't fallen down yet. I don't know if a second, or ten years passed like that before I was able to croak out of a bone-dry throat, "Wh-what about Loco and Lobo, the Cruz brothers?"

Charlie kept his eyes steady on the road for a couple of heartbeats, then said, "The Cruz boys died in 1962. Right at their driveway, along with Loco's wife, Alevaria, who was seven month's pregnant. He hit a bulldozer parked on the side of the road where the road crew was cleaning the ditches . . . Loco was so drunk he was seeing double, and he picked the wrong dozer. Loco and his brother will likely be there at the garage forever, drunk and unhappy, endlessly fighting and feeling the guilt and remorse you saw."

"Oh, God. That's, that's horrible. But Loco said he was waiting for the Sheriff, that he was going to jail in the morning."

"That's his conscience, his guilt speaking. He's trying to make amends for what he did."

I guess everybody makes their own prison, don't they."

"Yeah."

Charlie said nothing more, while I thought for a while.

"What happens now?" I said, my voice just a whisper. "Where are we headed?"

"We're going to a place called Bittersweet, on the other side of the desert. That's where you're going. I've got to go back to Montela."

"Whaddo I do in Bittersweet?" I said.

"Remember in Sunday school, about heaven and hell?"

"Yeah."

"Bittersweet is where the Great Spirit looks at your life, sees whether you had more good deeds or bad acts . . ."

I interrupted him, "I get sent to heaven or hell?"

"No, not exactly. We're all going to be reincarnated . . . as humans. The question is, how long it takes. If you have more good than bad deeds, you get sent back to life sooner. Or vice versa. If you've died doing a good deed or a heroic act, you can choose to have a job like I have, for as long as you want. I take the newest souls across the desert, to their reckoning, explain the procedure."

"Oh yeah," he added, "If you don't have a job and you're not an innocent . . . babies or children for example go back immediately . . . you have to wait in the waiting room."

"What's that?" I asked.

"It's like the biggest, oldest, noisiest, dirtiest bus station in the universe. Too hot in the summer, too cold in the winter. Not enough seating. The lunch counters are always closed. Forget about the bathroom. And there's always an announcement blaring too loud from the PA system that you can never make sense of."

The radio was on "Rhythm of the Rain" by the Cascades. I listened as it played, thinking about everything.

I thought about my life, wondered how many good acts I had next to my name in the big play book, how many bad ones. I thought about my wife, our son and daughter, the CU team. I found myself thinking about my parents . . . they'd both died a few years ago . . . I wondered if I would see them. My mind was out there in the passing lane, going at full speed, when Charlie started to brake and downshift.

"Coach," he said, "we're here."

I looked out; the desert was gone. We were sitting in a big parking lot, at a gateway that said "ENTER." It led to a huge gray building that I couldn't quite make out.

"What do I do?" I asked him.

"Just follow the arrows. You can't go wrong . . . stay on the path. It's all marked," Charlie answered.

"What if I don't go?" I asked. "What if I just stay at the gate?"

"You can," Charlie answered. "Nothing will happen."

"What happens then?" I repeated. "What if I don't move?"

"Nothing."

"Nothing?"

"No. But you can't go backward. You'll just stay there until you decide to go forward."

"So it's like being in limbo?" I asked.

"Yeah. Or purgatory. I stayed at the gate for a while myself."

"How long?"

"I don't know. Time is different here, it doesn't pass by. There's dark and light, but there's no day or night, no yesterday or tomorrow. There's only now."

"Only now?" I said, parrot-like.

"That's right. Time stops when you die. It stopped at 1963 for me. It stopped for you too. Now is all we have."

"Is that why you've got the '63 'Vette and vintage music?"

"Yeah. It's all I knew when my time ran out. When I died."

"Okay, Charlie, I know I have to go," I said. As I opened the door I thanked him, then said, "Is this your job, are you the only driver?"

"Oh, no," he said, "there's other Sky Riders too. But I never stop driving. I have to go now for another passenger in fact. His name is Caleb MacMann."

Shaking from stress and apprehension as I walked toward the gate, I swallowed my fear and stepped into the unknown, wondering if there's football where I'm going.

Acknowledgments

This is the place where writers confess, pay their dues to other writers, and thank all those who helped along the way. So here it is:

The idea for the book began forming like thunderclouds in my head when Carol Smythe, Town of Neversink historian and curator of the Time and the Valleys Museum in Grahamsville, New York, suggested Diane Galusha's seminal work, *Liquid Assets: A History of the NYC Water System*. One thing led to another and I found lots of material at Purple Mountain Press, most notably two of John Conway's books; *Retrospect: an Anecdotal History of Sullivan County, New York*, which inspired the Shanachie's story about the fly swatting contest, and *Dutch Schultz and His Lost Catskills' Treasure*, which gave me the idea for "The Practice of Artful Deception." Speaking of which, as my small homage to the writers, and screenwriters of the black-and-white gangster movies made in the 30s, 40s and 50s, of which I'm a fan, the postmaster's name, Frank Chambers, was John Garfield's character in **The Postman Always Rings Twice**, and "Mad Dog" was Humphrey Bogart's nickname in the movie **High Sierra**, where he drove a 1936 Plymouth coupe. My Mad Dog had a 1936 Chevrolet coupe. Did you catch onto either one? I hope so. And by the way, the next Shanachie story is from the lexicon of American tall tales. The drunken man and snake story has been told and retold, usually involving bees, spiders, snakes or such, who die after biting the drunk. The third tale about the British pound notes is from the family archives of Michael Curley; he swears it's true. The last piece in the collection is a ghost story called "The Destiny of Sky Riders." It's a heartfelt tribute to my high school friend, classmate, fellow football player and distant cousin, Charlie Grey, who was killed in a single car accident in the fall of 1963. He was seventeen years old. Our senior student body, consisting of just thirty-three students, and the entire high school, were devastated. Most of us had grown up together. Charlie is held dear by the surviving members of the Tri-Valley High School class of 1964 to this very day.

Although writing is a solitary pursuit, and a craft best suited to introverts, no book project can come to fruition without the assistance of others. I would like to thank all of the following individuals and proclaim my gratitude for their invaluable help in bringing this book to you. In no particular order, they are:

Mike Curley, Bob Will, Robert and Karen Curry, Susie Miller, Margaret Williams, Dick Ralston, Thomas McKenna, Betsy Cary, Larry Cary, Jeani Redding, Meg Versteeg, Skip and Joanie Mooney, Paul Kelley, Mary Coccetti, Dr. Richard Blade, Kirk Farber, Vickie Leigh Krudwig, Hayden Battle, Susan McKenna, my editor: Alison Auch, whose thorough and meticulous work is displayed on every page, Emeritus Professor of English at the University of Colorado, Colorado Springs, Alex Blackburn, for his erudite guidance, assistance and suggestions, and to Kathy Ralston and Linda Zabukovic for their editorial comments. A special thanks to Donald Kallaus, who shot the photos, designed the cover, and computerized the text. Don's help, assistance, and guidance, as well as his friendship of many years were invaluable. Last on the list, ever and always first in my heart, is my beautiful and supportive wife, June. Lover, friend, helper, confidante, she has been at my side throughout, always ready with a kind, gentle word of encouragement, spelling corrections and typing skills, as well as infinite patience with my endless rewrites. Without her help and hard work, I would not have been able to complete this project. The credit is half hers. Any errors are mine.

— JDM

BONUS PAGES:

Thanks for buying and reading The Neversink Chronicles. It is our hope that you enjoyed the book and will recommend it to others. Now, here's a sneak preview of our next scheduled Rhyolite Press publication. It's called The *Colorado Noir Chronicles*, which we'll be bringing to you in early fall, 2012. It will be more than 300 pages of the most noir stories you've ever read, all set in and around Colorado Springs, Colorado. Have a look . . .

The Aluminum Mistress

--- John Dwaine McKenna

The Aluminum Mistress

After they got to know her better, all the guys at the shop tried, but it was impossible to guess how long the old woman had been living on the streets; because she was stingy with personal information, wary and tough as a feral cat.

The first time she was spotted by Santos and Little Davie, she was rummaging through the trash cans in the alley out back of the Southside Tire Company. Santos, the parts runner, saw her when he turned to flick his cigarette butt away.

"Hey, check it out," he said, nudging Little Davie and pointing at the woman with his chin.

Little Davie, one of the tire busters, opened his eyes and eased his chair back down on all four legs from where he'd been leaning on the wall enjoying the sun, and said,
"What . . ."

"Check it out man. Over there." Santos pointed with his chin a second time.

The old woman had her butt pointed right at them as she leaned over into the trash, fishing something out. She was wearing men's work pants with a big stain on the right buttock that went halfway to her knee.

"Ugh," Little Davie said. "Got an ass on 'er like a pack mule."

"Whaddaya think she's doing in there?"

"Getting breakfast?"

"Naw, she's not," Santos said. "I bet she lost something."

"Looks to me like she lost it in her pants."

The woman straightened up and turned around, putting her left hand on the small of her back, where it ached. She was a medium sized woman, thick in the waist . . . the effect of a poor diet and being of post-menopausal age. She wore an old corduroy coat and her gray hair hung in greasy strings from underneath a navy blue watch cap that, like her, had seen much hard campaigning.

She turned and faced Santos and Little Davie.

"There ain't nothing wrong with my hearing," she said. "I ain't looking for breakfast neither. I'm hunting cans. Aluminum cans. Either one-a you heroes got any? Or are yez too busy running your mouths about old ladies out here in the alley. And why ain't you working?"

Santos was silent, watching the old woman as she pushed her three-wheeled bicycle down the alley toward them. There was a large cardboard box, tied on with rope behind the seat, half full of aluminum cans that rattled as she came up to Little Davie.

"And you . . . you oughta' be 'shamed of yerself, talking like that . . . I ain't got no ass like no friggin' plow mule neither. You eat, and kiss your momma with that mouth, boy? Well, doo-ya?" She said it just like Clint did in the movies.

Little Davie, who went about 340 and stood six foot seven inches tall, was out of his chair and backed against the overhead door as the woman came up to him, pushing her bike. With his head down like a five year old caught stealing cookies, all Little Davie could say was, "No ma'am. Very sorry ma'am."

"You got any cans?"

"Nuh—no."

"You got any?" She said to Santos.

"No, I don't."

"Can you get some?"

"Sure." Little Davie said.

"Save 'em. I'll be back tomorrow and get 'em." She said. "Name's Elaine. I gotta go. I ain't got no silver spoon in my mouth ya know. Gotta go."

She rode off, heading south down the alley with the box of aluminum cans tied on her bike.

Santos was lighting another cigarette when Caleb's voice came over the intercom: "Santos to the front desk. Santos to the front desk. Little Davie your tires are here. Time to go ta' work, Hoss."

Santos trotted off to the front counter to answer the owner's son's call. Caleb was a pretty nice guy, but it was a good idea to be respectful of him. Casting off thoughts of the old woman, *what was her name . . . oh, yeah . . . Elaine, that's it . . . Elaine.* Little Davie lumbered back to his station, not looking forward to changing a set of ten tires on the old Mack dump truck. They were industrial duty ten-hundreds, on twenty-inch wheels, the old fashioned 8-ply kind that have spring steel snap rings, rubber liners and inner tubes; the kind that have to be disassembled with a pair of 24-inch pry bars, a 3-pound hammer and 4-inch chisel, then reassembled outside, in a special cage made from 2-inch steel pipe set in concrete, just in case the thing exploded when a hundred and twenty pounds of air pressure went in. He sighed and looked up at the "halo" forming around the top of Pikes Peak . . . a bad weather sign. The Ides of March could get winter-deep cold, maybe even snow. No, he wasn't looking forward to the rest of the day. It was a nasty job. He sighed and gathered his tools.

In true Colorado Springs fashion, the implied bad weather never materialized. The clouds dissipated around the peak and disappeared. The following day was warm, the sun bright in a cloudless blue sky.

Little Davie stepped outside for his break at 10:15, same as he did every day, to the parking lot behind the garage bays by the alley. Drinking coffee from an insulated stainless steel mug, he nodded to Sonny Edmonds, owner of Southside Tire Company, who was washing his horse trailer.

"Hey Sonny, you're about to wear the paint off that thing."

"Naw. It's the horse piss does that." Sonny threw the sponge in the wash bucket and picked up the hose, started rinsing the sides and top of the trailer.

"You getting ready for the Range Ride?"

"It ain't 'til July, before the rodeo. How you bearing up, after all those truck tires yesterday?"

"Oh, just fine, Sonny, just fine. I got a couple blood blisters from the snap rings is all."

"When didja finish?"

"Little after six-thirty. Caleb and I were out of here before seven."

"I'll tell Caleb to give you a couple-a easy jobs."

"Thanks, you don't have . . ."

Little Davie stopped talking when he saw the old woman on the three-wheeled bicycle pedaling down the alley. She spotted Little Davie and headed straight to him.

"Girlfriend?"

"No. Well, sort of."

"You got cans for me?" she said.

320

"Yeah. Hang on a minute." Davie said and disappeared in the garage.

The old woman got off the bike and stood by it, watching Sonny. Behind the cats-eye tortoise shell glasses, her eyes were as bright and alert as those of a spring robin.

"Whatcha got in the box?"

"Cans. Aluminum cans. You got any cans?"

"No, not right now I don't."

"Well, if you get any, save 'em for me. I'll be back to get 'em."

"Okay," Sonny said. "I'll do that. Say, I'm thirsty. Think I'll go get a sodey-pop. You want one?"

"Sure, if you got orange. I only like orange."

"Okay. You watch my stuff. I'll go get us one."

"Don't take too long. I ain't got no silver spoon in my mouth. I gotta go."

"Okay. I'll be right back."

When Sonny came back with his R-C Cola and an orange drink for the homeless woman, she was teaching Little Davie the fine points of aluminum can crushing.

"See, what I do is twist 'em like this," she said, holding the can top and bottom and twisting them in opposite directions, collapsing the sidewalls. "Then I squash 'em with my fingers like this." She held the can at the top and bottom with her thumbs and fingers and squeezed the can down to less than half of its original height, showing remarkable strength in her hands.

"That's so I can carry more of 'em," she said, as Sonny handed the orange soda to her. "I'm not getting very many today. I think somebody's been watching me. Stealing 'em before I get there."

"You think so?"

"Oh, yeah, they're worth money you know."

"Really?" Sonny said, giving Little Davie a wink.

"Oh yeah, why I'm collecting 'em."

"Maybe I ought to keep 'em."

"You said you'd give 'em to me."

"Oh, yeah. Guess I did. What do you think, Davie?"

"I told her I'd save them for her."

"He did too. A bagful. I been showing him how to crush 'em."

"Well okay then. I guess we'll have to save 'em for you," Sonny said.

"Well I gotta go. I ain't got a silver spoon in my mouth."

Sonny said, "Hey, what's your name, so I know who we're saving the cans for?"

"Elaine," she said. "Name's Elaine. Be sure and crush 'em down. Don't let nobody else have 'em. I gotta go. I ain't got a silver spoon in my mouth you know. Gotta go."

"See you later."

Elaine disappeared down the alley, heading south, just as she'd done the day before. Little Davie drank the last of his coffee, watching her go.

"Looks like you've got a new girlfriend, Davie. The mistress of aluminum cans."

Little Davie shook the last few drops from his cup and said, "I think we both do."

...TO BE CONTINUED...

ABOUT THE TYPE

This book is printed in Adobe Caslon,
an updated version of the typefaces developed
by William Caslon in London, England during
the second and third quarters of the eighteenth
century. Caslon was the type favored by Benjamin
Franklin, and the first printed copies of the
American Declaration of Independence and
Constitution were set in it. Caslon is noted for
its distinct, old-style design and legibility.
It is one of the most widely used and popular
of all typefaces.

www.ingramcontent.com/pod-product-compliance
Lightning Source LLC
Chambersburg PA
CBHW021532250626
47154CB00006BA/2079